I SLAMMED THE COFFEE CUP INTO HIS FACE . . .

and he hesitated a half second to shield his eyes. In that time I had reached him, grabbed his wrist and pulled him over my outstretched thigh. He sailed away behind me and slammed upside down against the wall. He crashed down on his head and lay still. The second gunnie reached for his gun but I had mine in my hand in a moment and he pulled his hands away, holding them half up in surrender. The second oldest hood was watching me, open-mouthed. He had his coffee cup in his hand and I fired once, shattering it in his fingers.

He swore and pulled back. I stuck my gun back in the holster and turned to the English speaker. "Don't jerk me around anymore, *signor,* I'm good at what I do."

CHARTER BOOKS, NEW YORK

This novel is a work of fiction. Any references to historical events; to real people, living or dead; or to real locales are intended only to give the fiction a setting in historical reality. Other names, characters, and incidents either are the product of the author's imagination or are used fictitiously, and their resemblance, if any, to real-life counterparts is entirely coincidental.

This Charter Book contains the complete
text of the original hardcover edition.
It has been completely reset in a typeface
designed for easy reading, and was printed
from new film

HAMMERLOCKE

A Charter Book/published by arrangement with
Charles Scribner's Sons

PRINTING HISTORY
Scribner's edition published 1986
Charter edition/October 1987

ISBN: 0-441-31609-3

Charter Books are published by The Berkley Publishing Group,
200 Madison Avenue, New York, New York 10016.
The name "Charter" and the "C" logo are trademarks
belonging to Charter Communications, Inc.

PRINTED IN THE UNITED STATES OF AMERICA

10 9 8 7 6 5 4 3 2 1

For Ben Lawson,
who is 50% Barnao and 100% OK

▸ 1 ◂

It smelt like an ambush. It shouldn't have. This wasn't some littered alley in Londonderry, I was standing on thick wool carpet among furniture made from two-inch teak, talking to a secretary who bought her clothes in Paris and had her makeup applied the way they spray fenders in a body shop.

But she was the giveaway. She was flustered, as if I'd walked in and found her saving her boss the bother of going all the way down to the massage parlor to have his dreams come true. She had trouble meeting my eyes and there was tension around her mouth that even her million-dollar Max Factor makeover couldn't conceal. She tried a tight little smile and told me that Mr. Ridley was expecting me and would I knock and enter. Like that, knock and enter.

So I knocked on the ten-foot-high door but because of my suspicion I waited for His Master's Voice. Behind me I heard the secretary gulp down a quick breath.

A fat man's voice said, "Come," and I shoved the door open. It swung wide to my right but I didn't saunter in. I checked through the crack down the edge, then stepped inside and took a quick pace to the left, turning to face the door as it swung shut.

In the glimpse I'd had of the room I could see no menace. Herbert Ridley Sr. was the soft man with the tan, safely behind his desk, both hands on top like a banker turning down a loan application. The guy in front of the desk was harder but forty pounds past fit. He had on the kind of glen check suit that cops buy at discounts from tailors on their beats. From the strain under the left armpit I knew he was carrying. I still wasn't alarmed. Applying for a job isn't a capital offense, he wouldn't shoot me.

I went to the other chair and nodded at Ridley. He was smirking, the corners of his mouth twitching at his private joke, probably the fact that the other guy had a gun. I said, "I'm John Locke, I've come about the job of protecting your son."

Ridley went Hollywood on me. He swung around to gaze out of his window, putting his feet up on his Chippendale escritoire. Over his shoulder he said, "You're supposed to be tough, Mr. Locke."

I ignored him and sat down. He waited but when nothing happened he looked back over his shoulder as if I were in the back seat of his Mercedes. "You're supposed to be tough," he said again.

"Unless you're planning to barbecue me, it shouldn't be a problem," I told him.

Now he did a bully boy laugh and spun around in his chair, swinging his feet down clumsily. He looked at me and then cocked his head back and laughed again. "Suppose I told you that Mr. Sullivan here spent two years in Viet Nam."

I turned to Sullivan. "Did you get a tattoo?" I asked politely but he was too busy looking menacing to take any notice.

Ridley was starting to lose patience. He'd written himself some kind of scenario here but I was getting all the good lines—he didn't like that. "Sullivan was decorated twice," he said.

"Good for him, so was my mother's front parlor." I

stood up. "I'm not sure what you're talking about but get to the point. Do you need a professional to look after your son or not?" I've found it never hurts to be forceful. It lets them know you're a hardnose, which is the business I'm in.

Sullivan spoke now in a growl he'd perfected in the service, I guessed, hazing recruits. "Shall I throw him out, Mr. Ridley?"

Ridley ignored him. "Tell me about yourself, Locke," he said. Sullivan was edging to the front of his seat, ready for what he thought would be a pounce.

"I'm ex-Cambridge, ex-Harvard, didn't finish either, and ex-SAS." I had finished that one, seven years, two of them in Northern Ireland, one in the Falklands and a lot of other work including getting my picture on television as I swung in through the window of the Iranian embassy in London.

"And now you're looking for work?" Ridley purred. He was going to play the money game. He had lots, I had none, nah-nah-nah.

"Right."

"Well, what qualifications have you got?" He waited. Maybe he didn't watch television and had never heard of the SAS. I didn't bite so he sighed and pushed on. "What makes you think you could take care of my son?"

"He's going to Italy. I've been there, I know a Giotto from a grilled cheese sandwich and I don't eat spaghetti with a knife and fork. An example like me might be useful to an eighteen-year-old dropout."

Sullivan made another little push to the front of his chair but not quite to the point of balance, I still had him pinned if he moved. Ridley spluttered. "Who're you calling a dropout?"

"I did my homework. He's had two arrests for joy-riding, no convictions. He was last seen trying to finish grade thirteen at Jarvis Collegiate. His marks aren't out yet but his teacher isn't holding his breath."

Ridley straightened up in his chair. "So you've been

snooping, and I'm supposed to be impressed," he said, huffily. He should give up the Marlboros or quit balling his secretary and take up squash, I thought. Again I let him carry on and he did, blowing his surprise. "I've arranged a little test for you. With Mr. Sullivan's assistance."

"If it involves that cannon he's got under his arm, advise him against trying it," I said evenly. "If he goes for it I'll stick it up his nose."

Sullivan roared and sprang. At least he would have sprung if I hadn't hauled him out of his chair by the left wrist, tripped him over my foot and pinned him on the floor, face down, swearing into the deep pile. I locked his arm up his back and reached over his shoulder with my left hand. His gun was a U.S. Colt .45 automatic look-alike, an air pistol.

I stood back and let him get up while I uncapped the end and tipped out the little red paint balls inside, the kind that kids of all ages use in war games, if they've never been in the real thing.

Sullivan got up and dusted off his coat. He was angry but we both knew I could take him and he wasn't planning any more springing.

"An air pistol?" I said. "Why not a pop gun or one with a little flag that pokes out with 'Bang' written on it?" He didn't say anything so I slipped the pellets back into the magazine. Then I turned and fired at the Picasso print on the far wall. The paint round splatted all over it like tomato ketchup. Ridley howled with anger.

"You sonofabitch. That painting cost ten thousand bucks."

I turned and put two shots into him, splashing his beautiful vest and the tie with its yacht club insignia. He roared again, first at me, an unformed howl, then at Sullivan. "Gct him. You can't let him get away with this."

I turned to Sullivan. "I guess you buy your own suits,

so I'm not going to shoot you," I told him. "Just sit down."

I could see him working out the alternatives. Neither one was good. One way he got fired, the other way he got hurt. I guess firing was less painful. He sat and Ridley stood, swearing and swiping away at his ketchup stains with the sleeve of his Sea Island cotton shirt. I took the last pellets out of the gun and put them into my pocket. Then I dropped the gun on the floor beside Ridley's shining empty desk. "Don't call me, I'll call you," I told him and walked out.

Miss Lacquer was standing outside the door. I smiled at her. "You're going to be asked to get him a clean suit. Try not to hurry, a little humiliation is good for the soul."

She couldn't hold in her grin. "That was you, shooting?"

"Yes. It couldn't have happened to a nicer guy."

"A pity they weren't real bullets," she whispered.

I grinned and gave her my card, which is a natty blue color with the words "John Locke, Physical Assurance" and my phone number.

"Call when the laundry's done, maybe we can cook up a scheme to keep his hands off you," I suggested and walked out into the air-conditioned bullpen where a hundred computer gnomes were clicking and beeping away at their little terminals, earning Ridley the money to play games with unemployed bodyguards. I sighed at the thought. Nothing had changed. He still had money and I still didn't, but at least I wouldn't be stuck saying "yes" to the fat bastard.

▸ 2 ◂

Kansas City was in town that afternoon, trying to do it to the Blue Jays, so I spent a pleasant three hours down at Exhibition Stadium, baking gently over a couple of beers.

It was tied up at the end of nine, then Moseby snicked one along the third base line and it hit that little glitch in the artificial turf and hopped past Brett and Garcia made it home and put the Royals out of their misery.

While I waited for the crowd to clear I called my answering service. A woman had rung. Elspeth Ridley. I dialed the number and a Caribbean woman's voice said, "Ridley residence."

"Good afternoon, this is John Locke returning Elspeth Ridley's call."

"Hold the line, please," she said in an Islands singsong.

A chilled voice came on and said, "Hello, Mr. Locke. Can you come and see me, please?"

"Of course." I'm always polite to women, even if they're related to Herbert Ridley Sr. "When would be convenient?"

"At once," she said without inflection. Money was talking again. I glanced at my Rolex. It was five-forty, rush hour. Did she think I was a magician? "Where do you live?"

She told me the address, up in Rosedale where Toronto's old money sits gathering moss. I told her I would be there in an hour and went down to retrieve my Volvo.

The crowd had thinned enough for me to get out onto the Lake Shore and up Jarvis Street, then Mount Pleasant so I was able to make the five miles in forty minutes but I didn't want to look eager so I parked a couple of blocks away and walked out to Yonge Street to watch the homebound commuters. It's something I do to calm myself when my bank account gets low.

I stood and looked at all that fear on the move. All those tense people taking home full briefcases, just to impress their office manager or their client or some other whey-faced money-grubber, worrying into the small hours over dog food or real estate or computer time-sharing or some other 1980s' necessity. Sure they make money but the price is too high for me.

My wants are simple: excitement, travel, good food and beautiful women. I'd had it all in the army. Not food, of course. I've eaten mice, snakes, frogs, snails, all kinds of choice tidbits when I've worked under cover. But even the worst postings meant transit through interesting places, where there were women, who always seemed beautiful, and with the chance to eat better than it's possible to eat anywhere in Britain. No, I had no grudge with the army but I'd finally grown tired of keeping tabs on terrorists. I still don't understand them and they do business in places I'd rather not be. So I resigned my commission and brought my medals back to Canada. A free man, except for having to go hat in hand to a crusty-sounding rich old woman. I turned back. Everything has its price, especially freedom.

The maid was beautiful, light-skinned and fine-featured with a look in her eyes that said she didn't take her boss too seriously. She looked me up and down as frankly as I looked at her. "You can come in," she said and when I grinned she added, "any old time." It was the best news I'd had in a while.

Elspeth Ridley was a stiff-backed woman of seventy, sitting in a wheelchair in the conservatory repotting African violets. She put down the pot she was holding and spun her chair to face me, moving with a strength that showed she despised her body for letting her down. She dusted off her hands and reached out to shake mine. "Mr. Locke, thank you for coming." Her hand was strong and hard. I decided I liked her.

"My pleasure." She waved me ahead of her and rolled her chair through the doorway into the living room. She pointed to the sofa. "Make yourself comfortable. I was about to have a drink before dinner, would you join me?"

"Thank you." I sat down while she wheeled herself to the sideboard and got out the Beefeater. She had a bottle of Bushmills as well, a woman of character.

She built me an Irish on the rocks and herself a martini then turned her chair around and looked at me very straight. I sipped and waited. At last she spoke. "Just what did happen in my son's office today?"

"I was always taught 'never complain, never explain,'" I said.

She waved the comment aside. "I tried to teach Herbert the same thing but he never understood me. Now he's been on the telephone blustering away about lawyers. I'd like you to humor an old woman and tell me what happened." She left it at that, sitting up straight with her drink cupped in both hands.

"I suppose he thought he had to test me, if I was to be the bodyguard for his son. He had his security chief, a man named Sullivan, try to threaten me with a gun. I don't like that so I took the gun away and when I found they had it loaded with those war-games pellets I fired a couple of them in his office, to give him an idea of what guns are for."

She sipped her gin and said nothing. She would be one hell of a poker player, I thought. I bit into my Bushmills and waited. At last she said, "Where did you learn how to take guns away from men the size of Mr. Sullivan?"

"In the British army." I wasn't going to talk SAS again until I could see where it would lead me.

She inclined her head. "But you're Canadian, aren't you?"

"Born in Toronto but I didn't want to put on a green uniform and sit in Saskatchewan developing cirrhosis. So I went to Britain."

"Ordinary soldiers don't learn tricks like yours."

"I was a volunteer for a special unit."

She thought about that for a moment. "Which unit would that be, Mr. Locke, the SAS?"

"Yes, ma'am."

A man would have asked questions about the training or how many times I'd seen shots fired in anger or if I'd ever killed anybody. She said, "Did you hold a commission?"

I nodded. It was no big deal, just first lieutenant, the second rank up from the bottom but they don't give commissions out with the rations in the SAS, I'd had to give up my rank in the Grenadier Guards to volunteer. It didn't matter to Elspeth Ridley anyway, she was talking business. "So you know how to behave," she said with no flicker of amusement.

"Better than that, I think I understand the boy I'll be accompanying," I told her. It was more than money now, I wanted to work for this woman, she impressed me.

"What makes you so sure?" Just the right note of disbelief to keep me anxious to explain.

"From the checking I've done I get the impression he's a spoiled rich kid with not much ambition beyond having a good time. That could have been me, at his age."

Again she avoided all the time-wasting questions. "The world is filled with former delinquents, do you come from a wealthy family?"

"My father founded Locke Explorations." There, my pedigree was out.

She humphed, thoughtfully. "I've met him. A big forceful man of about my age. He was on the Symphony committee one year but left because he was never in the city, he was always in Ungava or wherever, looking for new ore bodies."

"That would be him."

"And you're the prodigal son." She sipped her gin and allowed herself a little laugh. "I like that. Let me tell you the problem."

I listened and she wet her whistle again and began to talk, slowly and calmly at first but I could feel the anger mounting in her speech. "Herbert, young Herbert, has been a problem for about five years, ever since his father left his mother. He was thirteen then, quiet, interested in painting. His father won the custody battle." She stopped and sipped again, gathering strength for the truth. "God forgive me, I helped him." I said nothing and she went on. "So. My son is the kind of man who suspects any trace of artistic ability is a sign of weakness. He took his son's paint brushes away and bought him golf clubs and tennis rackets, which the boy hated."

I could see the pattern coming now but she didn't stop for questions, looking up and past me, through the door to her African violets that allowed themselves to be potted and shaped the way the owner wanted. "The boy didn't throw a tantrum, he simply went along with his father's wishes, but I could see the resentment building. And then when he turned fifteen, he started the anti-social behavior that has persisted since."

"What kind of behavior? I already know about the cars."

She looked at me for a second. "You must be very shrewd, Mr. Locke, we kept it all very secret. But anyway, that was the least of it. He began pilfering, usually from women. When his father had one of his lady friends over, Squeak—" she stopped and waved one hand, "that's his nickname, Squeak would go through her purse and steal, not money but something personal."

"Missing his mother, I guess," I said. Let's hear it for the Reader's Digest school of psychology.

"Obviously," she said. "But his father regarded it as a sexual aberration and he beat him."

"And that's when he switched to car theft?"

"Among other things." She set down her glass and clasped her hands together. "For a boy of not quite eighteen he is very precocious."

It sounded pompous, unlike her. I asked, "What other things?"

She thought about that for a full minute while I waited, nuzzling my glass of Bushmills and wondering if I had chosen the right way to make a living. "Perhaps you might ask Louise, my maid," she said, "but I would prefer it if you didn't."

I let her off the griddle. "So the job of escorting him is not so much for his protection as it is for the protection of the great Italian public," I suggested.

She took it up gratefully. "That's exactly right, Mr. Locke. I, and my son, of course, have decided we needed a responsible, mature, strong adult to accompany the boy to Italy."

"Why Italy?"

"Italy is the spiritual home of all art," she said. "I want to rekindle the old desire he had for painting." I said nothing and she went on with anger in her voice. "I want to take his mind out of the gutter and point it upwards again, where he once was headed."

I set my glass down. "It sounds considerably more interesting than other assignments I've been looking at. How much would you pay for the service?"

She didn't hesitate. "I'm sure your other assignments would have paid well, Mr. Locke. However, my figure is one thousand dollars a week for the six weeks of the journey, plus all expenses, of course."

"Of course," I said and reached for my Bushmills, trying to keep my happy hands from trembling. Six weeks of first-cabin accommodation and enough extra cash to handle three more months of expenses. Praise the Lawd!

▸ 3 ◂

I refused a refill on the Bushmills and we sat and worked out all the details. The boy and I would fly out on Saturday, two nights away. We'd fly Alitalia direct to Milan and on to Florence. There we had three weeks' worth of rooms at the Rega, a discreet family-style hotel on one of the Lungarnos. The old lady looked up at me sharply when she fed me this last word and I nodded like a good little bodyguard and said, "Of course, on the river."

That pleased Elspeth Ridley. She could see I'd been to Florence so she talked about art for a while and I fed her some answers and she was certain I was the right guy for the job, which was a beauty.

Three weeks in Florence, a week in Venice and another week grabbing the best of the rest of the Renaissance: Ravenna, Pisa, Siena, then down to Rome for the last seven days.

Rome was disgustingly commercial, she told me. Herbert Junior would probably ignore the art and concentrate on its big-city pleasures once he got there. However, she believed it only fair to let him relax after five weeks of study.

I respected her for that insight. I'd already figured he would have earned himself a little howling after five weeks of cultural force-feeding. Now she'd made it part of the plan.

Then she raised the only snag she could see to the arrangement.

"It's quite possible that Squeak won't like you," she said.

"I'd be surprised if he did. But we'll get along okay," I promised. I wasn't bothered. I once baby-sat a defecting PLO gunman for a month, waiting for his buddies to turn up and deliver him to Paradise with their AK47s. I'd stayed awake for most of that time in order to send them on ahead of him. Compared with that episode, this was a snap. For six weeks of high living plus six big ones in the bank I'd entertain the little fart with card tricks if I had to.

She nodded, and then gave in and mixed herself a second gin, feeding me another Bushmills first. She tasted hers and sighed. "I wonder if I would need this if I didn't have any family."

"You can cross this particular grandson off your worry list for a while," I promised.

She sipped and nodded. "I think so. But it seems to me that you should really spend a day or two getting the measure of the boy."

"It would help. I don't even know what he looks like, so far."

"Well I think we should remedy that, at once," she said, getting the old snap back into her voice. "Yes. We need a rehearsal. Why don't you and he take rooms at the Windsor Arms, tomorrow night?"

"It's always a good idea to meet on neutral turf," I agreed. It was easy being agreeable now I'd got the job. Besides, I liked the idea. The Windsor Arms is small and old and expensive, home away from home for a procession of Hollywood stars when they're filming in Toronto, something which happens a lot. Lunch in their Courtyard cafe was an investment I made once a week, just to be visible among people with enough money to need bodyguarding. A freebie in residence was money in the bank.

"Good. Then that's settled. I'll get the reservation made and you can stay there tomorrow and spend Saturday morning picking up any odds and ends Squeak needs for the trip."

Not so good. I'd be trailing around with a shopping bag full of spare underwear. But what the hell, I'd have three good meals at the hotel before we left town.

We went on for another half an hour, at the end of which she did tricks with her checkbook and I was folding half my pay into my wallet.

She told me to pick the boy up at his house, at four P.M. the next day. He would be packed for the trip, she would take care of that part personally. And then she gave me the last instruction.

"Go to the Bank of Commerce at Bloor and Bay tomorrow and ask for Mr. Hawkins. He'll give you the traveler's checks you need for the trip. I would appreciate some kind of reckoning when you return, nothing fancy, but an indication of where all the money will have gone," she said. Then she rolled her wheelchair back, quickly, as if she'd found that a sniper had her in his sights, tired, suddenly, as if she'd been hoarding her strength to protect the boy before folding.

I stood up and gave her a formal little nod, the bow of the head an officer and gentleman gives the Queen. "Thank you for your confidence, Mrs. Ridley. I'll take good care of your grandson."

She smiled. "I know," she said, in a tone that told me it would be my ass if I didn't. She wanted value for money.

I gave the housemaid a wink as I left and walked out to my Volvo whistling "Happy Days Are Here Again."

My own apartment is the top floor of a triplex up in Moore Park which is one contour higher and one social notch lower than Rosedale. Most of the residents are aging WASPs who bought the big old houses in the fifties, or yuppie duplex-dwellers with Save The Whales stickers on their Audis—the tofu and racquetball crowd.

I would never have taken the apartment if I was still in the service. Access is by an indoor stairway or from a fire escape at the back of the house. There's no alternative way out and it's too easy to cover for a working spook to be comfortable in. But I've bought a couple of devices to help me if anything from my past life blows into town and right now I'm out of the anti-terror business so it suits me just fine.

On the ground floor there's a pair of gay architects who quarrel all the time and above them Janet Frobisher who works in radio. She's bright and attractive and I'm tempted to borrow cups of sugar from her but the old adage about not doing anything on your own doorstep has kept us at arm's length so far.

My place has its own locked door on the second level, with a flight of stairs from there to the top. I've earned myself enough personal black marks with the IRA and a number of other bad boys that I always do the trick with the hair on the door when I leave. There haven't been many terrorist attacks in Canada so far but those people have long arms and even longer memories, so it's prudent to maintain the old work ethic.

The hair was gone. I reached back to the holster I wear at the back of my belt and pulled out my equalizer. It's a Walther PP Super, 9mm caliber and dependable as daylight. I cocked it, clearing my throat explosively to cover the sound, and opened the door.

The stairs make a turn halfway up and there was nobody in sight so I eased up the inside of the stairwell, silently, and peeked around the corner, gun first, like a bird with a deadly beak. No worms. The top door was closed, nobody in the hallway. Maybe the hair had dried up and fallen off on its own. Maybe. But I've seen too many setups to take any chances. Keeping the gun up I climbed the rest of the stairs, humming noisily to myself, like a happy man with four or five drinks under his belt and nothing on his mind but his upcoming TV dinner.

I stood to the side of the door jamb, unlocking the door at arm's length in case the guy inside blazed away blind. He didn't and I slammed the door open and rolled into the room as if I'd jumped off a speeding truck.

He was behind the door, holding a baseball bat. I pointed the gun and snapped, "On the floor, face down."

He got down slowly, while I looked over my shoulder, through the space above the countertop into the dining room. I couldn't see anybody but that didn't mean he was alone. It wasn't a time to take chances. I stepped over and kicked him in the collarbone, the right collarbone; he'd been holding the bat right-handed. He yowled and writhed but didn't try to straighten up. I shoved his bat out of reach with one foot and went into the dining room and beyond to the bedroom, gun ready.

There was nobody else, not in the closet, or the bathroom, or even on the fire escape. I came back into the kitchen and sat on the stool. "Okay, sit up, slowly," I said.

It was Sullivan.

"Well. Took it personally, did you?" I asked him. "Or did the lovely and talented Herbert Ridley send you over here?"

Sullivan sat and cradled his right elbow in his left hand. The collarbone was broken. I wished it had been Herbert Ridley's and not his, but them's the breaks. He spoke, hoarsely. Pain has a way of cluttering up the voice mechanism. "Ridley sent me. He was madder'n a snake. He said he'd fire me if I didn't come over and pay you back for what you did."

"So you've tried. Now what?" I took the magazine out of the Walther and worked the action to get the live shell out of the chamber. Then I reloaded the shell and shoved the magazine back into the butt. Sullivan watched me, his eyes narrow with pain. I set the gun down and opened my booze cupboard. I took out the rye and poured a solid belt.

"You want water with this?" I asked and Sullivan's eyes opened up a crack.

"That for me?"

"Unless you're AA."

"Straight's good. Thank you." He dug the fingers of his right hand into the fabric of his glen check shoulder and reached for the glass gratefully with his left.

I watched him drink. He did his share of it, I judged. He bit it in half first, then set it down as confident as a married man with money in the bank. "This was nothing personal, eh," he said.

"Then why the Louisville Slugger?"

He shrugged, and winced as his right shoulder protested. He swore once then said, "Well I knew you were good. I figured maybe if I cold-cocked you I'd have a chance."

"Who let you in?" That was the big question. I'd put deadbolt locks on both doors when I took the place. He hadn't slipped them with his Visa card.

"Ridley arranged it. He has a contact at City Hall. Shit, he's got contacts everywhere, he's a wheel. Anyway, he found out who the landlord was and I told him I was a fire inspector."

"And you didn't have to show him any ID?"

Sullivan sniffed, then picked up his drink and took half of what was left. "Ridley arranged that, as well. I mean, this guy has juice."

I considered this. The clout didn't worry me, but the use of false ID meant a couple of phone calls, and that probably meant that Ridley's secretary had known about the setup. I wondered whether she had been pleased with the idea. That would be a pity. She'd seemed promising, if you like high-gloss finishes.

"So now I call the police and turn you in and we all go home."

He set down his drink. "You wouldn't do that, would you?" He was ashen. Fear again, I thought. Financial fear, the stick that drives civilians harder than physical fear drives a soldier. "Look, I've got kids. One's just started college. He's gonna be a chef, have a real future. He can't make it with me in jail."

I stood up in disgust. Not at Sullivan. He was caught in the same bind as the rest of the world. What made me mad was the thought that Ridley could ask for a guy to be hammered, then go home to his palace and drink too much Chivas and stay clean, even if the roof fell in.

"So what's going to happen when you have to tell Ridley you missed out?"

Sullivan tried another shrug, one-sided this time and less painful. "Maybe I can talk him out of firing me. I mean, you're good."

"I've got a better idea," I said. "Finish that drink and let's go."

He obliged without arguing and we went downstairs. I sent him ahead while I put my warning back in place, this time a shred of paper below the bottom hinge of the outside door. Then I joined him and walked out to my car.

He had to wait for me to open the door for him. His arm was hurting and wouldn't support its own weight anymore. I sat him in and we started off. I guessed he figured we were buddies now, a good jolt of rye will make brothers out of the most unlikely men. He sat back, letting his right hand lie in his lap like a dead cat.

"Where does Ridley live?"

"Up on the Bridle Path."

"That figures," I said. "What's he got, some transplanted English mansion with thoroughbreds in the back yard?"

"It's pretty fancy," Sullivan admitted.

It was. The Bridle Path is Toronto's biggest nonsectarian golden ghetto. It doesn't matter whether you're a Ridley or a Rosencrantz, or a Rajhput Singh, any old hobbledehoy with a million dollars or up for a house can rub elbows with the rich out here.

Ridley's place was typical. White picket fences with a discreet little TV camera at the gateway, a couple of acres of billiard table lawn and flowers like you see in jigsaw puzzles of English country gardens.

The house itself was a three-story pile with an honest-to-god portico big enough for a fleet of Cadillacs. I pulled in and instructed Sullivan. "Stick your right hand in your pocket. It'll hurt but not too badly. Go to the door and ask to see Ridley. I'll be behind you."

He tried one last plea. "He'll fire me."

"Not if you do as you're told. Hop to it."

He got out, painfully stuffing his limp right hand into his pants pocket, and walked up to the door. I waited until a houseboy came to the door then slipped out of the car and walked up behind Sullivan. He was cool. A little pain does clarify your thinking considerably. "This is my associate, Mr. Williams," he said and the houseboy gave me a snooty stare and told us to wait.

There was a big hall stand, capable of hiding a bull moose. I stood behind it as Ridley came down the hall to greet us.

"You shouldn't have come here," he said to Sullivan. "But anyway, how did it go?"

"Lousy," I said and stepped out. His face fell open and I stuck out my hand towards him as if I was going to shake his hand, only I didn't. I grabbed him by the testicles. "Wait in the car," I told Sullivan.

Ridley was gasping and his knees were giving out as I cranked up the pressure slightly. "Remember me?" I asked him.

He managed to hiss out one word. "Sure."

"What you did was illegal," I told him, speaking heartily, the army officer chewing out the hungover squaddie for being drunk the night before. "You could go to jail."

His knees failed but before he could fall I shoved him back against the wall. Between it and my grip on his handle he was able to stay on his feet, buckled but vertical.

"I just want you to know that your mother has retained my services to look after your son on his trip. I'll be calling for him tomorrow at four. After that he and I are going off together, knowing that you approve wholeheartedly. Understood?" A trembly nod. What Johnson said about hearts and minds following is true. I breezed on.

"Good. Now I have learned that you're threatening that meathead Sullivan with firing because he wasn't better than me, twice now. Is that right?"

This time he tried to shake his head but the lie was written in his eyes. I ignored him. "He was out of his class, Ridley. So you're going to give him a bonus for trying. I think a five percent raise should do it. Effective now. You got that?"

The nod was unqualified this time. He would have given Sullivan the house to get my hand off his equipment.

I smiled at him. "Good. And just to make sure that you keep your promise and don't try to play rough again, let me give you one more warning." His eyes were round but he said nothing. In fact you could give him marks for not squealing. "Unless Sullivan gets his raise and our feud is ended, right here and now . . ." I paused for effect and his tiny tormented mind scurried round and round its cage wondering what I would say next. I smiled again and went on. "I'm going to inform your mother."

Talk about hitting below the belt.

I let go of him and he stood up as I got out my handkerchief and wiped my hand, just for effect, to humiliate him further.

"It's all over. I'm sorry," he croaked. It cost him to say it but he was a whipped puppy. He meant it.

"Good. Now why don't you go out to my car and tell Mr. Sullivan about his raise?" I suggested.

He heaved himself away from the wall and walked

painfully out to the door and into the beauty of the summer evening. I followed him, enjoying the scent of his roses and the soft sobbing of a mourning dove in the lindens along his drive. I stood until Sullivan got out of the car and shook hands, very painfully, using his left hand to support his right. Then Ridley turned away, not looking at me. "Goodnight Mr. Ridley. I'll be by for your son tomorrow afternoon," I said.

He raised his head. "I'll make sure he's ready, Mr. Locke."

Sullivan looked at me with awe. "He's giving me a raise," he said. "What the hell did you say to him?"

"Nothing much. I guess you had to be there," I said.

I dropped Sullivan at the hospital and this time I called my answering service before heading home. There was one call, a Miss Pemberton. Her message was a warning, that I should expect callers that evening. It had come in at six-thirty. There was a phone number.

I rang it and asked, "Miss Pemberton, do you by any chance work for Herbert Ridley?"

Her voice was bright, kittenish, maybe she took off her stiffness with her office makeup. "I do. Is this Mr. Locke?"

"Right. Thank you for your advice, I've attended to the matter. It's a little late but I was about to go for dinner, have you eaten?"

"I was just going to start cooking. Would you care to come over here and share a pork chop?"

"Draw me a map and I'm on my way."

▸ 4 ◂

I was home by daylight and started getting ready for the trip. I packed one suit and a couple of pairs of lightweight pants plus a cotton windbreaker to cover my gun. Unless you're a cowboy or a cop you can't go around in public with your gun hanging out.

I debated whether to take it at all. My real assignment was to stop young Ridley from making a fool of himself in Italy. That might need nothing more than a quick grasp of his collar if he started leaning towards trouble. But on the other hand, his father was one of the richest of Canada's nouveau riche. If somebody put a snatch on the kid I could need some heat. I might as well go the distance and take the gun. That brought me to the second problem, how to get aboard Alitalia's squeaky-clean jumbo jet with 27 ounces of sudden death on my person.

I solved that one the way Ridley had solved his problem the day before, with clout. The head of security at Pearson International Airport in Toronto is an ex-RCMP anti-terrorist officer. I'd met him on a conference when I was in the army. A quick call to his office and he promised to smooth things out with Alitalia; they'd have a person on hand to get us past the metal detector without making all the bells ring. Without advertising the fact, the airlines are glad to have a trained armed man on board major flights. It's cheap insurance. As a bonus they would clear me for our Florence connection as well. Good news.

I called the answering service to let them know I would be away for six weeks, then I was ready. I lugged my bags down to the second floor landing and tapped on Janet's door. She opened it and stood there in her track suit with Mozart and the smell of good coffee pouring out the doorway all around her.

"Hi, John, going away?" She's a honey, tall and elegant with Irish red hair and eyes as green as the Mountains of Mourne. She has a friendly directness that maybe overpowers the guys who should be chasing her. Somebody should. I wished, as I always do when we meet, that she didn't live so damned close.

"Yeah. I've lucked into a good one, six weeks in Italy babysitting a rich kid."

"Half your luck," she said. She'd picked that up from an Aussie boyfriend who looked like a fixture until he made the mistake of slapping her. She decked him with a cast iron skillet and that was the end of that romance. She stood back. "I was just making some coffee, have you got time for a cup?"

"I'd love one. Thanks." I dumped the bags and followed her inside. Her place is one room bigger than mine and homey, the way only a woman can make it. Maybe one of these days I should get myself one of those things.

Janet stepped into the kitchen and came out with a tray with cups. "Black, right?"

"Right." I took the coffee and sat, enjoying her company. Hell, this could get habit-forming. She curled herself on the couch and sipped.

"What was the ruckus last night? It sounded like you were having the boys over for volleyball."

"I had a caller. A large gentleman wearing a baseball bat."

She frowned. "Is that hat or bat?"

"Bat," I said, and she mouthed an Oh.

"You're sure in an exciting line of work." She grinned. "I judge by the look of you that it was him hitting the floor, not you."

"Yes. No problem. But I'm going to be away for a while. I wondered if you could keep an eye on my place for me, please. I don't have any plants to water but if you could pick up my mail from downstairs, and if you see anybody hanging around or see the door open at all, leave a message on my answering service. Tell them it's top of the list. Would you do that for me, please?"

She laughed. "Try and stop me."

Well, that was my intelligence network in place for the trip. I'd already set the usual signals for myself, aligning the doormat with the door and tucking a shred of paper into the crack. I should be safe enough. But it was good to have Janet on my side.

"How's the big world of radio?"

"Boring as ever," she said cheerfully. "All the budget goes into TV. People have forgotten how to think, how to listen. Even our decision makers. We can't get the money we need to put on drama, can't even give a guy like you a tape recorder to pick up some sounds of Italy. Nothing but talk, talk, talk."

"Talk is cheap," I reminded her and she snorted.

I finished my coffee and had my idea. "I'm on a dummy run with this kid, tonight. We're in a suite at the Windsor Arms, checking whether we can coexist at close quarters. I wondered if you would like to have dinner with us? If you know any snotty-tempered eighteen-year-old girls, maybe you could dig one up for him."

"You realize this is Friday night. You're asking me to take a raincheck on talking to my plants," she said.

"I have the manners of a warthog, but my heart's in the right place."

"Yes," she said. "About eight inches south of your navel." We both laughed and she told me she would call her script assistant. "She's a student at Ryerson, with us for the summer. You'll like her. She impresses easily."

"I don't get no respect," I said. "Listen, thanks for the coffee. You want me to pick you up or shall we say eight o'clock in the Courtyard?"

"I'll see you there. I'll probably have to drive out beyond the black stump to pick up Lindie."

I stood up, shaking my head. "Beyond the black stump. You realize that bloody kangaroo chaser set your vocabulary back about fifty years?"

"I know." She uncurled from the chair, stretching like a cat. "But the bastard was good value when he was sober."

"Ah, love," I said and kissed her on the nose.

I put my bags in the trunk and drove to Bloor Street. It's Toronto's Fifth Avenue. At least, one short stretch of it is. Either side of that, east and west it turns into ethnic alley, Italian to the west, Greek to the east, out where it's called Danforth. Mid-town you have to pay about eight dollars a minute for parking but I checked into the hotel and let them worry about the car while I walked over to the bank to talk to Mr. Hawkins.

He had a pleasant surprise for me, in the shape of ten thousand U.S. dollars in traveler's checks. All in my name. I did all the signing and thanked him and he looked me straight in the eye, a trick he could do just fine as long as we were both sitting down.

"This is a lot of money, Mr. Locke."

"About thirteen thousand Canadian at today's exchange rate," I agreed.

He humphed and took his glasses off and peered at them as if wondering what he looked like when he was wearing them.

"Yes, well what I mean is, Mrs. Ridley is an old and respected customer of ours." He let the statement hang there like a mild threat.

"And she's a new but highly respected client of mine, Mr. Hawkins, so never fear. I'll take care of her cash."

He put his glasses back on, nervously. "Yes. Well, you understand," he huffed.

"Of course." I smiled a ten-thousand-dollar-plus-exchange smile and stretched out my hand to him. "I appreciate your concern for her, she's a most remarkable woman."

I walked back to the hotel and checked the room. It was a suite on the top floor with a view to the west, down on some of the treetops that make Toronto such a pretty town. I sat for a few minutes, asking myself again why Ridley would ever have advertised for a person to take care of his kid in Italy. Maybe he'd been hoping for some pretty little comparative art co-ed who would show him the sights by day and screw him into an understanding of his position as a rich kid by night.

Finally I decided against questioning divine providence. I went next door to the Danish place where they serve the best curried herring in Canada and bring the frozen schnapps to your table in an ice-wrapped bottle. Bliss.

Maybe it was the aquavit, or maybe I was starting to get over the fear of looking gift horses in the mouth, but after lunch I decided to check behind the Ridley facade. I went back to my room and called a friend of mine, Martin Cahill, as sergeant in the Mounties, the RCMP.

We exchanged the usual banter and then I told him, "I'm just off to Italy, bodyguarding a rich kid."

"Talk about coincidence," he said. "I was thinking of having supper at the Pizza Hut."

"Yeah, well, I don't like the vibes I'm getting from the kid's father. Name of Herbert Ridley. He's the head honcho for Ridley Enterprises and something called Goliath Holdings in Calgary."

"Doesn't ring any bells," Cahill said. I could imagine him standing there, rubbing his big Irish jaw, frowning. "So, you think he's a rounder, what?"

"No, but he's playing some game or other. I mean, people go on trips to Italy all the time without hiring bodyguards. I want to know if he's super rich, or if he's got problems he hasn't mentioned. I mean, if the kid is in danger, I'd like to know ahead of time."

"Yeah. See what you mean." The line hummed while he thought then he said, "I'll have a word with our financial guys, they know who's doing what to whom. Jimmy Mahood, he's been in Calgary the last five years, if there's any hanky-panky, he'll know."

"'Preciate that, Martie. It's worth a bottle of Bushmills."

"Great idea. Think of it yourself didya?" We laughed and he said, "Call me in a couple of days. I'm working the day shift, off on Tuesday, Wednesday next week."

"I'll call you from Florence."

"Name-dropper," he said and hung up.

At four P.M. sharp I drove to the Ridley place and pulled under the portico. The big front door opened first bounce of the bell. I was expected. I gave the houseboy my card and said, "I'm here to collect Mr. Herbert Ridley Junior."

"Yessir," he said, sizing me up. "You're expected, come in please."

"Thanks." I stepped inside as he waited for me. "What's your name, please."

"Kim Lee," he said, surprised. I nodded and ushered him on.

He led me down the long parquet hall to the kind of sitting room they showed in Brideshead Revisited. Ridley senior was there, with a synthetic-looking ash-blonde in her thirties and the kid, who was pretending to read People magazine and had his back to me.

Ridley stood up, warily, it seemed to me. He waved at me vaguely and said, "Dear, this is Mr. Locke. Mr. Lockc, my wifc."

I gave her a big smile and a polite nod and told her I was delighted to meet her. From the interested look in her eye, she might have been delighted to meet me under different circumstances. She sounded Southern, Georgia possibly, but well schooled in some Yankee college. She gave me a sweet magnolia smile and said, "Are you going to take real good care of our son?"

The best that money could buy, I thought, but I kept it down to, "Yes, ma'am."

She turned up the kilowatts on her smile, then turned them off as she addressed the back of the head in the armchair. "Herbie, say hello to Mr. Locke."

He put down the magazine and turned around, as enthusiastically as he might have done for a dentist. "This is bullshit," he said in a drab little voice.

His stepmother did a Scarlett O'Hara thing with her hands and said, "Where do they learn this language?"

Ridley junior stood up. He was about five-ten, one-eighty, with the beginning of his father's softness in face and body. Only it still looked like puppy fat on him. Six weeks of basic training and he could be whipcord. He had off-blond hair, negligently long, and a bored expression. He was wearing blue jeans and loafers that could have handled a shine and a T-shirt with a Canadian flag made from a marijuana leaf instead of a maple.

I was being tested, by him and the others. I took it one step at a time. No sense sticking out my hand and being snubbed. Instead I smiled and said, "Hello."

He ignored me, but my face was intact. He was trying to stay even. His stepmother bustled over and kissed him on the cheek and his father put a buddy-buddy arm around him. "Have a great trip," his father said.

"Sure," Herbie said. He pointed at me. "My bags are at the bottom of the stairs. Put them in the car."

Test time. Both parents were watching, Ridley senior with just a hint of a smirk on his face. I was bought and paid for. Now I would have to show the proper servitude.

"With pleasure," I said and turned towards the door and called, "Kim Lee!" in a parade ground voice.

He was there in five seconds. "Yessir?"

"Mr. Kim. Would you be kind enough to take Master Herbert's bags out to my car, please?" I asked, smiling into his soul.

He was shaken by the request coming from a visitor but he didn't flinch. "Yessir," he said and vanished.

I turned and stuck out my hand to Ridley senior. "Well, goodbye sir. I'll have your son back, safe, sound and well informed in six weeks' time."

He accepted my hand, carefully. "Thank you," he said quietly.

I turned to the stepmother who was looking at me like I was a portion of pecan pie. "Your servant, ma'am," I said. A little Southern courtesy works wonders.

"A real pleasure, Mr. Locke," she cooed. "Ah'm looking forward to seeing you again." She squeezed my hand and I smiled again and turned to Herbie.

"Here we go," I said, and waited for him to buckle and move.

He went, slouching to break a sergeant-major's heart. I beamed at the parents one last time and followed him. I hadn't gone ten steps before I could hear the urgent clipping of the stepmother's heels on the parquet behind me, then the scuff of the father's desert boots.

They both stood on the doorstep and waved as we drove out, me waving politely, Herbie slumped in the seat as if he'd been filleted.

I drove without speaking and at last he broke down and opened up on me. "This isn't gonna work," he said.

"I've heard that song before," I told him cheerfully. The job was getting more interesting. It would be worthwhile if I could turn him into a human being before we returned. That way I would have earned his grandmother's money.

A Lamborghini came south on Bayview, cutting me off. I stayed in my lane, checking the mirror as I drove.

Herbie straightened up a little. "Why'd you let him do that?" he sneered. "This shitbox too slow to keep up with him?"

"Cars impress you, do they?"

That startled him. I'd questioned his credentials. "They impress anybody with any brains," he said.

"Would you remember that car if you saw it again?" I asked and he snorted.

"Of course I would."

"And this one? Would you remember this?"

He laughed out loud. "Nobody notices a crapcan like this."

"Exactly," I said and smiled as the Lamborghini was waved down ahead by a cop on radar surveillance just north of Sunnybrook hospital.

"What's that s'posed to mean?" Herbie asked, but he wasn't sneering.

"In my business you can't afford to be conspicuous," I told him.

"And what business you in?" he asked. Obviously his English grades at Jarvis were not going to be high.

"I'm a bodyguard," I said. "I look after people too rich or busy to look after themselves. Which is why you will carry your own bags on this trip. That way I'll have a hand free if somebody gets pissed off with your arrogance and wants to punch you up the throat."

He thought about that in silence for a while then asked, "How far do you reckon to go to look after me?"

"As far as it takes," I said.

He leaned back, thinking. I sneaked a quick look at him. He had the absorbed air of a little boy contemplating a battle between a cobra and a mongoose. "Like I mean, if somebody threw a grenade at me, you'd jump on top of it, right?"

"That's my usual practice," I said. There was a short pause while he worked that one out, then he laughed.

"Smart guy, huh?"

"The smartest."

I parked underground at the hotel and we went up to the room, Herbie carrying the heavier of his two bags without complaining. I guessed he wasn't going to waste time on a scene when there was no audience around to appreciate it.

The bell captain saw us once we reached the lobby and we let a boy take the bags. He took my key and unlocked the door with a flourish. Herbie walked in and looked around contemptuously. "What a dump," he said.

The bellboy flashed an anxious eye at me. Poor reaction meant poor tip. I gave him a couple of bucks and he heartened. "If there's anything you need, sir, just ring."

He left with a little bow and Herbie mirrored his bow and imitated his voice. "If there's anything you need, sir." He threw his arms out despairingly and slumped on the couch.

I ignored him. What I needed was a six-mile run but it didn't seem smart to leave him so soon. He would take a cab back home and I'd be apologizing. No, I could run in Italy. Here, I was a jailer. I looked at him. His eyes were straying to the TV. Within moments he would be watching reruns of *I Love Lucy*. But it gave me an idea.

"We've got three hours to kill to dinner. You fancy a movie?"

He raised his shoulders an inch, but it wasn't a refusal.

"Okay. Let's go."

He rolled off the couch and pulled himself as close to vertical as he ever got. The soldier in me resented his stance. It was meant to be an insult, and on this ex-officer, it worked.

"You're not that tall," I said and his head whipped around in surprise.

"Howja mean?"

"Only tall men need to slouch. Guys like John Kenneth Galbraith."

He didn't know the name but that didn't matter. I'd gotten through.

"So who needs to go around like they've got a broomstick up their ass?"

Now he had my attention. "Where'd you hear that expression?"

He shrugged again, slouching an inch lower, proving his point.

"It doesn't matter. It just means you've been exposed to some old sweat and I don't think your father's ever been in the service."

"Him," he said and the contempt filled the room.

I locked the door and we went down and out to Bloor Street. We lucked into the right time for *Jewel of the Nile* and I bought the tickets and we were two hours closer to dinner.

When we got back to the room he fell on the couch again and said, "Order me a sandwich, I'm starving."

"We've got a date for dinner downstairs," I said. "A friend of mine is bringing a girl who works for her."

He turned face down into the cushion and swore. "I'm not gonna sit in some dumb restaurant."

"You're going to be doing a lot of it in Italy. I thought this would be good practice, and the food downstairs is excellent."

He lay there without moving. I left him and opened one of his suitcases. He had a good pair of light gray slacks and a Lacoste shirt. I took them out and draped them over the back of a chair.

"Take a quick shower and get changed," I told him.

He ignored me for perhaps half a minute, then turned his face up and said, "You serious?"

"Absolutely."

"I'm not showering and changing for a couple of stupid broads."

"You've got thirty seconds," I said.

He sneered. "Then what?"

"Then you're under the shower, only if I run it, it will be cold."

"What makes you think you could put me under the shower?" He was still sneering but he was interested now.

"If I had to, I could put Muhammad Ali under the shower," I said cheerfully. "Of course, I might have to kill him first, but you'd be no problem."

He sat and I glanced at my watch. "Fifteen seconds."

"I was gonna shower anyway," he said and went into the bathroom.

"Would you like a drink?" I called after him, "I was going to order a beer."

He stuck his head back around the door. "I'll have a screwdriver," he said, and pulled his head back in.

I rang room service and ordered a couple of Heineken and an orange juice. It arrived as Herbie finished showering. I signed for the drinks and took the juice and his clean clothes into the bathroom.

"Here, and put these on," I said.

He reached for his T-shirt. "I'm more comfortable in this," he said.

I took the T-shirt off him and tore it in half.

He said "Heh! What the fuck gives? You just tore up my shirt."

"It offends me," I said, "and when I get mad, I act. When you're a little older you'll realize that you don't mock anybody's flag," I told him. "Smoke all the grass you want, but don't mock Canada."

He laughed, an ugly putdown sound. "What're you, some kind of patriotic freak?"

"I'll buy you a nice Mickey Mouse T-shirt tomorrow, it's more your speed," I said. "Meantime, put these on. And here's your orange juice."

"I ordered a screwdriver," he said.

"You requested one," I corrected him. "But you're too young."

"I've been drinking for ages," he roared.

"Yeah, and look where it's got you." I shoved him lightly out of the room and got under the shower.

I was quick, in case he decided to get cute and make

a run for it. He hadn't. Instead he had opened one of the beers and was watching TV.

He waved the beer at me, in case I'd missed the fact. "This stuff is godawful. How can you drink it?"

I took the bottle off him, leaving him his half glass. "Did you ever think, the reason you drink vodka is that you're too young to appreciate drinking, you want the effect without the taste?"

He didn't have an answer for that so he went on watching TV while I slipped into my suit and put on a tie. "Pretty fancy," he said. "You planning to get into this broad's pants?"

I sighed. "Choke down the last of that beer and let's go downstairs," I said. "And one more thing. While we're in company you will act like a gentleman or I will take you outside and kick your ass good, you got that?"

He sniggered. "Getting to you, am I?"

I laughed along with him. "Not really, it's just that you're the first prisoner I've ever had that I've been told not to kill if he got ornery."

▸ 5 ◂

Dinner was surprisingly pleasant. Janet looked gorgeous and the girl she had brought along was bubbly and nice. Herbie behaved himself. When we were offered a pre-dinner drink he looked at me first and said he fancied a Heineken so we both had one while the women had white wine. He also had a glass of wine with his meal and that was that. By ten o'clock we were through, with no blood on the tablecloth. But I knew he wasn't going to leave it like that. I was waiting for the other shoe to drop.

It was still warm outside, close to eighty, one of those soft Toronto nights when you wouldn't choose to be anywhere else in the world. I didn't fancy heading back upstairs to put in three hours watching TV so I asked the girl, Lindie, if she could suggest somewhere to go.

"Oh yes," she almost squealed. "I'd love to go to Grungie's. They have a great band." She appealed to Herbie. "Electric Jam, d'you know them?"

I thought he flinched but he said, "Yeah, they're great."

Janet looked at me. "Bach it won't be."

I winked at her. "Let's try it, you're a long time dead."

We got a cab and found the place, which sported a strong smell of grass and was infested with more Mohawk haircuts than have been in one place since the battle of The Little Big Horn. I turned and shrugged at Janet: "I hope the U.S. Cavalry's within hailing distance, the natives look restless."

She laughed and pressed me forward. "Onward to the fountain of youth," she said. The band was the usual hairy bunch of louts, all trying to beat some sense into their guitars but there was draft beer on sale so all was not lost.

Lindie was ecstatic. Her blonde curls were bobbing as she nodded in time to the upfront rhythm. "Aren't they great?" she squealed. Herbie's head was twitching to the music as well so I looked at Janet and shrugged. She swallowed a giggle and we squeezed ourselves around the end of a table that wasn't quite full.

There was a napkin dispenser on it so I pulled one out and tore off a couple of small pieces for ear plugs. Janet gestured and I did the same for her. It made things tolerable. I ordered draft beers for everyone and we sipped while the kids grooved. Conversation was impossible but I was able to look at Janet, who was well worth the trouble.

I also looked around the club. Old habits die hard. The place was as squalid as any bar in Belfast and if I'd been there I would have chosen some spot with my back to the wall. That wasn't necessary in law-abiding Toronto but I wanted to know where the heat might come from if Herbie decided to pull any stunts.

The bouncer was obvious. He was around six-two, two-thirty, with the chest development that said he pumped iron three hours a day. He had a bouffant hairdo that made him six-six and he was wearing a summer suit with a tie knotted but not snugged up into the collar which was an eighteen by the look of it and not quite big enough. He looked like the kind of guy who would buy season tickets to *Rambo*.

After a few minutes, Herbie excused himself. I debated going with him but decided he needed a little space so I watched to see that he went to the washroom. It was downstairs so he couldn't squeeze through a window and leave me with egg on my face. I noticed him speaking to the bouncer as he went out and saw the guy follow him with his eyes, a puzzled look coming over his blank face.

Then Herbie came back and he was the life of the party, bending forward to tell Lindie something that made her giggle helplessly. And then the bouncer was at the table.

He stood on the far side, beyond Herbie and the girl but he was speaking to me. "Hey. You."

I looked up at him without answering and he repeated himself. "You. You in the suit."

"What's on your mind, friend?"

"I don't like your attitude," he said. Even above the roar of the music I could hear that he was imitating Stallone.

"What's wrong with it?" I glanced at Herbie who was suddenly concentrating on the band, drumming his fingers and beaming.

The bouncer came around the table to stand beside me. "The little guy says you figure I'm gay."

"Don't mind him. He'll say anything when he's drunk," I said, but I drew my feet up ready to act if he swung.

He did, but before he could complete it I had drop-kicked him in the testicles, but lightly. He sank to his knees, clutching his groin, making fish mouths.

"This man is drunk," I said loudly. "Come on, let's go, this place is disgusting."

Janet was on her feet in a second, then Lindie. Herbie was still sitting, staring at the bouncer. I reached down and grabbed him, apparently by the shirt, but actually giving him a finger and thumb horsebite under the armpit. He yowled and straightened up and we made for the door through the chorus of screams that sprang up behind us.

I whispered in Herbie's ear, "Any more tricks like that and I'm going to let the guy tear your ears off, okay?"

He didn't say anything but I could feel him trembling under my arm.

We took a taxi back to the hotel and walked the women down to Janet's car. I took her key and unlocked it and put them both in. Then I bent down and gave her a kiss, not as quick a kiss as I'd expected. Her mouth was soft and she put her hand on the back of my head and held me for a long moment. It was much more satisfying than the kisses I'd had the night before.

She let go at last and said, "Thank you for a very interesting evening, John. I'll see you when you get back."

"For sure. Take good care of yourself." I winked at her and she grinned and drove off.

Herbie and I headed towards the elevator. He went straight to bed and once I was sure he was asleep, I went into my room and undressed, leaving the door open so I'd hear him if he tried to sneak out. He didn't and I was soon asleep.

I woke up at five, as I generally do, and looked in on Herbie. He was out cold, sleeping like a baby. I left him and put on my running gear, took my keys, and went down to the car. I drove it home through the quiet streets as the sun came up, parking in my usual spot to the left of the garage, then ran back to the hotel, the long way, down Mount Pleasant to the waterfront across to the foot of University and back up to the hotel. It's only four miles so I made a couple of quick tours of Queen's Park to round it out to six and was back to the suite before Sleeping Beauty had come out of his coma. I showered and then woke him up around seven thirty and got our last day in Canada started with bacon and eggs in the room.

We shopped and had lunch and headed out to the airport at three thirty to give us lots of time for the six o'clock flight. Herbie was subdued all day, sullen rather than penitent but at least he didn't pull any stunts. We checked in at the Alitalia counter and the girl asked us to wait a moment, we were expected. Herbie looked at me. "What's this, we getting the V.I.P. treatment? I didn't think they knew my old man in Wopland."

"Hold your silver tongue," I told him. "They don't."

One of the pilots came for us, a movie-star in uniform. He clicked his heels and asked, "Signor Locke?"

"Yes, and this is Mr. Ridley."

The pilot beamed politely then ignored Herbie and led us through the crew entrance, flashing an ID for the security people. They let us through and we were in the lounge. The pilot left us and went back to his pre-flight checks and I pulled Herbie into the duty-free store.

"I'm going to pick up a bottle of Irish," I told him. "Have you got a camera to take with you?"

"A camera?" His scorn was an inch thick.

"You're going to be around some of the most beautiful paintings and buildings in the world. If you don't take a camera you'll be sorry later on, when you're trying to remember them."

He sighed. "Listen, this isn't my idea, eh. Like none of it. My grandmother wants me to look at a lot of dumb paintings but I'd rather be on Cape Cod or someplace. Okay?"

"Stick with me," I told him patiently. They have Bushmills Black Bush in duty-free shops, so I picked up a liter for myself then went to the camera counter and got a Pentax for the kid. He tagged along, more to question my purchases than to be agreeable. The camera made him curious. "Why don't you get an automatic?" he wanted to know.

Contact! It was the first sign of animation he'd shown, even if it was negative.

"They're fine for people who don't have any imagination. But if you want depth of field or backlighting or anything at all tricky, you have to make decisions an automatic doesn't allow for. Trust me." It wasn't time to lecture him but even though he sniffed and pulled away, I could see he was interested. Maybe his grandmother was right, an artist was lurking beneath the slob.

Next we went to the bookstore and I picked up a collection of cryptic crossword puzzles while he got the latest blood-and-thunder paperback. And then we waited and finally we were aboard the first class section and on our way.

The service was spectacular and so were the hostesses, two ripe Latin charmers with eyes carved out of anthracite. I'd made a point of sticking Herbie next to the window so he couldn't get cute with the girls who danced attendance on me because of the gun they knew I was wearing. I had moved it to my left hip. You can't fly nine hours with a pistol in the small of your back.

We had an excellent dinner with a couple of glasses of Asti Spumante and by midnight, Herbie was asleep and I was working through the second of the London Times crosswords. One of the girls was attentive enough that I was tempted to set something up in Florence but decided against it. You're working, Locke. You'll have to fit in your assignations around your assignment, not vice versa.

We had an Italian breakfast of rolls and *caffelatte* and touched down in Malpensa airport at nine thirty. We took our luggage and transferred by bus to Linate for the hop to Florence. Maybe because of jet lag Herbie had nothing to say on the trip. He looked around him at the bustling, excited Italians with typical WASP scorn but didn't bother making any snide remarks. At Linate we were once again ushered past security and within an hour we were in a taxi amidst the Sunday morning traffic of Florence.

Florence is a deceptive city. It doesn't have the grandeur and sweep of Rome, nor the menacing hyperactivity of Naples. Most of its grandeur is indoors and its people are laid back and friendly. You could almost be in some well-preserved English town, except for the sunshinc and thc occasional glimpses of magnificent churches. From the cab, traveling down unremarkable main streets between warm old buildings of brick or Tuscan limestone, before you've seen the inside of the museums, you could wonder what all the fuss is about. So the place has been in business for seven hundred years. So what?

This must have been Herbie's first impression. He recovered his confidence. "This place is a dump," he said. "Look at all these crummy old places."

"Yeah. They haven't changed a bit since Columbus was a cabin boy."

He looked at me. "I didn't know he was a Wop." The cab driver spoke good English and I saw his eyes dart to the mirror at the word.

"Listen, Herb. If you want to go home again with a full set of teeth, I suggest you drop that kind of talk for the duration of your stay. Understood?"

He sucked his teeth like he was taking inventory and lay back in the seat, bored, bored, bored.

The Rega is a comfortable place, about three hundred meters up river from the Ponte Vecchio which we passed on the way. I noticed that the jewelry shops were all closed but the bridge was jammed with street vendors. Herbie looked at them and snorted. "What is this, schlock city?"

"Not during business hours. Some of the best jewelers in the world have stores on the bridge," I told him but he shrugged. Maybe an earthquake would have got his interest, but I doubted it that day.

The hotel was comfortable. There aren't any look-alike North American chain hotels in Florence and this place had probably been doing business for three hundred years but they'd spiffed it up with a bar on the ground floor and an elevator which we took to the top where we overlooked the river. Again we had a suite and I let Herb pick which room he wanted. Not that he wanted either one. He slumped face down on the bed like a drowning victim while I unpacked my gear.

"Hang your clothes up, it'll get the creases out," I told him but he ignored me. I took the opportunity to shower and change and when I came back out he was sitting up on the bed, legs and arms folded, the body English statement that nobody was home.

"This is bullshit," he said. "Did you see all those people out there, thousands of dumb tourists with nothing better to do than walk around some Wop town when they could be on a beach somewhere."

"Most of them have saved for years for the opportunity," I said easily. "Now are you going to shower or are you coming out like that?"

"Coming out where? I'm staying here," he said. It was another test. Was I going to drag him by the collar with his heels making grooves on the floor? I thought not.

"Suit yourself, I'm going for a drink."

I went to the door and he lashed out with another attack. "Is that all you do, drink? What're you, a wino?"

"Beer mostly," I said cheerfully and went out. I wasn't sure he wouldn't make a run for it, not with any purpose in mind but just to embarrass me if his grandmother should call and ask to speak to him, so I went only as far as the bar on the ground floor and had an espresso. Within fifteen minutes he was down. He hadn't showered but that didn't matter too much. At his age you can't really tell.

I called out to him, "Hi, in here," and he came. That was surprising, but not very. He'd spent so much of his time being superior that he felt vulnerable in a place where people didn't speak his language. He flopped into the chair next to mine and asked, "What's that, more booze?"

"Espresso. Want a cup? It'll keep you going a while."

He shrugged so I called the waiter and ordered. "What's the big deal about keeping going anyway?" he asked.

"It's the best way to handle jetlag. We'll try to adapt to the pattern here. We can have an early night, but you do better if you try to fall into their rhythm." I was tired myself but I've done enough traveling to know the ropes.

He shrugged again and ignored the waiter when the coffee came. I said, *"Grazie, Signor,"* and Herbie sneered. I was beginning to recognize why. He was breathtakingly ignorant and aware enough of the fact to act superior. "Why'd you say that? He was just doing his job."

"Manners cost nothing," I told him. "Drink it and we'll head out for a look around."

He sighed. "Look at what?"

"Finish your coffee," I told him. "I'll show you."

He sipped it and pulled a suffering face. I watched, without comment, listening to the crisp ripple of an Italian conversation in the lobby. I don't speak the language but I've been in the army long enough to recognize authority when I hear it. Then the manager of the hotel came into the bar, moving on tiptoe, the way people seem to around trouble. Behind him was a thirtyish man in a a gray suit of some metallic-looking material that changed color as he moved. He had a bushy moustache and was holding a passport in his right hand, tapping it impatiently against his left thumb. The passport looked Canadian. The man was unmistakably a cop.

The manager smiled at me, nervously. "Signor Locke, this is Tenente Capelli." He dropped back and the *tenente* took over.

"You are John Locke?"

"That's right. Is that my passport?"

He ignored that one. "Signor Locke, can you come with me, please?"

"Where to?" I didn't get up.

The *tenente* shrugged. "It's not important. I understand you have a gun with you, a *pistola?*"

Herbie looked at me with new respect. I nodded politely. "That's right, *tenente.* I have a permit to carry it."

The *tenente* gave me a smile you could have cut up into ice cubes. "An Italian permit?"

"No, Canadian."

He expanded, opening like a flower in the warmth of his own righteousness. "You will have observed, Signor Locke, that you are in Firenze, not Montreal. Your permit is not good in Firenze."

"And you want me to turn the gun in?"

He sighed. Maybe Herbie was infectious. "Of course. Italy is not the Wild West, Signor Locke. Italian people do not need guns to walk around the streets."

I smiled, amiable as ever. "Do you have some identification, *tenente?*"

That made him stiffen angrily. I guessed he was a wheel in town, everyone was supposed to know him by sight. But I didn't. After a pause he pulled out a little leather folder, flipped it open and showed it to me. It was official enough, a good likeness, a thumbprint and his rank, Tenente Giacomo Capelli. I noted that he was with the Polizia, the city department, not the Carabinieri, which is federal.

I stood up. He was tall but I was taller and he didn't like that. He said nothing as I unbuckled my belt and pulled it free of the loops on my pants and the holster in the small of my back. I held the holster with my left hand and brought it around. He reached out his hand to take it but I didn't give it to him. You don't hand over guns that way, not in the army. I took it out of the holster and slipped the magazine out, then opened the action and handed over the gun.

He took it and closed the action then held out his hand for the magazine. I was flipping the rounds out, one by one, with my thumb. He clicked his fingers impatiently but I kept on until all seven were out, then handed over the magazine.

"The bullets," he said. He was enjoying himself. There's a lot of sexuality about guns and disarming people is good for the macho character.

"You'll get them when I have a receipt with the serial number of my weapon on it," I told him.

He snorted but produced a notebook and took a property receipt from the back of it. He made it out and handed it to me. I nodded thanks and checked the number. It was correct and he had his name and rank on it and it was signed properly, the same way his ID had been. I handed over the shells and he slipped them into his pocket. "When you leave our city I will let you have the gun back, but not the bullets," he said. There was no arrogance now. He'd done his job, he was going. A professional, I reckoned, grudgingly.

"I'll look forward to it."

He turned on his heel and went out without speaking. Herbie was sniggering. "You sure told him," he said.

"Don't worry," I promised. "If anyone tries to shoot you, I'll show him this receipt. That'll cool him out." My mind wasn't on the conversation, I was wondering how the grapevine had heard so soon that I was tooled up. Either the *tenente* had a direct line to airline security at the top level, or else someone in Canada had given him the word. It changed everything.

▸ 6 ◂

Herbic didn't finish his coffee and after a few minutes more we went out onto the street and wandered down towards the Ponte Vecchio. It was one of those glorious cloudless Tuscan days with a sky so blue you wished you could paint. The city was crowded but it wasn't a menacing busyness, it was more like walking into an entertainment ground with everybody on holiday. The locals were zipping around in cars and on swarms of little Vespa scooters, but there were tourists everywhere. The space against the river wall in front of the hotel was lined with tour buses, German, French, English, and there were dozens of Americans and Canadians on the street, wearing the pastel shirts and pants that make them stand out everywhere in the world, all chattering to one another excitedly, half drunk on the atmosphere.

The streets in Florence are mostly narrow. Except for the piazzas and the main thoroughfares the biggest you find is barely wide enough for traffic after the endless cars are parked down both sides. We didn't pass a spot big enough to park a bicycle. I figured that

Italians who are driving around are just looking for a place to park. It's the national sport, bigger than cycle racing. But it was fun to be out amid so much bustle.

Herbie ignored it all. He had his hands stuffed in his pockets, making a point of looking dead ahead, shutting out the sights. Nothing was going to impress him, he'd decided.

I walked a pace or two behind him on the narrow sidewalk, studying the rounded shoulders and the overlong mousy hair. He was no different from a thousand other middle-class misfits I had met, except that he was under my charge and away from all of the stresses that had turned him into such a chronic sorehead. I felt sorry for him and his anger and decided to do what I could to shake him loose.

We found our way along the network of narrow side streets, jostling through the noisy, friendly crowds until we came to the Piazza della Signoria, the biggest square in town. I'd caught up with Herbie by now and was chatting to him as we walked. Not lecturing, just pointing things out. He was still ignoring me but it was becoming an effort. He was beginning to feel the warmth of the city and was excited, despite himself. Typically, his comments were sneers, but at least he was noticing things. He waved at the statues. "What is this place, Queer City? All these guys with their dorks hanging out?"

"Quite a few of the artists kicked with that foot," I said, "But it doesn't take anything away from their talent."

"Buncha fairies," he snorted, but he couldn't tear his eyes away from David.

"That's just a copy," I told him, "the real one is inside, away from the acid rain. It'll take your breath away."

In one of the open air rcstaurants a tourist had thrown a crust for the pigeons and immediately hundreds of them swooped around until one of the waiters ran out and anxiously shooed them away. Herbie laughed. "Wants to keep the pigeon shit out of the spaghetti," he said, "Although how the hell they'd tell the difference I don't know."

We wandered around the square, among all the tourists and the locals, many of them spectacularly pretty girls. I saw that Herbie was looking at them, shyly. What do you know, I thought. The kid wants a girlfriend. I wondered what kind of hassles he'd gotten into with his grandmother's maid and the other women. Probably put his hand up their skirts, I imagined, although it didn't seem like something he would do, so far in my acquaintance with him. He didn't seem sexually unhealthy. Ignorant and unpleasant a lot of the time, but nothing pathological.

We found the Savonarola marker and Herbie looked at me curiously so I told him the story.

"Savonarola was a priest who got the locals annoyed. He preached that art was decadent, poetry and paintings were the work of the devil. This was at a time when the Renaissance was just rolling and all the rich people were surrounding themselves with beautiful things. So after a while they got tired of his badmouthing and they tried him and hanged and burned him and a couple of his disciples, right here."

While I was talking Herbie pretended to ignore me, his eyes darting everywhere but as we walked on he asked suddenly, "How come everybody was so goddamn churchy? I mean look at this place, there's priests and nuns everywhere."

"Religion has always been very real in this city. God is part of the scenery. But besides that, a lot of people, particularly anyone with talent, went into the church so they could live comfortably while they got on with their painting or sculpting or whatever."

He frowned, then tossed me the question clumsily, not looking at me, embarrassed by the subject. "Yeah, but that meant no screwing, eh?"

"Some of them were dedicated enough that they didn't mind. Some had girlfriends anyway and some were gay. But in the meantime they didn't have to play politics to stay alive. They lived in the monastery and did their thing and nobody killed them, as long as they didn't get the world in an uproar like Savonarola."

An Italian boy of about Herb's age roared by on a scooter with a pretty girl hanging around his waist. Herbie started back, then swore. "Sonofabitch nearly hit me."

"Teenaged arrogance," I told him. "There's a lot of it going around."

We found an indoor restaurant on the edge of the piazza where there was a spare table and went in. I didn't have to persuade him, he was becoming more docile and I was starting to wonder whether I was needed at all. So far he wouldn't have put any strain on a maiden aunt.

He said he wasn't hungry but accepted prosciutto with melon and a glass of red wine along with me. We could see out onto the square and he couldn't keep his eyes off the crowds, the girls particularly. That was the answer, I thought. If I could line him up with something soft, my worries were over. It didn't have to be sexual, by the look of him he wasn't ready for that yet, he wanted somebody to care for him. Nobody at home did, except for his grandmother, and she didn't see enough of him to make a difference. I figured he probably had the same daydreams that sell so many copies of *Playboy* but was ripe for the holding hands in the moonlight treatment, if it could be arranged.

We were eating our ham when a guy about thirty came into the restaurant and stood at the doorway looking around like a bright-eyed bird. He was wearing an open-necked shirt and black slacks but he had the lean look of a lifelong grifter, somebody who gets by on his wits, but only just. I judged him to be either a tour guide or a tout for some store or service in the city. You see them everywhere although they're less obvious in Europe than they are in the Arab or South American countries.

He finally settled on us and it was as if a light had gone on behind his eyes. He straightened and smiled and came to our table beaming. *"Signori."*

I nodded at him. Herbie went on eating.

"Signori," he said again. "You are American, yes?"

"No," I said and he made that explosive little sound with his lips and threw his hands up.

"Then you are from Canada. Perhaps from Toronto. I have a cousin in Toronto. He is in the plastering business there."

I don't like touts of any kind but the guy was working, so I was polite to him. "*Signor*. I don't wish to be rude but we are having lunch."

He bowed from the waist and straightened up again, an apology in human form. "A thousand pardons, *signor*. My name is Mario Di Tursi. I am in the travel industry. It is my work to welcome visitors to our city."

"I appreciate that, *signor,* but I would appreciate a little privacy until we have finished our lunch." There was a sharpness to him that had my hackles on edge. Nobody else was being accosted, so why us? I'm not the kind of person who attracts touts. I guess they don't see me as an easy mark. There's something in deportment that discourages panhandlers and muggers. Was he appealing to the kid? And if so, why?

The waiter was watching us from his place near the wine bin. He looked nervous, wondering if the guy was going to have an adverse effect on his tip.

Di Tursi didn't take the hint. He pulled out the vacant chair beside Herbie. "*Signor*, with your permission."

"You don't have permission, Mr. Di Tursi. I would appreciate it if you left, right now."

He stood up, fluttering his hands in apology. I stared at him until he took the hint and bowed and backed himself right out of the restaurant.

"Why'd you lean on him like that?" Herbie asked. He was interested, at least Di Tursi had done that much for us.

"Nobody else is getting bugged," I said. "How's the ham?"

"Okay, I guess." His plate was empty. "I never had it with melon before."

"Don't your folks take you out to Italian places in Toronto?"

He humphed. "I wouldn't go out with them," he said, and added the clincher, "even if they asked me."

Poor little rich kid, I thought. Give him a day or two of attention and he'd come right around.

"Do you see much of your father?"

"Naah. He's always at the office or out of town. He's got deals cooking everywhere. This year it's real estate, last year it was oil. He's always looking to make another buck."

"That's what business is all about," I said but he snorted again, bitterly.

"Then business is a crock," he said. "How much goddamn money do you need for Crissakes?"

"More, usually," I told him. "If you go into the family company, that's going to be your life."

"Yeah, well I'm not gonna make myself a slave, like him."

A heaven-sent opportunity for some of the Locke charm. "What would you like to do instead?"

He closed that door with a bang. "Nothing," he said. "I'd like to spend the money having a good time."

"That way lies alcoholism and suicide," I told him. "You have to get excited about something, whether it's business, danger, art, something. Man wasn't made to lie around eating peeled grapes."

"How would you know?" he sneered. "You've had to work all your life, you think it's the only thing there is to do."

I laughed. "Fifteen years ago that could have been me talking. I was a spoiled rich kid, just like you."

He sniggered as if I'd told him a dirty joke. "You? Rich? Then how come you're working for my old man?"

"This is what I like to do," I said. "Not necessarily babysitting but traveling and eating well and running into the occasional donnybrook."

"Bullshit. If you had money you'd be on a beach, same as me." He was certain of it.

"Have it your own way." I finished my prosciutto and reached for the wine bottle. "Want some more of this?"

"Naah." He waved me away, then stood up. "Let's get outa here."

"Sit down, I'll call the waiter and get the bill." I wondered if he would sit down, but didn't let my concerns show. If he thought he could make me jump by making arbitrary decisions, life would be miserable for the next six weeks. I just beamed, not begging or commanding and he sat. The waiter bustled over and I said, *"Il conto, per favore, signor."*

Herbie shook his head. "What is this shit? You know about ten words of the language and you make like you're a native, who're you fooling?"

"Not a soul," I agreed. "It's just politeness, if you give the pleasantries in anybody else's language, they'll help you with the tricky bits. If you don't they're liable to be stone deaf if you have a complaint."

"Yeah, well you don't have to worry, you picked up a bundle of money to take care of things."

"I'm earning every nickel."

I paid and left a little change for the waiter and we left. We were both starting to flag, the glass of wine along with the heat and the jetlag was reaching us. Whatever it was, Herbie yawned. "I wanna sleep," he said.

"Why not? Just an hour, most of Italy closes down

for noon anyway, we'll do the same. We've got three weeks to check out all the artwork."

"Three weeks!" Herbie said. He made it sound like a sentence.

We were about halfway back to the hotel, walking Indian file through the crowds on a side street when I saw the girl coming towards us. She was devastating. Tall for an Italian, slender and regal, as gorgeous as a sailor's dream. She was wearing a light green summer dress that floated around her as she moved, striding confidently along the outside of the sidewalk on the opposite side of the street. She was carrying her purse in her left hand and as I watched her, enthralled, a Vespa hurtled alongside and the driver reached out and grabbed it from her, dragging her sideways so that she sprawled in the street as she lost her grip on the purse.

I reacted automatically, lunging three strides across the street to cut off the Vespa and clothesline the rider with my left arm straight across his throat. He tried to duck but I bent my knees to match his movement and my arm hooked him off the machine which skidded across the roadway making people on the other side scream and scatter.

My arm was pulled but the man was down, struggling to find his feet as I rolled him prone and pinned one arm up behind his back.

The girl was on her feet and she ran up and grabbed her purse, babbling in Italian. The only words I made out were *"Grazie mille, signor."*

"I'm sorry, I don't speak Italian," I said, looking up at her. She was beautiful, flushed and excited as she clutched her purse with both arms.

"Signor, thank you. You were so brave."

It's hard to look modest while you're still wearing your shining armor but I just shrugged. "Do you want to turn this man over to the police, *signora?"*

"My purse. I have my purse. The *polizia* will do nothing." I wasn't sure if she was right but I didn't want to get involved in court appearances so I straightened the guy up and patted him down until I found his wallet. He was squirming and swearing at me in Italian. I made out *"cazzone,"* which meant he thought I was an oversized sex organ but he shut up when I increased the upward pressure on his arm, bending him in half.

I flipped the wallet open with my free hand and offered it to the girl. "Check his name, anyway, it will maybe scare him a little."

Then, surprisingly, Herbie was there. "I'll do that," he said.

He took the wallet and leafed through the contents. "There's something here says Paolo Catena."

A crowd was gathering and I was starting to feel a little conspicuous. "Toss it on the ground," I told Herbie. He looked at me in surprise but I nodded at him and he did it. I let go of the kid, who was about twenty-two and, as he stooped to grab the wallet, booted him firmly in the seat of the pants. He fell full length then scrabbled to his feet and ran for his scooter. Within seconds he was around the corner.

The girl was still standing there, holding her purse in both hands and looking at me. I stuck out my hand. "John Locke, *signora,* delighted to be of service."

She took my hand and held it firmly. I noticed she was wearing about a quarter pound of careless gold in bangles and chains but she had no rings. "My name is Carla Fontana, Signor Locke, and I am very grateful that you were so brave."

My left arm was sore from the impact of the kid's chest, but not enough to slow down my eye for the main chance. "Anybody would have done the same thing," I told her. "Perhaps you would be kind enough to join my friend, Herbie Ridley, and me for a drink or a coffee."

Herbie was staring at her and she turned on him and smiled a smile bright enough to give him a tan. "I would be honored," she said.

A knot of tourists had gathered around us, anxious to get in on the action. One of them was a middle-aged man wearing a Yankees baseball cap. He said, "That was quick thinking, fella. You a cop?"

I didn't want to hear his war stories so I smiled politely and said, "Not exactly," and took the girl's arm. "Let's go in there." I pointed to the nearest restaurant.

The three of us edged through the crowd that was blocking the entire street now and went into the restaurant. The help fell over itself to find us a table and we sat down. "What would you like?" I asked and she beamed. "I think a cappuccino, please. But please, I pay. What would you like?"

Herbie and I had a beer, she had the cappuccino and she sighed, as if she had just finished a sprint. "In all my life, this has never happened to me," she said, then shrugged and pouted to make her point. "In Firenze, it does not happen. In Roma, yes. And in Napoli—" she let the sentence dangle and made the flipping motion with the fingers under the chin that means disgust.

Herbie was still silent. I think the kid was awestruck, probably with the girl, who was a traffic-stopper, but maybe at the speed of my reaction. It didn't bother me, I was looking to promote a closer acquaintance. "You live here, in Florence?"

She nodded. "Yes, I am a . . ." she paused to hunt for the word, "a teacher of art."

"And now it is summer, are you on vacation?" I asked, and sipped my beer.

She nodded. "During the summer, I sometimes show people the art in our city."

I wondered how that line of work could provide the kind of jewelry she was wearing but this was one gift horse I didn't intend to look in the mouth. "Herbie is here to look at the art in Florence. We are here for three weeks."

I let it sit there, giving her all the opportunity she

needed to back away gracefully. She said, "Three weeks. That is excellent. So many visitors come for a day. They see David and some of the paintings and they buy purses and glassware and they go home saying they have seen Florence. To see Florence takes a lifetime."

"Well, if it's not to pushy of me, I wonder if you have a little time to show us something of your city. We would, of course, pay you for the service."

She gave us another one of her heart-slowing smiles. "It would be a great pleasure."

She had almost finished her coffee and I was well down my beer. It was time to move. "We are staying at the Hotel Rega," I said. "John Locke and Herb Ridley. If you were free tomorrow, perhaps you could meet us there, after breakfast."

"I will be there at eight thirty," she said. "And now, I must go home and change. I am dirty from falling."

"Until tomorrow then, *signora*," I said and stood up. "And thank you for the beer."

"Thank you, Signor Locke," she said. "I have all my money in this." She held up the purse like a trophy, then opened it and took out a change purse. She rummaged in it and brought out ten thousand lire which she dropped on the table. Then she held out her hand to me. "Until tomorrow."

I took her hand and she squeezed mine. "And please, do not call me signora. My name is Carla."

"*Domani*, Carla," I said. "Come on Herbie, let's go."

He finally spoke when we were on the street. "Jeee zus! Did you get a look at her?"

"For sure," I told him, "you figure she can show us around better than that creep in the place we had lunch?"

"She can show me around the goddamn world," he said. Playboy forever!

"Yeah, she's a dish. But I also think she's a grifter," I said.

"You mean, like a phony?" He was shocked. The bad guys are always ugly in the fairy stories he watched on TV.

"I think so," I said. "For one thing, she's not a native Italian."

He stopped, astonished, and I turned to wait for him. "What the hell makes you say that, just because she speaks good English?"

"Partly that. As good as her English is, she shouldn't have to think twice to find the word for teacher."

"Yeah, well, she was shook up. Like she'd just been mugged." It was reasonable enough that I questioned my own judgment, but there was another fact to add to the pot.

"The other thing is, no Italian ever drinks cappuccino after midday. They drink espresso. Cappuccino is for breakfast or for tourists."

He started to move again, slowly, drawn along by the discussion. "You sure about that?"

"Sure as you're born."

"Then you mean she was just pretending. Why'd she do that?"

"Unless I miss my guess, somebody knows you're in town and is trying to get next to you. That would explain why the police knew I was carrying and they disarmed me. Somebody must have told them. And it also explains why that guy tried to pick us up in that restaurant. And, when that didn't work, they staged that little charade so we'd feel all paternal about Carla Fontana."

Herbie frowned. "You really believe all that? Shit, you're suspicious."

"I believe it enough to call the *tenente* who took my gun and ask if she's got a record," I said. "Let's get back to the room and do it."

He caught up to me with two jogging steps, then slouched again, walking in time to my steps but back in his familiar negligent mold. "But if you think somebody's tryin' a pull something, why'd you ask her to show us around?"

"If she does, we'll know what their moves are. If we don't, they could try something we're not prepared for," I said. "And anyway, that's one hell of a nice-looking lady."

"Sure is," he said. "I hope you're wrong about her."

▸ 7 ◂

I called the desk from the room and they connected me with Tenente Capelli. He sounded peeved, either I had torn him from the noontime embraces of Signora Capelli or he figured I was going to argue with him about my gun.

"Tenente Capelli."

"Tenente, thank you for taking the call. This is John Locke." He didn't cut in or sigh loudly enough to be a distraction so I sailed on. Herbie was watching me from the couch where he was sprawled with his feet up on one end. *"Tenente,* I am a professional bodyguard in Canada and the reason I am here in Florence is to protect Mr. Ridley."

"You have no permission for the gun," he began but I flagged that one down. If I had been on my native heath I would have made a joke about it but I figured my sense of humor would lose something in translation, like his temper.

"No, I appreciate that and I'm sorry you had to come and get it. The reason I'm calling is that I am anxious to find out if a person who has contacted us has a criminal record. I assume that you, as a professional policeman, share that interest."

"Possibly," he said, but his interest was rising.

"It's a woman, five-six, about one-fifteen pounds, that would be fifty kilos. She's very good-looking, around twenty-eight, seems wealthy, and she gave us the name of Carla Fontana."

"The name is not known to me." He sounded huffy again.

"I was wondering if it might be possible to check your files, *tenente,* and and see if you have a listing for such a woman."

"And what am I looking for, Signor Locke? For a thief?" He was acting disgusted with me. "What makes you so certain that your companion is attractive to a thief?"

"*Tenente,* he is from one of the wealthiest families in my country. In the past, before the Polizia broke up the Red Guard, there were incidents in Italy. It is my job to prevent such an incident. I am requesting your assistance."

"You are at the hotel?"

"Yes, room six-fourteen."

"Wait," he said and hung up.

Herbie parted his feet so he could get a better look at me over the end of the couch. "What'd he do, tell ya to shove it?"

"He's calling back," I told him. "Go ahead and snooze for an hour, I'll wait."

"Suits me," he said and turned over so he could lie face down on the couch. Inside a minute he was asleep.

I spent the time usefully. I got the hotel to make another call, to Rome, to Guido Vona. Gina answered and I chatted with her about the kids for a minute until Guido could grab the phone. He was as excitable as ever, his English still as heavily accented.

"Eh, John, you're 'ere, in Roma?"

"Not quite, but closer than I've been since '82. I'm in Florence at the Rega Hotel."

"At's nice. On business?"

"Kind of. Listen, I wondered if you were still working at the old trade?"

"Bakin' bread," he said, very carefully. Maybe phones were still tapped in Italy, even though the Red Guard was sewing mailbags for the next twenty years.

"Of course," I said heartily. "I was wondering if I could get a special order from you. I'm expecting a party. Maybe you could make a delivery to me, the same as last time would be perfect."

"Thatsa lotta money, Johnnie, everything's so *caro.*"

"I could go as high as five hundred mille. I admire your cooking so well."

"I'm busy right now," he said carefully. "It take some time to see you."

"Yeah, well, tomorrow would be good. I'll pay you for your travel."

"Hokay. I see you atta hotel, four o'clock, *domani.*"

"Thanks Guido. My mouth is watering," I said. *Ciao.*"

"Ciao," he said and hung up to contemplate where he could get me a nice clean piece. With all the guns left behind in mainland Europe during the war I figured he would make himself at least half the five hundred thousand lire, that would pay him a hundred and a quarter U.S. dollars for his night's work and expenses for his drive. And I would be back where I'd been before the *tenente's* visit.

I sat and put my feet up, staring blankly at the telephone. My Mickey Mouse code wouldn't fool the police for a minute if they were on to Guido's sideline but he was straight except for the guns and he never sold to terrorists, just honest robbers. Probably he wasn't exceptional enough to rate a permanent tap. He had helped the police on the Red Guard thing, cautiously, of course. That was when I had met him, when I was seconded to Rome to act as bodyguard to the British Ambassador, after his regular guy was caught in bed with a handsome souschef from the Embassy kitchen at a time when the General Dozier kidnapping had all the foreign dovecotes in Italy fluttering.

The phone rang fifteen minutes later. It was Capelli.

He sounded more interested this time. "I have no Carla Fontana, but there is a Carla Dezotti who sounds the same as you say." He sounded grudgingly respectful for my sharpness in picking her out.

"Do you have a photograph, *tenente?*"

"Yes, can you come and look at it?"

"I could, but I don't know whether somebody is setting me up. If I come to see you, they might suspect something."

He sniffed impatiently, so I tried the other alternative. "Perhaps you could come by for a drink or for dinner this evening? People would think I was just trying to get you to give me my toy back."

"You are a nuisance, Signor Locke," he said. "But you make sense sometimes. I will be there at six. In the bar."

"I appreciate that, *tenente.* And tell me, what has this Carla Dezotti done?"

"She is the associate of a man called Pietro Scavuzzo in Milano. He is someone we are watching."

"The plot thickens." I said and he cut in with exasperation.

"What is that?"

"It means, things are beginning to come together. Tell me, does your file say that this *signorina* is from North America?"

Now he sounded impressed. "How did you know that?"

"Just a hunch. I'll see you at six, and thank you for your trouble."

"I think you are a lot of trouble," he said and hung up.

There was nothing else to do for an hour so I changed into running gear and hit the street. Heading upriver, away from the city center, it was possible to find enough space to move and I put in a fast forty minutes before coming back into the hotel a soggy mass of righteous muscle. I was hoping to pick up my key without being noticed. Despite what fulltime jocks think there's very little less exciting than a steaming athlete. There was a woman at the desk, talking to the manager who was explaining something in rapid-fire Italian. I glanced at the woman, automatically. She was in her late thirties, six or seven years older than I am but you'd have to be an expert to know it. She was pretty. Not beautiful, like Carla-what-ever-her-real-name-was, but blonde and wholesome and obviously North American. One of the maturing ex-model types you see in corn-flakes commercials.

I walked up and suddenly the manager broke off. "Signor Locke." I turned and beamed, she was looking at me as well. "Yes, *signor.*"

He came around the counter, all pinstripes and anxiety. "*Signor,* this lady is Signora Ridley. She wishes to talk to you."

I'd seen Signora Ridley at the family palace and this wasn't her, neither was she an old lady in a wheelchair. But I smiled and said, "Mrs. Ridley, I don't believe we've met. I'm John Locke, can I help you?"

She didn't smile, she looked anxious and natural, not out to win me over with synthetic syrup. "Mr. Locke. I'm Herbie's mother," she said.

I didn't let my surprise show. "How do you do? We weren't expecting you, this is a pleasant surprise."

The manager was standing to one side like an anxious stage manager in the wings. She gave him a formal little smile and turned back to me. "The surprise is mutual. I always stay here when I'm in Florence." She was carrying a handsome red leather purse and she held it up to explain. "Leather goods. I run a little chain of boutiques in Canada but I come here often on buying trips. How did you come to choose this hotel?"

I grinned. "It's making more sense to me now," I said. "Elspeth Ridley sent us here. Arranged the reservation ahead, from Toronto. I guess she was hoping this would happen."

She turned back to the manager and spoke to him in Italian. He made an ingratiating little grin and answered her. She nodded and came back to me. "Yes, Guglielmo got a call from Elspeth; she asked him to make sure I found out about Herbie's being here."

I spread my hands, indicating the running gear. "I'm not very presentable right now, but we have a suite, I can be invisible while I change, please come on up and see him. He's catching up on some missed sleep."

"You're sure you don't mind?" There was iron underneath the charm but she kept it well hidden. "No, it's a real pleasure. I figured Mrs. Ridley senior was a fan of yours, from what she said, now I can see why."

Now she gave me a smile. "You're very gallant, Mr. Locke."

I led the way to the elevator. "Call me John, please, I'm working for the family and it's more friendly anyway."

"Fine, and I'm Catherine. People usually call me Kate." She had a voice to match her looks, firm and confident and attractive. It seemed to me that Ridley senior must be as big a twit as he looked if he'd traded in this model on Pitty-Pat Peachfuzz.

The elevator was European and slow and we had enough time in it for me to contemplate telling her she didn't look old enough to be Herbie's mother. But I realized she was matter-of-fact enough to tell me she was sixteen when she had him and leave me to pick the bones out of that so I talked shop instead. "Did Elspeth explain to the manager why I'm here?"

"No, she said that Herbie was in the company of Mr. Locke, but that was all."

The elevator stopped and I let her lead me out. "I'm supposed to be keeping an eye on him while he gets a look at the art."

"Does he need a fulltime person to do that? Couldn't he have come with a group or something?" she asked curiously.

"His grandmother thought not," I said, and added the obvious question. "Have you seen much of him since the divorce?"

She faced me as I unlocked the door. "I haven't seen him since he was fourteen." Her voice hardened. "It was not my idea, Mr. Locke, but the Ridleys are a very difficult family."

"I know," I said and ushered her in.

Herbie was still asleep, lying curled on his side. Except for his ghostly juvenile stubble he looked the way he must have as an infant. I crouched and spoke to him. "Herbie, wake up."

He woke and tried to focus on me. "Wassup?"

"Sit up, son. Your mother's here to see you."

He sat up and put his feet on the floor, rubbing his eyes. Then he looked up and his eyes widened. "Mom," he said, in a wondrous voice.

I don't think they heard me excuse myself. I went into my room and had a glass of water, then poured a good belt of Black Bush and took it into a long tub. I normally only shower but I wanted them to have some space. Then I dressed in gray slacks and a red shirt that had vacation written all over it and went back into the sitting room.

Herbie had been crying but he was dry-eyed now, sitting across from his mother who was in an armchair. I stood and waited until they both looked up at me. "I'll be downstairs in the bar," I said but Kate Ridley shook her head.

"Please join us, John. Herbie and I have been talking and I thought we might decide now how I can fit in with your plans."

"That would be great," I said and sat down in the other armchair.

"I'm here for another week, leaving Sunday morning," she said. "I have appointments every morning this week but the rest of my time is free. I was hoping to share the time with Herbie."

Surprisingly, Herbie spoke first. "Hey, neat," he said, fourteen years old again, his Mom was taking him on a picnic.

"Would you have any objection to my following you

around?" I asked. "I don't know if Herbie told you bu I have reason to believe that there are people in Florence who know he's here and are showing an unhealthy interest in the fact."

She nodded. "He mentioned that. No, I would like it if you could join us."

"My pleasure." Good. My paycheck was secure and I would get to eat dinner with a very attractive woman, better and better.

"Herbie says you've made some agreement with a guide to start showing you around tomorrow."

"We could change that, if you like, or just retain the guide for the mornings, while you're busy."

"That would be best," she said. "There's so much to see here that probably mornings on and afternoons off is the best way to avoid getting overloaded with impressions."

Herbie said, "We've got plenny a time to see the paintings next week, why can't I come with you in the mornings?"

She smiled. "It would be very boring. I spend my time arguing prices in Italian. You'll be better off with Mr. Locke. The paintings will blow your mind. You might feel like starting up again. You were good as a little boy."

Herbie shrugged but he didn't dismiss the idea as he would have done automatically for his father. I decided we would buy him some paints the next day. In the meantime I was in the way here. The love in the room was almost tangible. How the hell she had kept away from her son for so long was a marvel. No wonder he'd been such a pill away from her.

"I'm expecting to meet a man in the bar downstairs," I said. "Now our arrangements are made, why don't you two chat a while? Perhaps we can all have dinner together later on."

"Fine." She was probably a very good businesswoman, I decided. She made decisions quickly. This one was already complete. "We'll join you around seven,

Thank you.”

. “Would you like some refreshments? All me Irish whisky. I can order something up, ou like?”

“Good, I’d like a Campari and soda and Herbie will have a Coke, please.”

For the next couple of minutes I did my aged retainer act, phoning the desk and signing for the drinks when they arrived. Then I nodded to them and went out, locking the door behind me. I didn’t want any sneak moves while I was sitting downstairs over a bottle of Peroni.

I had my book of crossword puzzles with me and I nursed a couple of beers all afternoon while I battled with clues like “Quiet hymns for goddesses.” I was congratulating myself and penciling in “Nymphs” when Capelli arrived. He looked laid back this time, his off-duty demeanor, I guessed. We shook hands and the waiter hustled over. He ordered scotch and water, unusual for an Italian. Either he had spent time overseas or he was modeling himself on cosmopolitan cops.

He raised his glass and I lifted mine. “Thanks for coming, *tenente*. Did did you bring the picture?”

He pulled an envelope from his pocket and handed it to me. “Is this the woman?”

I opened the envelope and slid out the picture. It showed Carla sitting at a restaurant table with a fifty-five-ish sugar daddy type, mustache, bald head. She was laughing and had one hand on his arm. The implication was all there.

“Yes, that’s the girl, is this the man you mentioned?”

He reached for his picture, put it back in the envelope and back into his pocket. “Yes, that was taken by a woman who works for us in Milano. She is very interesting, your friend.”

“What do you know about her?”

He sipped his scotch. “Twenty-seven years old. Born in Chicago. Her father was a prominent Mafia man. He was killed last year, shot in his car. The girl was by then married to another Mafioso and a week later he died also. A bomb in his car. She left Chicago, lived in New York for a few months and came to Roma. She met Scavuzzo and moved with him to Milano. He keeps her in an apartment and they are together often."

"And he's with the Mob?"

Capelli nodded, an almost imperceptible shift of his eye level. *"Sí.* He is connected to the Paolone family in New York. We believe he is their contact here for drugs. They do not come into Italy but the shipments are arranged by Scavuzzo."

"Any record of kidnappings, extortion, the usual rackets?"

"Extortion, yes. It happens everywhere. Kidnapping, no."

I took a mouthful of beer. "That's interesting. It seems to me that the only reason for getting next to Ridley would be kidnapping. His father is rich and maybe he expects trouble of this kind, otherwise he wouldn't have looked for a bodyguard."

Capelli shrugged. "Kidnapping is not common any longer. In Corsica it is still done, but not here. I think the Getty boy stopped it."

I remembered that one. Getty's grandson kidnapped, his ear cut off as warning and still no ransom paid. If a guy that rich won't play ball, it's going to make this kind of crime unpopular as well as unprofitable.

"Well, I can't think of any other reason why she would have put herself in our way," I said.

"And in what way was that?" He seemed amused. "She came up to you and said, I am a guide, I would like to work for you?"

"Not exactly. She had her purse snatched by a kid on a Vespa. It happened across the street from us. I helped her and we got friendly from there."

He looked down into his drink like a witchdoctor examining chicken entrails, stirring the ice cubes with his swizzle stick. "That would be more like Scavuzzo's plan," he admitted. "You feel like a hero. She is beautiful and you do not question anymore."

"That's the way I read it."

He looked up again. "And what arrangement did you make with this woman?"

"I asked her to show us around. I figure that if they're after the kid they'll work through her, try to get her to distract me and put the snatch on the boy. At least I'll have an idea what I'm working against. I imagine she will try to separate me from the kid, then arrange for him to vanish while I'm off with her somewhere."

He nodded. "Exactly. You are good at your job, *signor.*"

"I'd be even better with my gun," I tried but he shook his head.

"My *maggiore* himself told me to get your gun."

"Where did he hear? The airline knew about it, would they have reported the fact to the police?"

He shrugged. "The *maggiore* does not tell me who tells him. Only I know it must be someone important. He does not have his ear in ratholes like me."

"And can you do anything for me?" I wanted some backup. It would be good to know somebody was watching us, in case Herbie got sidetracked while he was on his way to the washroom or a store and I was expected to stand and wait with Carla. Not that waiting around her would be a hardship.

Capelli said, "I can spare a man, one man, for daytimes. You understand we cannot do more. But my man will follow you, as long as you walk. He will stay behind you while you are with the girl."

"That would be fine. If it is a setup, she might try to send him off somewhere, if your guy stays with him, I'll act normal."

"Good," he said and finished his drink. By now, people were coming and going, mostly Americans, the women lusting for the moment when all the leather stores would be open, the men O.D.'d on churches, looking for a bourbon if they could find one. One or two couples came into the bar, but mostly they went right upstairs. At seven o'clock Capelli drained the last taste of scotch from his melted ice cubes and stood up. "My man will be outside the front door tomorrow. Just walk where you are going and he will follow. Do not look around, ignore him."

"For sure. And thank you, you're being very good to us."

He grinned sourly. "Good to me also. What do you think would happen if the boy is kidnapped? I would be working day and night."

"It won't happen," I promised and we shook hands. He left and I went back to the elevator, tossing the room key lightly in my right hand. Like most European hotels, the Rega attached its keys to great brass ornaments. This one was a chess knight and it must have weighed half a pound. No way you'd walk off with it.

The elevator was at the far end of the floor from our suite and I paced quietly down the corridor and listened automatically at the door. I heard nothing for a moment and was about to put the key in the lock when I heard an unmistakable whimper. Somebody was hurting Kate Ridley.

▸ 8 ◂

Silently I took out my Buck claspknife and flipped it open, turning away from the door to muffle the click as the blade set. Then I put the key in the door and turned it. I tried to be silent but the mechanism clattered so I flung the door open and leaped into the room. There were two men there. One of them was holding a gun on Herbie who was sitting far back in the armchair while the other man was trying to mount Kate Ridley who was lying on the floor with her mouth taped and her arms tied behind her.

I flung the heavy key at the man with the gun and he fired wildly once before I drove stiff fingers up his nose, tearing it half off his face. He screamed and dropped the gun, grabbing his face. The other man was scrambling to his feet, pulling another gun. I kicked him on the point of the elbow and he roared but changed hands with the gun. Before he could complete the move I slashed him above his good elbow, cutting the tendons to his hand. He dropped the gun and tried to run but I kicked him again under the left buttock where the sciatic nerve crosses the bone and he collapsed.

Herbie was bawling like a calf. "He was going to rape my Mom."

"It's okay. She's not hurt." I flicked her dress down over her loins and rolled her over to cut the rope off her wrists. She stood up quickly, tearing the tape off her mouth. She was trembling all over, shaking like a car running on one cylinder.

She tried to speak but no words came. I took hold of her and held her close, bumping her back softly. "It's over and they're both going to jail for a long time," I said. "Call the police."

She picked up the phone and dialed and I went to examine the first hood I'd attacked. He was moaning and I bent and took his hand away from his nose. It was flapping back from his face and streaming blood. I told Herbie. "Bring a towel for this bastard, Herb, he'll dirty up the carpet."

I glanced at the other man. He was sitting up, rocking gently, his arm bent tight to control the bleeding. He was no threat any more.

While Herbie went into the bathroom I picked up both guns. Both were Berettas. I slipped the magazines out and worked the action on each to take the last shell out of the chamber, then I set them aside and listened to Kate. She had her composure back now and was speaking rapidly on the phone. She was speaking Italian so I gave up trying to follow and sat and watched while Herbie gave the towel to my first victim. He buried his face in it, sobbing.

"Serves him right," Herbie said angrily. "Serves them both right. I hope they die."

"They'll probably wish they had when they get in jail." I imagined Italian prisons were as bad as those anywhere else, worse, if you include the big underground pen in Naples.

"What happened?" I asked him.

Herbie turned away from the man, frowning, trying to concentrate on my question. "We heard the key in the door and we thought it was you coming back," he said. "Then they came in, with their guns out."

So they'd had a key. I made a note to tell Capelli that. It made it sound like they'd had inside help. "What did they say?"

He shrugged. "I don't know. It was in Italian."

His mother hung up the phone and sat down in an armchair, keeping a wary eye on both men. They had given up struggling and were sitting quietly, nursing their hurts. The man I had cut was bleeding badly but he had pressed his handkerchief into the cut so I ignored him. I noticed that he had closed his fly as well. He would regret that rape attempt all his life. If he hadn't stayed for that, they could have got away.

Kate Ridley spoke. "They told me, 'don't move lady and you won't get hurt, we want the boy.' So I sat still and then that one—" she indicated the man who had tried to rape her—"he got some rope out and the tape and tied me up. While he was doing it I could see in his eyes that he was getting excited and he told the other one that I was a good-looking woman and he was going to have some fun. Then he tore my pants off and then you came in."

"They're amateurs," I said. "I was afraid that the Mob was trying to snatch Herbie but Mafia soldiers wouldn't have done what they did, they would have taken Herbie and gone. These are amateurs."

Capelli said the same thing twenty minutes later. "Neapolitan pigs," he spat. "This does not happen in Firenze, Signor Locke. We are a good town, a peaceful town. These two are southerners. We will find out who sent them."

"Whoever it was, they used a key."

"Did they?" He frowned. "I will ask them where they got it."

I didn't envy either one of them the next four hours in his company but I didn't say anything. He went on. "You are a remarkable man, two *banditti* with guns and you stop them." He shook his head in disbelief and made the quick little shaving motion of the hand down the chin that means "shrewd move."

"I need my gun," I told him. "We've been in town six hours and this happens. I must have my gun back in case it happens again."

"That is not possible," he said.

His detectives were clearing up the mess. Two neat plainclothes men, handcuffing the two prisoners and looking to him for the next order. He waved them off and spoke to them in Italian. They nodded and left, marching proudly behind their prisoners. Cops everywhere love a good clean crime with all the ends tied up tight.

Capelli picked up the guns from the couch. He examined both of them without speaking. Then he looked up and said, "Of course, if you should happen to find a weapon and then forget to give it to me until you leave Firenze, that would be different." He put one of them into his pocket and stood up, leaving the other gun and magazine lying on the couch. "For now, I will take away the gun that was used in this crime and I will call you tomorrow and tell you when we have to ask you to come to the court."

Herbie looked at the other gun and blurted, "They both had guns, both of them," but the *tenente* ignored him. He bowed formally to Kate Ridley. "*Signora,* on behalf of the people of Firenze, I offer my apologies for this. Good night."

He went to the door, nodded again and left. I went after him and put the chain on the door. Then I came back and picked up the gun. It was the better of the two. The other one had been dirty, the one the first man had fired. This one was bright and properly oiled, a good working piece. I slipped the magazine into it and went into the bedroom to try it in my holster but the Beretta was too small to fit properly so I slipped it into the right pocket of my jacket and brought the jacket and the bottle of Irish back into the sitting room.

"Would you like a drink?" I asked and Kate Ridley nodded. Then suddenly the dam burst and she collapsed into herself, sobbing helplessly. Herbie stood and looked at her, his own eyes filling with tears, then sat on the edge of her chair and put his arms around her. "It's okay, Mom. It's okay. Nobody's going to hurt you. John's here. You're safe."

I let them hug and rock and weep for a minute or so while I built a couple of solid drinks then took one over to her. "Here's what you need," I said.

She sat up and Herbie let go of her. She dashed at her eyes with her arm but took the drink. I gave her my handkerchief and she wiped her face and sniffed and handed it back to me. "Thank you," she said.

From the face she pulled at the taste I guessed she was no whisky drinker but it helped calm her. "I think you should stay here tonight," I suggested. "I'll get them to put a cot in here for me."

She looked at me, not focusing properly but she answered at once. "Yes, please. I would like that."

I sipped my drink and put the same question to her that I had put to Martin Cahill in Toronto. "If I may ask a personal question, just exactly how rich is Mr. Ridley senior?"

She shook her head, a tight little motion, almost a shudder. Her color had come back, full and high in her cheeks. She looked beautiful enough to bite. Hell, she couldn't be that much older than I was.

"He controls the company holdings. They're mostly in real estate these days, shopping plazas and office buildings across Canada and the States. I guess the value would be around five hundred million altogether, but I doubt if he could round up half a million dollars of his very own. He's on salary, plus bonuses and so on, but it's all family money. He doesn't own that much."

"Then why is Herbie so attractive to kidnappers?"

She frowned and formed her sentence slowly. "In the

past he had some dealings that I didn't like. It's part of the reason I left him. I'm wondering if he is involved with someone, owes them money or whatever and they're out to punish him."

"That would explain the attack on you. A couple of hired hoods wouldn't know that you weren't the current Mrs. Ridley. Maybe they were trying to hurt him through you."

She laughed, a short angry bark. "Fat chance," she said. "He'd love to see me humiliated. Even my little success in business annoys him."

I glanced at Herbie. He was watching her as she spoke. If there was any respect in him for his father it didn't show. We could have plotted his assassination without Herbie's lifting a finger.

I checked my watch. It was eight o'clock. "Listen, it's getting on to dinner time, could you eat anything?"

She shook her head, then stopped. "I'm sorry, you two must be famished. Why don't I order something up?"

"That would be good. And have them bring your things down here while you're at it. If that's possible."

She managed her first smile since the incident. "I have to get my toilet things, they'll mix everything up. I should go down to the room."

"Well let's do that now. Herb, you can come with us and make yourself useful." After the attempt to snatch him I wanted him in my sight, full time. He stood up at once.

"Yeah, good idea."

We went down to her room and waited while she put her things in her bags. There wasn't any clutter in her room. She seemed to be one of those efficient women who manage to stay attractive without making it their life's work. We waited for a bellboy to come and move the bags then rode up with him. He was small and cheerful but he looked at me with great respect. I imagined I was famous downstairs. He looked at me out of the corner of his eye, and at Kate, then back at me, maybe figuring I was going to get a warrior's reward. He didn't know I was hired help, like him.

Kate ordered for us from room service. It wasn't the dinner we would have got in any of the restaurants within a block of the hotel but she was still shaky and I was tired, not as sharp as I should be. The wine was good and we had a glass each with our meal and then the bellboy brought in a cot for me. We watched in silence as the housemaid made it up for me when I tipped her and she left.

After that we talked for half an hour or so about the next day. Left to me, Herbie and I would have left right away. I would have hired a car and driven to Rome, or maybe Venice. We could have sunk out of sight in the sea of tourists, coming back to Florence later, quietly, checking in to some other hotel. But his mother's presence changed that. He was so childishly glad to see her and she was in town for only another week. We had to stay.

"That's it, then," I said at last. "We'll do the sights tomorrow, whatever's open, a lot of the museums are shut on Mondays. Then we'll meet you for lunch and take it from there."

"Fine," she said. She looked at Herbie, whose eyes were drooping shut. "Time for bed, Herbie. You've got a lot to see in the morning."

He stood up at once, docile as a kitten. "Okay, Mom. G'night."

She kissed him and they hugged and when they let go of one another he surprised me. He came over and stuck his hand out, awkwardly. "G'night John. An' thank you."

I stood up and shook his hand heartily. "You're okay, Herb, and you're welcome." He ducked his head in clumsy acknowledgement and went through the door that divided the sitting room from the bedrooms and bathroom, closing it politely behind him.

"He's a good kid," I said and sat down again. The jetlag was catching up with me and I was tired but she was the boss.

She said, "He hasn't been, not recently. He was telling me. Joyriding in other people's cars, ducking school."

I wondered if he had mentioned the other activities, probably not, a boy wouldn't talk sex to his mother. I shrugged. "I was much the same at his age. Worse, I think. I got away with it for the same reason he has, my father was loaded. But I pulled a lot of stunts in my time. I didn't straighten up until I was in my twenties. He's ahead of schedule."

She was interested. "I wondered, watching you fight like you did, where does a man like you come from?"

"From the army, most recently. I spent seven years as an officer in Britain."

She nodded. "That would make sense. Were you a paratrooper, a commando or something? You fight brilliantly."

I guess I wanted to impress her so I said, "I was in the SAS."

She sat up straight. "Were you?"

"Yeah. It was something I had to prove to myself, whether I could do it or not, some men can't take the training. I did."

"What was it like?" She was genuinely interested so I shelved my weariness and said, "Pretty strenuous. They make you cover forty miles of rough country, carrying a pack full of bricks. And when you get to the other end, you have to go through a battle simulation. You have to go for days sometimes with no sleep. Stuff like that." I didn't want to give her the details. Old soldiers can be a bore.

"And did you see any action?"

I was surprised by the word. Most North Americans would have used the word "combat." I turned it into a question. "You said 'action,' does that mean your father or somebody was in the War?"

"Right. Dad was with the Princess Patricia's Light Infantry in Europe, Italy mostly, that's why he encouraged us all to learn Italian. He didn't talk about the war much, sometimes to my brothers but that's where I picked up the word."

"It changes you," I said and closed the subject.

She pulled her feet up under herself on the couch, the move a wife would make while talking to her husband. "Do you think Herb needs that kind of training?"

"Probably not. His grandmother says he used to paint. I'd suggest we get him some paints. It would be better if you did it, then when he gets back home he can sign up with an art college, the Ontario College of Art, if his marks are good enough. What he needs is something to love. Painting might be it."

She smiled at me, for the first time since we had met it was a truly feminine smile, testing me. "And what do you love, John?"

"That's a hard one. I guess I'd say freedom, the freedom to live the way I want, preferably with some travel and adventure and good living. That's why I left the army. You get the adventure but you don't get much good living."

"And freedom means no wife, I suppose." She wasn't teasing me, it was like being observed by an anthropologist. I felt like a Borneo headhunter, naked except for a bone through my nose and a bamboo jock strap.

"It has so far," I said carefully.

She looked at me for a long moment, then got up. I stood up at once and she came over to me and held out her hand. I took it. "I want to thank you for what you did. You saved me from—" she left it at that and turned away.

I said, "Good night, Kate." She paused at the door to turn and smile without speaking.

I checked the door. The lock and chain were secure, the inside catch pressed in the lock. I'd already checked all the windows. They were six stories up from the street, no ledge, no fire escape, overhung by a wide cornice that would prevent anybody but an Alpine climber from swinging in from the roof. I frowned at that thought, remembering the Iranian embassy in London. We'd gone through those windows in seconds. But they wouldn't try those kinds of tactics. Any attempt on Herbie would be a covert operation. We were as secure as we could be.

I waited until Kate Ridley had used the bathroom then went in and did the same then came out and stripped, turned off the light and got into bed.

It was narrow, like an army bed, and the traffic noises under the window reminded me of London in the days when I had been in the Guards, before I volunteered for the SAS. In a minute or so I was asleep.

The click of the door, opening softly, woke me like a bomb blast. I sat up, grabbing the Beretta, but it wasn't the outer door, it was the door that led to the bedrooms. I relaxed and let the gun sink.

It was Kate Ridley and in the faint light from the street, reflected down from the ceiling she seemed to be floating towards me in her wispy nightgown. She came to the bed and took my arm. "I'm cold," she said harshly.

I stood up, still holding the gun and she clung to me, her body like soft fire against my bare skin. I kissed her and she returned the pressure urgently. "Come," she commanded and took my hand. I followed silently into her room and she closed the door. Her bed was warm but she trembled when she got into it with me. I slipped the gun under the pillow and held her, pressing her firm little breasts against me. She gasped and we kissed again, deep soft kisses that melted her. I reached down and caressed her, stroking the inside of her thighs and then her moistness and she came almost at once.

"I want you now," she hissed and I raised her legs and entered her from the side, still stroking her and she gasped again.

It was a long time before she slept, her hair damp against her forehead, her body soft and relaxed at last, her horrors forgotten. I kissed her gently on the cheek and fell asleep.

▸ 9 ◂

I woke early and went back to my own bed without waking her. Then, at around six, I put on my running gear and went in to Herb who was stirring already, still operating on Canadian time, awake hours earlier than usual.

"I'm going for a run," I told him. "Come and put the chain on the door when I'm gone and don't open it until I answer—" I tried to think of a code word that would make sense to him. " 'Jays,' when you say 'Blue.' Got that?"

"Sure. Hey, cool," he said.

I gave him the gun. "Don't use it but point it if you get suspicious, point it at the door and call the desk, ask them to send a man up to see if there's a prowler. Okay?"

"Okay," he said. Like most men he was happy to have his hands on a gun. I expected he would spend the next half hour standing in front of a mirror, making stern faces at himself. Until his mother woke up anyway.

It was cool on the street and only the locals were about, trucks driving down to the market place and storekeepers headed in for an early start. It was noisy and cheerful and exciting. I was slow after my hard night but I took off along the Lungarno, down past the Ponte Vecchio and the next couple of bridges before crossing to the quieter side and putting in a solid twenty minutes before turning back. Even in that short time the crowds had thickened and the restaurants were open. Workmen were snatching a quick espresso before starting the day and everywhere there was the happy bustle of a people who have been doing essentially the same things in the same place and pretty much the same way for generations. I was glad to be here.

Herb was on cue. He called, "Blue," through the door and I said, "Jays," and he let me in.

His mother was up and dressed. She smiled at me and Herb caught it and looked at me suspiciously. I wondered if we would get away with another night like the one before, now he was rested and would sleep normally. And I wondered if it was in the cards anyway. Maybe it was just what the bellboy had been thinking, the warrior's reward. Ah me. All this and a thousand a week as well. Life was being generous to John Locke.

"Good morning, John," she said. "You're energetic this morning."

"Every morning. It's a habit," I said, ducking the opportunity to ask her coyly whether she had slept well.

"I think we should go down for breakfast," she said. "There's lots of time. You can dress in my room."

"After a long shower," I said and went on through. Maybe it was being in Italy, maybe it was euphoria but I sang in the shower, all that I could remember of "Thy Tiny Hand Is Frozen." When I turned the tap off I could hear Kate laughing in the other room and I grinned at my faux pas while I shaved.

I dressed and slipped on my light jacket. Herb had set the gun on the coffee table in the sitting room and I dropped it into my pocket. Kate was working at a file folder and she looked up and smiled at me. "You're in fine voice this morning."

"I'm no Pavarotti but Italy inspires me," I said and we both laughed. Herb didn't. I wondered how much he suspected. Right now I was a hero. If he found out I was sleeping with his mother he might get all righteous on me and life could be difficult again. I'd have to play it very carefully.

We chatted for a few minutes, while we waited for the breakfast hour to begin in the coffee shop. I was wondering whether we should notify Herb's father about the attempted kidnapping but Kate disagreed. "No, it will worry Elspeth."

Now Herbie chimed in. "No, don't. They'll only want me to go home again."

Kate and I exchanged a quick glance. Waddya know? The kid was enjoying himself here.

We went down to the restaurant at eight and had *caffelatte* and rolls. Herbie even went so far as to try *"Buon giorno"* on the waitress, a motherly little woman in the traditional black. She beamed at us, probably thinking we were one big happy family, which was right in one way but nothing the Pope would have approved of.

After breakfast, Kate picked up her Florentine leather briefcase and said, "Well, I'm a working girl for the morning. See you at one o'clock, in the bar here."

"Right. Have a good morning." I stood up and Herbie waved and said goodbye and we were back to where we'd been the day before.

"Let's head out and get a paper while we're waiting to see if Carla shows up," I suggested.

"They have Canadian papers here?" Herb wondered.

"No, but the *Herald Tribune* will have the ball scores in it. The Jays were playing the Brewers yesterday, I want to see what happened."

"Okay." He waited while I signed the bill and we left. I looked all around for signs of a tail but I didn't see anybody. Either Capelli hadn't been able to get a guy assigned or he'd found one who was invisible. Either way it didn't matter much to me. I figured the kidnap artists had done their dash. I didn't count on any more trouble. I was prepared for it, watchful and ready but not convinced it was going to happen.

In the meantime, it was much easier being with Herbie. Today he was a different kid, interested in everything. Naturally, like any boy, he looked over the wall at the river. "Not very deep is it?"

"Not now, but it floods badly every now and then. They had a bad one in the sixties, it took them years to repair the damage to the books and paintings in some of the museums. It was a good thing in one way. It made them start cataloguing all the stuff they have in the city, what it was, where it was. It's made it easier for scholars."

"Really?" he sounded interested.

"Yeah, and the river, it's the Arno, was a big obstacle to the Allies during the War. Hitler had all the bridges blown up when his troops retreated. But someone talked him out of blowing the Ponte Vecchio. It's been in business for around five hundred years. Some guy on his staff saved it for the Italians. I guess he realized that the War was going downhill for the Germans and they shouldn't make any more enemies for peacetime."

I'd wondered if Carla would show. She could have come anyway, but when she didn't it confirmed my suspicions that the threat was over.

We took a couple of minutes to look in the store windows on the bridge. One of them had a wonderful display of coral, necklaces and other pieces laid out with a symmetry that made them look like a cake. Herbie studied it, trying to read the artfully placed little tag on one necklace. "That looks nice. I'd like to buy that," he said.

"For your girlfriend?" I knew it wasn't but flattery never hurts.

"Naah, for Mom."

"She'd like anything you bought, but I'll bet that's expensive. Why not pick up something in the market? She'd like it just as much."

"I like that one," he said and went into the store.

He was out again a minute later. "Shit," he said. "You know how much they want for that?"

"Too much?"

He laughed. "For sure."

I got the Trib from a street stall in the Via Del Proconsolo and we found a restaurant and sat and ordered espresso while I read the scores. The Jays had won and were still five games ahead of their division. At last, Toronto had a winner.

Herbie was restless, gazing across the street at another jeweler's. "I'm gonna look in there," he said.

I followed his gaze. The place looked respectable. It was thirty yards from my chair. "Go ahead, I'll wait here," I told him. He had to have breathing space and I didn't figure anything would happen on the street in broad daylight. But I set the paper down anyway and watched as he crossed and went inside. He was in there long enough for me to finish my coffee. Then he came out again and looked across at me, triumphantly holding up a little bag. I tossed some bills on the table and set out to cross the street to meet him. And then a car slammed to a halt alongside him.

I was across the street in three seconds but it was too late. Another car roared in behind them, trying to hit me. Three men tumbled out and came for me. I didn't even have time to draw my gun. I kicked the first one in the kneecap and he dropped but the second one was already on me, holding me around the head. I stomped on his instep and swung him towards the third one who was trying to slash me with a long narrow-bladed knife. He missed, cutting the guy holding me, making him scream and let go. Then all three of them scrambled to get back into the car while I spun around, pulling my gun to tackle the others.

I was too late. They had Herbie in the car and it was

pulling away, already fifteen yards ahead of me. I dropped to one knee to fire at the tires but a giggling pair of girls jumped into the street, right in my line of fire. I swore and pelted past them but by then the car had gained another twenty yards, too far for me to be certain of hitting the tires and a miss could have killed any of fifty people within three degrees of my aiming line.

I made a note of the license and whirled to face the other car. It was squealing around to turn away from me but at that moment it was broadside, shielding the world beyond from a shot if I missed so I fired twice, tearing the front tire off track and he slammed into a store front in a brilliance of broken glass. I covered the twenty yards in about five steps, dived into the store front and reached into the car to grab the driver by the collar, jamming my gun into the side of his head.

The store clerks were screaming in terror and the other men were trying to get out. I swung my gun at all of them and shouted, "Keep still or I shoot." Maybe they didn't speak English but they understood the gun. They froze. I shouted, *"Polizia, molto pronto,"* and the manager grabbed the phone. He dialed and jabbered and I stood there, ankle deep in shards of glass, surrounded by wonderful wedding dresses, trying to work out where we went from here.

▸ 10 ◂

The first cop on the scene was a traffic guy, one of the Vigili Urbani, the traffic police. They don't handle crime but they carry guns and he pulled his when he saw mine. I let go of the collar on the man I was holding and used the hand to point to all four of them. "*Banditti,*" I said and kept my gun on the driver. The cop poured a torrent of Italian over me but I told him, "*Canadese, non parlo Italiano,*" and he switched to clumsy English, no better than my Italian. I gave up and told him, "Tenente Capelli, *polizia, pronto, per favore,*" and he crunched over the broken glass and took the phone away from the manager of the store.

A crowd had gathered around the window, screaming, chattering, pointing but nobody tried anything. Then the cop came back out and drew his own gun and covered the occupants from the other side of the car. I glanced at him, he was young and smart and he loved having that piece in his hand. He looked like he'd never held it in public before and he gestured with it negligently while he spoke to the men in the car. Over the top of the car I told him, "Other *banditti* have taken my friend, Signor Ridley. They were driving a red Fiat, license FE 8242. Can you report that?"

He frowned and said, *"Che?"* and then a woman in the crowd screamed at him, I guessed she was translating for me. He backed away from the car and grabbed the phone again.

By the time he was off the phone I could hear the braying eee-ah, eee-ah of the approaching police car and then the real help arrived. They were two uniformed men but one of them spoke good English and I told him what had happened. He went back to his radio and called in and soon Capelli was there. He looked pale and tired. I guessed he'd been working late on the guys from the hotel.

"What happened?" he asked me.

I told him while the uniformed men handcuffed the men in the car and sat them in the rear seats of the two police cars. The one I'd kicked couldn't bend his leg. I guessed his kneecap was gone. They had a lot of trouble fitting him into the seat and it took a lot of shouting before he was inside, half lying across his buddy. Meantime, the store owner had arrived and was screaming at the Vigili Urbani man, obviously wanting to know who was going to pay for his window.

Capelli said, "I tried to telephone you at the hotel. I knew this would happen."

"How, *tenente?* Did those men talk last night?"

He nodded impatiently. "They sang, like birds. They told me there is a contract out to kidnap the boy. Not to harm him, to get him and hold him."

"Who put it out?"

"They haven't told me," he said grimly. "Not yet."

I had put my gun away by now and we stepped out onto the street where one of the uniformed men was asking the crowd what they had seen. It was like something from an opera. Everyone had an opinion. The air was thick with rapid Italian and a lot of arm waving was going on. Capelli took me over to his car. We stood at the front of it and he said, "The Neapolitans had heard in Roma. They came here at once and got a key from the hotel and waited. They were working with a third man, a driver."

"And what about these guys?" I indicated the pair in the back of his car. "Where do they fit in?"

He frowned. "I know all the criminals we have in Firenze. I think they are from somewhere else." He stooped and spoke through the window at the men in the back. One of them was silent but the other one, the one who had been cut, was feeling sorry for himself and he showed his wounded arm and rattled off a long speech. Capelli listened, then cut him off and turned back, sighing. "They want me to arrest you for hurting them." He grinned. "But I recognize him, he is from Milano, I have arrested him before in the Festival here, he is a thief. I do not think he works for anyone important."

"What about the getaway car? I gave the number to the first man on the scene."

He dropped his shoulders. "It was stolen here, in Firenze, this morning. My men and the Vigili are all looking for it but it will be left somewhere, very soon."

"Damn." I'd expected as much, professionals wouldn't use a traceable car but it was the only lead we had.

Capelli held out his hand. "I must ask you for the gun which you found under the couch in your room this morning and were coming to give to me," he said.

"I guess so. But will your *maggiore* let me have my own back now?" I took out the Beretta and unloaded it and handed it to him.

He took it, and the magazine and put them into his pocket. "I am not sure. The *maggiore* is a good policeman but he does not help you. He would not let me put extra men on duty with you. He says that Americans are too excited, there will not be another kidnap."

"Much he knows," I said. "If we'd have had another man here we'd have stopped them." I felt like a trapeze artist who had just missed the bar. I wished Capelli's man had been there to be my safety net.

He shrugged. "I am sorry. When I asked for the man for you I was told no. All our men are working on a pickpocket investigation. The *maggiore* was worried about missing wallets. Now we have a missing boy." He paused.

"We will take a statement from you and then you should go back to the hotel and wait. We will put a tap on your telephone and try to trace anyone who calls."

"You think they will?"

He opened the car door and sat down in the driver's seat, wearily. "I know they will. The contract says the boy is worth one billion lira to the men who take him. That's half a million American dollars."

"Jesus. His father doesn't have that kind of money."

"He will need more, much more. These pigs are only the workmen. Once the contractor has the boy he will want to make his own profit."

I swore again and he shrugged and indicated the seat beside him. "Come. We must go to the station and take a statement."

It was the typical police station, if you discounted the doorway that looked as if it belonged on some cathedral. Uniformed officers were typing, checking reports, talking on the phone and doing their best to look busy and there was the underlying smell of disinfectant and urine that let you know there was a drunk tank somewhere close by. Capelli turned the prisoners over to one of the uniforms and then led me out back to the detective squad room. It had a couple of old desks with typewriters and overflowing ashtrays and there were mug shots taped to the fine marble walls.

"Sit," he said and I did. He wound a piece of paper into the typewriter. "I will type this in Italian, you will trust me that I am doing it right?"

"Sure." I started giving him the story and he rattled at the machine with four fingers, pausing from time to time to gaze at the wall and think of the proper translation. We were almost finished when the phone rang. He answered it and said "*Sí*" a couple of times, then beckoned to me with one finger. I stood up.

"The *maggiore* will see you now," he said.

The *maggiore* was a wheel. His office was as big as a squash court, filled with antique furniture and a couple of good oils, reproductions from some of the Renaissance paintings I had brought Herbie here to see. The man himself was not tall but he had the assurance of rank. He looked about fifty-five. His hair and mustache were gray and he looked up at me out of stone-gray eyes. I got the impression he could happily have worked for Mussolini. Not a man to fool around with.

"Signor Locke?"

"Yes, *maggiore*." Politeness was vital. If he decided he didn't like me I'd be in one of his cells within minutes and it would take all the civil servants in Ottawa a year to get me out.

His English was stiff and formal as if he'd learned it from a diplomat and he wasn't comfortable with it. He paused often between words. But his accent was clear. A proud man.

"Tell me about the man who employs you, this Signor Ridley."

"He's a wealthy man, he controls a company with maybe five hundred million dollars in assets. But he does not have a lot of personal money. He will not find it easy to raise a ransom for his son."

He didn't say anything. He reminded me of my colonel in the SAS. I felt the same respect. This was a man who dealt only with facts. He had a kidnap on his hands and what could I do to help. Not a lot, by the sound of it, so he wasn't wasting words. I was glad he was in charge.

He spoke to Capelli in Italian. Capelli answered, standing very erect, not gesturing. I felt his arms must be breaking under the strain of staying still.

The *maggiore* swung his head back to me, like a hawk contemplating its breakfast. "The *tenente* tells me that three men tried to hold you but you held them."

"I was lucky they didn't use guns, *signor.*" He had sounded as if he were impressed but he said nothing more. He stood up and walked to the window, a stiff strut that would have looked pompous if I didn't know how much clout he had. He looked down into the quiet side street. "This has never happened before in Firenze." He swung back and stared at me as if it were all my fault. I could feel the cell doors swinging open.

He went on. "The *tenente* tells me you also stopped two men last night, two men with guns. You seem to be very lucky, Signor Locke."

"I was in the army, *maggiore*. I am trained to fight. I am a bodyguard."

He shrugged. "You say." He sat down again. "As a policeman I wonder how it is that one man can do so much damage and still the man he is guarding gets away."

You could have etched your initials on the atmosphere in there. I realized that I was a suspect. It made sense. Any copper would have thought the same thing. A sudden rush of violence in a town as free from crime as rural Vermont. This was the test and I kept my mouth shut and waited.

Capelli spoke now, respectfully and slowly, in Italian. The *maggiore* listened, listened, gazing at the bust of Caesar he had on his desk. He could have been Lorenzo the Magnificent hearing a request for a drop in taxes while he knew he still had a palace to finish.

When he spoke again he ignored Capelli and spoke to me. "The *tenente* thinks you are a good man," he said. Three cheers for Capelli. I'd buy him a whole bottle of Johnny Walker once we got the kid back. If we got the kid back. "He is setting up the operation to find the boy. Work with him. Do as he says. Do not try to find the boy yourself. Do you understand?"

"Yes sir." Seven years of army training almost made me come to attention as I answered. This was a guy you obeyed.

He waved us away and picked up a folder. Capelli

nodded, a quick bow of the head and then nodded to the door. We left.

"Shit. That man is scary," I said.

"He is a good policeman," Capelli said. I could see he was breathing fast. He didn't get called in there for compliments, that was certain. He'd been as uptight as I had.

"What happens now?"

"Now the work begins," Capelli said. "We will get men working among our contacts. And we are looking for the car. Perhaps when they changed, someone saw them. Perhaps."

"You think he'll still be in Florence?"

He opened the door of the squad room and ushered me in. "Of course. We have already put up roadblocks on all the roads out of town, everything is being searched. And I will talk to the men you arrested. I don't think they will know where the boy is being taken. They were hired to stop you from protecting the boy. The men in the other car are different." He sighed. "It is a big nuisance, Signor Locke."

"Call me John." It was the least I could do for him.

"Okay, John. Today we cannot keep it from the newspapers. It will be everywhere by noon. What will you do?"

"I guess I'll go back to the hotel and wait. I have to tell his mother. And I guess I have to phone Canada and tell his family there."

"She will not do that?" Capelli was surprised.

"They're divorced. She hasn't seen the boy for four years. Her ex-husband is remarried."

"Indeed," he said and I could see his policeman's mind whirring.

"You don't think she's involved, do you? Hell, those hoods last night tried to rape her."

"I don't know who is involved," Capelli said. "But she appears and all at once we have two kidnap attempts, one of them successful."

"Hell, no. She's straight arrow." He frowned at the

expression and I explained. "She's clean, she thinks the world of her son."

Did she? I wondered. Was I thinking with my brain or my glands? Who could tell?

It took only a minute or two longer and my statement was finished. I signed it and left. Capelli offered me a ride but I needed space so I walked back to the hotel, writing the script for the most painful phone call I'd had to make since the last time one of my squad was shot through the head by an IRA marksman. That had happened often enough that I had developed a formula to minimize the pain on both ends of the line. This one I had to think about.

It was six P.M. Toronto time but Ridley wasn't home. He was out in Calgary. His wife said she would contact him for me. She was honey and molasses on the phone but I told her nothing. I thanked her, hung up, and waited. After ten minutes the phone rang.

"John Locke speaking."

"Yeah, Locke, I was called out of a meeting for this, what's the big deal?"

"I have bad news, Mr. Ridley."

"The kid's been busted for goosing some Italian broad, a nun likely. Right?" The anger poured out of the phone like molten lead. "Goddamnit. You're there to look after him."

"It's worse than that. Since we arrived in Florence there have been two attempts to kidnap your son. The first one failed. I stopped the men who tried it. The second time they used more men, seven altogether. I stopped four of them but the second car, with Herbie in it, was gone before I could hold them."

"Kidnapped? You've lost my son? The bigshot SAS hero lost my son." He hadn't paused for a second. I wondered whether he was more pleased at my embarrassment then worried about Herbie. He took the phone down from his mouth but I could hear him telling whoever was in the room. "My son's been kidnapped. I hire a bigtime bodyguard to take him around Florence, the quietest city you'd ever want to visit and the boy is taken right out of his hands."

Why? I wondered. Why was he saying all of this? Did he really hate the kid that much? Would he even bother trying to raise a ransom? Was he glad that the final loose end of his first marriage was tied up? What a cold-blooded bastard.

He brought the phone up again and said, "So what are you doing about it? What's happening?"

"The police have the number of the car that took Herbie. They also have the four men I stopped. They are talking to them now. If they know where Herbie is, we will have the answer soon."

If I expected any congratulations on stopping four hoods, I was whistling his bride's favorite tune. I'd failed. That was the stick he was beating me with.

"Do the police have any ideas? Does this happen a lot?"

"Not in Florence. But the men I caught yesterday said that there is a contract out to kidnap your son. The price they were promised is one billion lire, that's about half a million dollars."

"Half a million dollars?" His voice ran up so high only the dogs in Calgary could hear him. "Half a million bucks?" How in hell do they expect me to find that kind of money?"

"I'm wondering how they knew Herbie was here." It was time to add a little muscle to the argument. I'd taken my kicking. Now it was his turn. "The police are asking exactly who knew the boy was coming here." I was winging this but it was coming clearer as I spoke. "And they also wonder if you have been contacted by anybody in Canada who might have a grudge against you or want to hit you for money?"

He almost laughed at me. His anger was a bray. "I'm sitting in a real estate office in Calgary. How many fucking Mafia people do you think there are in Calgary for Crissakes? And what right does some greaser cop have suggesting that I'm involved with those scumbags?"

"These are the kind of questions the RCMP will ask you, the answer may help. Please think hard, Mr. Ridley," I said, reminding myself that I had not mentioned the word "Mafia" before he used it. When he didn't speak I threw him the obvious question.

"Will you come over here to handle the transaction yourself?"

"Of course I will." Again he dropped the phone and did some poor-mouthing about the ineptitude of John Locke. Anger. Anger. Anger. Where was the fear? He lifted the receiver again and said, "I'll be there on the first flight. Where are you staying?"

"The Hotel Rega, it's on Lungarno delle Grazie. And, one other thing, Mr. Ridley. The first Mrs. Ridley is here. She's in town on business. She contacted us yesterday."

"You keep that bitch away from my son," he said, then added, "Goddamnit. She must have done this," and clattered the phone down. Nice guy!

After I'd sat and thought for a few minutes I called the front desk and asked them to look out for Kate Ridley in the bar at noon and send her right up. The chances were that she would hear about the kidnap before then. Nothing much has happened in Florence since the flood of '66. News of a kidnap would spread fast. She would probably run into reporters when she reached the hotel.

After that I sat and tried to form a plan. I'd done everything I could. Dammit, I'd stopped one kidnap attempt and put four men inside on the second one. And Herbie wouldn't be harmed, not for a while anyway, not until his loudmouth father arrived and started saying he wasn't going to pay. After that, if he was dumb enough to say it out loud, anything could happen.

Finally I settled down to the fact that I had lost the

boy. Instead of getting mad, I thought about what I could do to get even. The only idea I had right away was to call Martin Cahill back in Toronto and see if he'd found out anything. It made more sense than studying the wallpaper any further. I could have written a doctoral thesis on it by that time. It had small blue flowers on a gray background. Very restful. I calculated there were twenty seven hundred and some flowers on the north wall. Very productive, Locke. I picked up the telephone with real enthusiasm.

Martin was at home. "Just about to eat the expense account TV dinner," he said. "Wondering how the poor people are doing over there in Italy."

"Not good. My kid was kidnapped today."

"Really?" He dropped the joking. "What happened?"

I filled him in and he listened without commenting. Then he said, "This smells."

"You've checked out the kid's old man?"

"Yeah. An' the news is not good. According to Jimmy Mahood, the Ridley business is stretched thinner'n a jar o' jam in a family of twelve. Ridley invested in oil, heavily, a couple of years back when OPEC was turning the screws. He got greedy. Then the price started coming down and he was stranded. He's had to do everything short of kite checks to keep afloat."

I thought about that one for long enough that he asked, "You still there?"

"Yeah, just wondering what that means at this end. He likely can't afford a ransom for one thing. The kid's in big trouble."

"Well, I don't wanna make your day altogether but it gets worse. Apparently some of his real estate dealings have been with the Bonaventura Corporation. They're legit, on the face of it, but we happen to know that the principals are all Mafia heavies, guys from Montreal."

"Whichever way I look at this it comes up ugly," I thought out loud. "Mafia, Italy, kidnap, short of cash. Sounds to me like he might have gone in over his head on a six-for-five loan. Now he can't pay and the Mob is leaning on him."

"They'll have to find some way of getting it out of the kid," Cahill said, his voice suddenly distorting in and out on some atmospheric wave. "Because they won't get much more'n kind words out of his dad."

"If that. Anyway, thanks Martin. I'll be around with a bottle of Bushmills, soon's I get back."

"Better you should take me to Kentucky Fried Chicken," he said in disgust. "I just burned my goddamn Salisbury steak. Shit. I'm gonna have to get married again." He hung up on my laugh.

I sat and thought about his news. It didn't make things any easier for me, or for Herbie. There was no doubt about it. I was going to have to get the kid back, without payment. But even as I thought about it I was wondering, Why did a man as hard up as Ridley invest a couple or three grand in sending his kid to Italy? Don't get suspicious, Locke, I reminded myself. His grandmother sent him. She's probably paying for all of it, just as she's paying for me. But still the same question nagged. Why Italy? Why now?

The phone began to ring about an hour later. Newspapers. I hung up after each one and called the desk to try to get them to weed out reporters but my lack of Italian held me back so I took the calls one after another. And then, at noon, Kate Ridley came in.

I heard her coming up the corridor. I knew it was her from the babble of Italian that followed her like a swarm of mosquitoes.

The door was unlocked. She came in, not quite weeping, and asked me: "Is it true?"

"Yes. I'm sorry. There were two carloads of men, one to get Herbie, one to stop me. I stopped one group but the others got away with Herbie."

The tears spouted from her eyes. She walked blindly over to the window, her face streaming. I didn't presume on the night before to hold her or try to comfort her. I was furniture, a chair that had given way and hurt her kid.

The phone rang and she snatched it up. Then she put it down again without speaking. "A reporter," she said and sighed a long shuddering sigh and began to calm herself.

I left her alone while she went into her bedroom and got tissues to wipe her eyes. I'll bet Ridley's new wife would have repaired her makeup. Kate didn't. She came back into the room and sat down. "What are we going to do?"

"The police told me to wait here. They believe the kidnapper will call with a ransom demand. Capelli is coming over to join us in a little while. They're going to put a recorder on the phone. I guess they'll also shut the reporters up."

The phone rang again. Another reporter. I hung up.

"His father will have to be told," Kate said. She was sitting with her knees together, toes neatly pointed, contained and business-like. She would be strong.

"I've already phoned him. He's in Calgary but he should be here on the first flight."

"Will he bring money with him to ransom Herbie?"

"I'm not sure. The police said that the men last night had heard there was a half million dollar bonus for taking Herbie. That means the organizer will probably ask more than that."

"Why?" she looked at me wide-eyed. "How can you be so sure?"

I lifted my hands, a lost gesture. "I'm not sure, but if they're offering big money to the foot soldiers, they're expecting bigger money themselves."

"He doesn't have it." She shook her head, a rigid little shudder, like some strange modern dance movement. "He doesn't have that kind of money. Where will he get it?"

"He'll get it, and Herbie will be released." I wasn't so sure myself but this wasn't the time to make her any more fearful.

There was a tap on the door. I went to it but it opened and Capelli walked in, swinging the key. "Excuse me. I think you will not open the door and I have news."

"What news?" Kate Ridley asked in a hiss.

"We found the car that was used to kidnap the boy. Two of the three men were in it."

"Did they say where my son was?" she whispered.

Capelli sighed. "I am sorry, *signora,* they said nothing. They were dead."

▸ 11 ◂

"Dead? How?"

"Shot," he said, "I think someone did not want to pay them the money from the contract."

Kate Ridley gasped. Her face went milk-white and she started to tremble. I reached her in one step, catching her as she collapsed.

I laid her flat on the floor and put a cushion under her feet. Capelli made an urgent little popping sound with his mouth then swore softly in Italian. "I am a fool," he said.

"She'll be okay," I promised. "Don't worry about her. Quickly, while she can't hear. What do you think's happened to the boy?"

"He has been taken by somebody with organization, somebody big. This somebody sent the *banditti* to capture him, knowing perhaps that you would stop some of the men. Then he paid them in lead instead of gold."

Kate Ridley stirred and her eyes opened.

"Can you sit up, Kate?" I asked her and she nodded.

We supported her as she sat up, then half lifted her

onto the couch. Capelli said, "A thousand pardons, *signora.*"

She shook her head and gestured, dismissing his concern. "What about my son?" she asked.

The phone rang and I answered it, leaving Capelli to explain.

"John Locke, who's calling please?"

"Signor Locke, it is the desk. A man has come to see you. He has a delivery, a cake. I told him what has happened but he says it is important."

"It is, thank you for calling. Tell him to wait in the bar."

I hung up and spoke to Capelli. "I have to go downstairs, I'll be ten minutes."

He frowned. "What is happening?"

"Nothing to do with the case. I'll explain later." I went out, finding a uniformed man outside talking to a striking-looking brunette with a notebook. She abandoned the cop and latched on to me.

"Signor Locke, yes?"

"Signor Brown," I said and smiled and walked quickly down the corridor but she clip-clopped after me on high heels.

"*Signor,* a moment of your time, please."

She got into the elevator with me, still talking. I beamed at her and took no notice. She had to be a TV reporter, I guessed. Her makeup was perfect, she was ready to step in front of a camera at the drop of a hint.

"*Signor,* what is happening in there?" She was burning a smile like a thousand-watt light bulb, charm enough for a whole Miss America pageant.

"I don't understand, *signora,*" I said and then stood and smiled, counting the floors down to the ground while she tried all the tricks they taught her in journalism school.

The lobby was full of people, TV cameras, men and women with microphones. They saw the attention the woman was giving me and swooped after me like wasps. I ignored all of them and went into the bar.

Little Guido was sitting at a corner table, lighting a cigarette. He had a grappa in front of him. He looked up in horror as the TV cameras came in and quickly put a newspaper in front of his face.

As I walked towards him another uniformed policeman worked his way through the crowd and ordered them out, making sure that he was in front of the TV cameras while he did it. He shooed them all out and shut the door. I made a note to slip him ten thousand lire when I left.

Guido took down his paper and reached for the grappa. "Mother of God. John, I don' want alla these people look at me."

"Don't worry, Guido. We'll get you out the side door when you leave. Did you get my order?"

"Sure." He picked up a package from beside him. It was an ornate cake box, the kind that contains a Panforte, the airy sponge cakes they eat in Northern Italy, big enough to contain the cake in a plastic bag with a lot of loose sugar. You shake it all up before you open the box.

I took it, feeling the heft of a piece inside. The barman came out from behind the counter, all eyes and eagerness. I pointed to Guido's glass. *"Due, per favore, signor."*

He went back to the bar, doing his best to watch us while he poured two grappas. I peeled off three traveler's checks and signed them with the pen that materialized instantly in Guido's hand. He noted the denominations, all $100 and allowed himself a small smile. *"Bene,"* he said.

The barman came back, carrying the drinks in one hand and a cloth in the other. He set down the drinks and started swabbing the already spotless table. Guido spoke to him rapidly and he answered and shrugged but took the hint and went back to the bar to practice his pout.

"What flavor did you bring me?" I asked.

"Is no the same asa last time," Guido said. He

picked up his new grappa, and took a quick snort. "Is your favorite."

"The one I always have at home?"

"Sure." He made a modest little shrug. "We trya please the cliente."

I raised my grappa and toasted him. "Here's to business," I said and we both chugged the drinks down. I opened the box and took a quick look inside. He'd got me a Walther. I stood up, the box comfortably under my arm. "Thanks Guido. Get the barman to show you out the side way. I'll keep these others away."

We shook hands. He had a good handshake, warm and strong. Then I dropped some bills on the table and turned away, keeping ten mille in my hand, rolled up small.

Outside the bar it was a zoo. All the reporters were talking at once and the uniformed man was answering questions, speaking rapidly and stroking his fine mustache for the women's sake. He was having fun. When the crowd saw me he became number two on the hit parade but I smiled at him and shook his hand and the bill disappeared. I hoped the few bucks would be enough to quench his thirst. He made a way for me through the crowd and pressed the elevator button grandly. The elevator arrived and I was just stepping in when I heard a familiar voice above the babble, calling my name. I looked around and saw Carla Fontana, working through the crowd like a running back. "Signor Locke," she called. "You remember me?"

"Of course. Come on up." I stood aside and the cop held the elevator door for her and she was inside, as beautiful as I remembered, glowing with exertion.

It was no time for games. "I didn't expect to see you today," I told her.

She was Joan of Arc, heroic, unappreciated. "Why not?"

"The boy's gone. It was him you were looking for, wasn't it?"

Italians can outshrug the entire world. She could

have made their Olympic team. "I'm afraid I do not understand, *signor.*"

"We can discuss it in the room. I'm glad you showed up."

I stood aside to let her go ahead out of the elevator and down the corridor. She seemed to know which room. The same uniformed man was on duty and he straightened up to his full height when he saw Carla. He was still an inch shorter than her but Italian men are used to that. He was proud as a bantam rooster.

I tapped on the door and called out, "John Locke."

A detective opened it. Two of them had arrived since I'd left. One of them was fitting a tape recorder to the telephone. Capelli was supervising. He looked up and saw Carla and his jaw dropped minutely. Then he straightened and spoke to her in Italian. Kate Ridley watched them, following their exchange as if it was a tennis match.

I nodded vaguely at everybody and went into the bedroom to open my cake box. Guido had done me proud. It was a Walther PP Super and a full box of 9mm ammunition. I loaded the gun and put it into the holster then slung it on my belt, moving the location this time so it was at my left side, butt forward, ready for an across the body draw. Quick draws don't matter much outside of western movies but this positioning would save me a second or so and the boys played rough in this country.

I topped it off with the cotton jacket and came back out of the bedroom. Capelli said, "I think you should hear what Signora Fontana has to say." I wondered why he was using her alias. Probably, like a good copper, he hadn't shown all his cards yet.

Carla spoke in English. "The news is all over town, all over the country by now." This didn't surprise me so I waited.

She touched her hair, a courtesan's gesture that showed she didn't earn her keep teaching art. She was somebody's little bon-bon. "I was telling the *tenente* that I knew already that there was going to be an attempt to take the boy."

"How?"

She smiled patiently. "I have important friends. One of them told me that the boy was coming and that his father was very rich. Everyone in a certain group knew all about him."

"Is that why you set up that little drama in the street yesterday?"

She dismissed the question with a wave of her hand. "I have already told the *tenente*. It was my friend's intention to protect the boy. He owes the boy's father a favor, something about business in Canada." I glanced at Kate Ridley. She was staring at Carla the way you'd stare at a snake.

Carla said, "My friend asked me to make your acquaintance. Then when you were so quick, I reported to my friend that the boy was safe, you're a very resourceful guy." Her American accent was emerging, second by second, as she opened up and dropped the camouflage.

"A nice story, Carla. But I've got a couple of questions. A: Is it true? and B: If it is, why are you here now?"

She smiled a languorous smile, the feminine equivalent of the British expression "Don't get your knickers in a knot, everything's taken care of." "My friends are anxious to honor their debt to the boy's father. They asked me to come and see you because you already know me. You would let me in. They want to help."

"The police are already working on it," I said. The phone rang and Kate Ridley answered. The detective was watching his recorder. She spoke quickly, then hung up. Carla ignored it all. "The *tenente* is a good man but he has to work by different rules. I have already spoken to him and he has accepted."

Capelli nodded once and I cheered up. The Mafia could open doors that would be locked to him. If it wasn't a Mafia kidnapping and they owed Ridley senior, this could be useful. Very useful.

"What can they do?"

"My instructions were to talk to you and see if you needed help. After that, if you think they can help, I go back and they do what has to be done."

"I'd like to come with you," I said.

She pulled a mocking little face. "And you would know where to look? Your Italian is good enough to ask questions?"

"No. But I have some skills that might be useful."

She lifted her shoulders. "I will take you," she said. "After that it is up to my friends."

I looked at Capelli and nodded towards the bedroom. He came with me and we shut the door. "Does she know you're on to her?"

"Of course. A Mafia *nobile's* mistress. She knows we know her."

"You figure she can help us?"

Now he did his shrug. God, it was infectious, a form of Italian St. Vitus's Dance. "If it gets the boy back faster, yes it is a help. If it does not, it does no harm. They came to me, I am not in their debt."

"Okay then, I'll go with her and we'll take it from there. No way can I sit around that room waiting for telephone calls."

He had noticed the cake box and he picked it up, tossing it from hand to hand like a basketball. "Your friend the baker, he sells good things."

"The best," I said carefully. I'd seen his *maggiore*, I didn't want Capelli to be forced to lie to him about my gun. He saved me the trouble, changing the subject. "Remember you are lying down with pigs. Expect to get dirty."

"I've lain down with worse in my time," I told him. "You look after things this end."

We went back into the sitting room and I spoke to Carla. "The *tenente* thinks I should come. Let's get to it."

"Good," she said simply. Then she went to Kate

Ridley and squatted down in front of her. "Mrs. Ridley. Try not to worry. We will find your son."

"I pray God you do," Kate said quietly and her voice had knives in it.

The same reporter was outside the door again. God alone knew how she had sneaked out of the crush downstairs. Carla solved the problem for me. She spoke to the policeman and he started asking the reporter questions. She shrieked at him, all her charm blown away in anger as we walked away and she couldn't follow.

We took the freight elevator to the basement and out the back. There were people standing around, report ers possibly, but Carla put her hand on my arm and chattered away to me in Italian, laughing and preening, and the men did nothing but ogle her, ignoring me completely. When we were around the corner she pointed to a Mercedes coupe. It was double-parked and one of the Vigili Urbani was standing in front of it, looking doubtful. She paid him for his courtesy with a brilliant smile and he melted, looking at me the way I'd look at a sweepstakes winner. Business, just business, I wanted to tell him. Right now I had other priorities.

We got in and she pulled away, moving easily, fluidly, not with the kind of brio you find in male Italian drivers. I tried the obvious question. "Where are we going?"

"You'll see," she said. She opened her purse with one hand and took out cigarettes, offering them to me first. I shook my head but pressed in the lighter for her. She took a cigarette and lit it, waving the lighter afterwards as if it was a match. Every gesture was a little larger than life. I guess she had to be part actress in her work. Her boyfriend expected the best performance possible.

She drove for about twenty minutes, whirling me through the traffic smoothly, using the power of the Mercedes the right way. If she was as good in bed as she was behind the wheel, Scavuzzo was getting his money's worth.

We stopped on a street of old limestone houses with the same moneyed feel you recognize in the Upper East Side in New York, except that these places were lower, only three stories high. She parked the car in a laneway beside it. There were other cars there, two Mercedes and a Porsche. Money talks. I guessed it was conferring inside. "Come," she commanded and walked briskly to the front door of the nearest house, making no attempt to be friendly anymore. I rated only as much charm as was needed for camouflage.

I followed and Carla let herself in. A babble of Italian voices in various male registers was coming from a room to the left of the door. She pushed it open carelessly and walked in. Four men were sitting around with coffee cups. Two of them hustled to their feet, feeling for their guns when they saw me but she turned them off with a spout of language and they settled down. I got a look at them all before I approached the table. The gunmen were young, beautifully dressed in light suits. The other two men were older, one of them in his fifties. They were both dressed less showily. They were the heavies, was my reading.

The oldest one said, "You are called Locke?"

"That's right." I looked him over. He had a friendly face, if you discounted the eyes which lay in it like stones in a puddle. He laughed shortly and spoke to the others in Italian. The second heavy pursed his lips and gave an approving little nod. The two gunmen narrowed their eyes and looked snotty. I guessed he was telling my war stories for me.

"You're fast, Signor Locke," he said, all but his eyes smiling.

"Not fast enough, *signor*. They got the kid." No need to act macho, the muscle men could do that for all of us.

"And that's why you're here?" It was more statement than question so I tried a mock-Italian shrug. "The *signorina* said she had powerful friends. Right now I could use some friends in Firenze."

He humphed and translated then asked me, "Coffee?"

"Please," I said and he told one of the gunnies to oblige. The guy didn't like it but everybody else outranked him. I thanked him gravely and sipped and waited.

The oldest one did all the talking. "We hear that there were two cars. You stopped one of them, four men." He looked around at the gunmen and repeated it in Italian for their benefit. It still didn't make them love me but it gave me some kind of status, they relaxed a little. Then he asked, "You heard what happened to the others, the men who took the boy away?"

"I did. It sounds as if the boy is in danger."

He shrugged, then sipped his coffee. "Not if his father has money. They want money, not the life of the boy."

"And you can help me find the boy, *signor?*"

Another shrug. "Of course. Nothing happens in Firenze that I do not hear about. We will find him."

"Good. His mother is at the hotel, she is worried."

He frowned and spoke to Carla in Italian, then to me again. "His mother is here, in Firenze?"

"Yes. It's a coincidence. She has business here, she buys leather goods for stores in Canada."

He sucked his teeth. "But Signor Ridley has a wife in Canada, this is another woman?"

"His first wife, they divorced, five years ago." I hoped he wasn't a devout Catholic, it wasn't likely but in the cradle of the Renaissance they have more than their share of religion.

I needn't have worried. "No matter, our business is with Signor Ridley."

"I understand Signor Ridley has friends here," I said. It wasn't very profound but if Ridley had markers to call, I wanted to know about them.

He ignored me. "And you have come here because you want to help us look for the boy?"

"I have some skills that could be useful."

He translated this and the second heavy nodded slightly. The other two scowled and suddenly one of them was talking, pouring out a torrent of anger. Not that his tone was any guide. Italians can sound angry when they're talking about the weather, hot Latin passion, I guess. Only this guy was for real. I imagined he was telling the others that I was a big useless WASP twit not worthy of unlatching his Gucci bootstraps. When he finished both the heavies were grinning and I guessed what was coming.

One of them spoke to him and he stood up, looking grim.

"If you've told the pretty little boy to try me out, tell him not to, because I'll hurt him," I said.

The oldest one said, "You talk a lot."

The kid stood up. He came around the table slowly and I stood up to wait for him. Maybe they expected me to pick up a chair but I didn't. I just held my coffee cup, as if I'd been interrupted in the middle of enjoying my espresso. He was eight feet away when he drew his knife and flicked out the blade.

I slammed the coffee cup into his face and he hesitated a half second to shield his eyes. In that time I had reached him, grabbed his wrist and pulled him over my outstretched thigh. He sailed away behind me and slammed upside down against the wall. He crashed down onto his head and lay still. The second gunnie reached for his gun but I had mine in my hand in a moment and he pulled his hands away, holding them half up in surrender. The second oldest hood was watching me, open-mouthed. He had his coffee cup in his hand and I fired once, shattering it in his fingers.

He swore and pulled back. I stuck my gun back in the holster and turned to the English speaker. "Don't jerk me around anymore, *signor,* I'm good at what I do." I stooped and picked up my own coffee cup from the carpet.

Carla was crouched over the man on the floor. He was out past cold, his eyes open. "You've killed him," she said.

"I've winded him, and made him feel foolish. That's all. Get me some more coffee." It wasn't fair of me but it was the right thing to do then. The atmosphere was as butch as a wrestler's locker room. I held the cup out towards her and she took it and went to the espresso machine, not speaking. I made a note of that. I owed her one for this.

I bent and checked the guy on the floor. His eyes fluttered and he focused on me. I gave him thirty seconds then stuck out my hand. He took it, reluctantly, and I helped him up. I sat him in a chair and told the English speaker, "Tell him, please, that I bear him no ill will, he was doing his job." It's easy to be magnanimous when you're holding all the aces.

The boss spoke to him and he nodded. I picked up the man's knife, folded it shut and handed it to him. He disappeared it into his pants pocket and tried a faint smile. I slapped him lightly on the shoulder and sat down.

Carla put more coffee in front of me and I thanked her politely and sipped. "Right," I said to the boss. "Now that you've tested me, can I come with you?"

He took out a cigar and lit it carefully. *"Si,"* he said at last. *"Si,* we have work for a man like you, Signor Locke."

He got up then and we all stood up respectfully. I didn't begrudge it. Respect never hurts, especially to a man who can order you shot if he doesn't like you. He and the other older man left the room and the rest of us sat down again. Carla spoke to me. "I told them you were good."

"It's my only trick." I beamed at her. "Sorry about

the coffee, it was necessary at the moment."

"Forget it, I know these people better than you ever will. It was the right thing to do," she said, and added, "but don't try it again."

"Ma'am, I am a pussycat around bright women," I told her and she laughed.

"Now you're catching on," she said.

She spoke to the others in Italian and one of them left the room. "We'll have to wait a while. I've sent Giacomo for some cards," she explained.

"Good idea," I said. I didn't think so. Long years in boring English officers' messes has cured me of card playing forever but I needed to make nice for a while, cards would help. It might take the bastards' minds off trying other games on me, like the old knife in the back trick. This way I could keep my eyes on them. I sat back and waited until Giacomo returned with a deck of cards.

I picked myself a new chair, with its back to the wall, and let them teach me their card game. It was a form of blackjack called *sette-mezzo*, seven and a half. They played with a cut down deck, only face cards and ace through seven. It's an easy game and I'm no dummy but I was eighty-two thousand lire in the hole by the time the younger of the two heavies came back into the room.

The others stood up as he spoke rapidly in Italian. Then the men nodded and Carla turned to me. "There is news. The boy has been located. We will go and get him."

"Why not call in the police?" I asked her. It's what any North American would have done but she greeted the idea with a sneer.

"The police would take all the credit and Mr. Ridley wouldn't know how hard we had worked on his behalf," she said.

"Okay, so what happens now?"

"Now we wait until dark and then go and get him."

"Just like that?" I mocked her.

"It may be more difficult than that, but you will have a chance to show how good you really are, Mr. Locke," she promised. Then she laughed, a nasty bray, like a tenor sax vibrato. "If you're good enough," she said. "Because the people who have him are very good indeed."

▸ 12 ◂

My gut did its customary flip-flop at the thought of solid risk. It's always that way, when you get briefed on the operation while you're snug and warm and miles back from the front line. All the men I served with were the same. You react by making jokes or falling silent but your stomach is contracting against the slam of imaginary bullets and your heart is racing. Later, when the chips are down and you're fighting automatically, the way you've been trained to fight, the fear goes away, but the briefing always chills you. This one was worse than usual. I'd be going in with a couple of play-acting amateurs instead of a squad of men trained as well as I was.

But you don't let it show. You get on with your job. Mine was taking care of the Ridley family so I said, "Let me phone Mrs. Ridley. She's worrying about the boy," but Carla vetoed that one.

"She can do the 'my hero' number when you take the kid back," she said and laughed. "She's quite a looker, did you get lucky?"

I looked at her as she stood there, safe behind the twin fences of her beauty and the protection of her scumbag boyfriend and I snapped back, "did anyone ever tell you you're a class act?" She opened her mouth to answer but I cut her off. "If they did they were lying."

She took it coldly but calmly. "Brave talk, Locke. Remember, I'm your ticket to the kid. Any more crap and I'll throw you to the wolves."

She was right, she could have done it so I said nothing. The others were watching her in polite astonishment. I guess she was always courteous around them. As Scavuzzo's mistress she could afford to be gracious to the poor people. This snarling was out of character. Giacomo, the man I'd decked, looked at me carefully. Maybe he assumed there was something between Carla and me. It's the first assumption any guy would make, especially in Italy. I wondered if his suspicions would be reported back to Scavuzzo, and if so, how it would affect Carla's tenure. Ah well, that was her problem, if her body needed guarding, she could pay me to do it.

Since there was nothing to do but wait we were fed. One of the young guys went out and came back with bread and olives and prosciutto and a bottle of wine. The food was good but I stayed away from the wine. If the competition was as sharp as we figured I didn't want to be sleepy come nightfall.

Afterwards we sat in a beautiful room among lovely pictures and antiques and played their dumb card game until it got dark outside. Carla drew the drapes and put the lights on. Then the old guy came back in. He beckoned to me and I went out after him, down the hallway and back to a big comfortable den with heavy furniture. He led me in and shut the door behind us.

"My friend is going to instruct the others. I wanted to speak to you," he said. He was smoking a thin black cigar that smelt like a burning barbershop.

"You've got two different plans, one for them, one for me?" It sounded like a setup and all my receptors were tingling. I was here to get Herbie back, not to wind up dead in some crummy scheme.

"It is the same plan, in two different parts," he said easily. He spat out a shred of tobacco, then put his cigar back in his mouth and waved towards the couch. "Sit down."

I sat and he sat behind his desk. "The boy is held by a man called Mazzerini, not by him, of course, by his men, his *soldati*. They are in a warehouse."

"Is it empty?" I've done enough house-to-house searches in Ulster to know the chances of getting killed in a building full of hiding places among piled crates.

"Probably not," he said. "But we think that the boy is in the cellar. There are no windows, nobody could hear him if he shouted, it is the best place for him."

I thought of Herbie, lying in the dark, wondering how the police were ever going to find him. It didn't sit well. "How many *soldati?*" I asked.

He shrugged. "Four, five maybe. We have no way of telling."

It still didn't smell right, so I pushed him. "How can you be sure that the boy's there?"

He took his cigar out of his mouth and stared at me. I guess he didn't get asked many questions. "You worry a lot," he said.

"I've been in a lot of worrying situations, *signor*. I've found it pays to be careful. How did you get the information?"

"One of the men in the warehouse talks to me. He called after he had finished his work. He says they drove in with the car and the boy was in it. They took him to the back office. The cellar is underneath."

"Did he get a look at the boy?"

"He says the boy walked to the office. He was afraid but he was not hurt."

"So what's your plan, and what are the two parts?"

Now he grinned, yellow teeth clenched on the cigar. "Can you keep your mouth shut and listen good?" he asked.

"Right to the end."

"Okay." He set the cigar down in the heavy ashtray and started talking business, looking at me the whole time without blinking.

The plan was straightforward. Carla would drive up to the front of the warehouse and make a fuss. She would have some story about being promised delivery of a parcel and its not having arrived. She would be wearing something delicious and most of the boys in the band would probably crowd to the front to check the view. If she could convince them to open the door, one of the soldiers I'd been playing cards with would rush in with a sawed-off shotgun and take charge. Meanwhile the other guy and I would be on the roof, breaking in through the skylight. We would start our entry as soon as we heard Carla laying down the law outside.

"And you think they'll believe some woman is coming after a parcel at that time of night?"

He shrugged. "The *signora* is rich. Rich people get what they want in Italy. The men will argue but they will listen."

He could be right, I thought. If they were dedicated socialists they would be glad of the chance to swear at a rich bitch. If they weren't, she might con them into trying to find the package. Either way they would open the door.

"That might get the door open, but it still won't work."

"What makes you say that?" He blew smoke and looked bored. He gave the orders, he didn't listen to suggestions.

"You need more men. Eight would be ideal. Two on the roof like you said, three front, three back. You blow the doors and pour in."

He snorted. "Blow the doors. An' I suppose the people on the street don't hear? They don't call the *polizia?* They don't look, see what's 'appening?"

He had a point there. This was my first nonmilitary expedition. We didn't have any authority to go into that building. Unless we were in and out in seconds we'd be in a gunfight with the *polizia,* probably the Carabinieri, with the nubby little grease guns they parade around with in the airports. I had no choice. I did it their way, even if their way was a Chinese fire drill, or I didn't do it at all.

I didn't let him off the hook too easily. I took him through it a couple of times and it always came up the same. It wasn't much of a plot but it was complete, as far as it went. And then I asked him my own questions. "Okay, what do we do with the guys inside? Are you taking handcuffs or tape to tie up your prisoners?"

His face was like a rock. "We do not take prisoners."

"Then you can count me out. I didn't come to Florence to shoot a lot of Italian fish in a barrel."

He struggled with that one, spluttering angrily. "Fish in a barrel? You mean you will not shoot these men who have taken the boy and killed other men?"

"Not in my job description," I told him and stood up. "Either you order something to secure prisoners or I take you with me to the police." I stood up and put my hands on my hips, flopping the jacket open so he could see my gun.

He looked at it, pursing his lips angrily, then waved one hand. "All right. We got tape. You take tape."

I would have liked better equipment than he'd suggested. The tape was only part of it. I would have liked the stun grenades we'd used on the Iranian embassy in London. Drop a couple of them into the warehouse and you could walk in with no opposition But I doubted that he could have got them so I called it quits and nodded. "In that case, I'm ready when you are."

"Good." He stood up too and stretched out his hand. I shook it and he said, *"Buona fortuna."* I'd have believed him a little better if he had managed to avoid that snaky grin of his, but what the hell, this plan made more sense than sitting around in the Hotel Rega, waiting for the phone to ring. What other choice did I have?

I went back to the sitting room. The two heavies were cleaning their guns. One had a Beretta, the other a U.S. Army Colt .45. Useful if we had to hit the wall of the warehouse from inside.

I took out my own piece and borrowed their gear, cleaning out the smoky barrel and oiling the mechanism properly. It was a newish gun and had been looked after. I wiped it dry and put it back in my holster, remembering that the load was short one round. I'd had a full magazine plus one up the spout. Now there were only seven rounds left. It should be enough. If it wasn't, I was in deep trouble.

The evenings in Florence are as noisy as the days. People don't finish work until seven or eight and then they head out for dinner around nine. Even the quiet street we were on was rattling with chatter and the endless popping of Vespas and little cars until ten o'clock. Then we moved.

The two hoods split up. Giacomo dropped the sawed-off shotgun in a plastic bag and got into the tiny rear seat of Carla's Mercedes. Savario, the other gunnie, carried a roll of heavy strapping tape and a coil of rope in another plastic shopping bag. He came with me in a Fiat. The only extra equipment I'd been given was a flashlight. That and my Walther would have to take care of me.

Savario spoke no English but Carla had gone over the plan for us. If she was angry at me she was too professional to let it show. The way she explained it we would climb onto the roof of the place next door. It was higher than the warehouse and we would drop onto the roof then down through the skylight on our handy-dandy Alpine rope. I would go first and make for the ground floor back. Savario would follow.

The plan had more holes than a Swiss cheese but I figured to be able to hook Herbie out of his cave singlehanded, once I was inside. Savario could follow and tape up the casualties. The biggest anxiety I had was that Giacomo would get in the front door with his shotgun and blast me. He played in a rough league and I had made him look small. It depended on how much value his boss put on my hide. Maybe it was enough to keep Giacomo's finger off that trigger.

The warehouse was on the edge of town, about a mile from the place where Herbie had been snatched. If Capelli had been telling the truth about roadblocks they must have been set up farther out, where the street turned back into highways. We saw a few cops on the street but no other signs of official action.

Savario was a good wheelman. He drove past the place at the same speed as everything else that was moving, pointing it out to me with his thumb, then he went up three blocks before turning off and heading back towards the rear of it.

The rear was another street but Savario had the key to the building we wanted. He parked the car a block away and we walked down to the office building. He let us in and locked the door behind us. It was like something out of Charles Dickens. The door had a big deadbolt lock on it and it was wooden and high, not like the modern glass doors of North America. Once we were in we were out of sight.

I headed for the stairs but Savario put his hand on my arm. "*Ascensore,*" he said cheerfully, and followed up with what could have been the Italian for "why walk when you can ride." I grinned politely and followed him into the old-fashioned cage.

The owners of the building must have been pretty laid-back about burglary. There was no alarm on the door that led to the roof. But then, why bother when guys like Savario had keys to the front?

I tied our rope in a highwayman's hitch to a ring in the wall, then we let ourselves down the fifteen feet to the roof of the warehouse and I jerked the other end of the rope and it untied and fell into my arms.

The roof of the warehouse had two low risers in it and there was a chimney beside the skylight, ready-made for anchoring our rope. We coupled it and waited, nursing the pry bar Savario had brought in his bag, until ten-thirty-eight when we heard the ugly screaming of Carla's diversion out front, right on cue.

Her involvement was the only sensible part of the scheme. It wouldn't have worked if she'd been a man. Somebody would have come to the window and told his fortune for him. But Italians could give me pointers on chauvinism. They wouldn't doubt that she was genuinely looking for something. They expected women to act stupidly. They would come to the window only to explain why she was nuts but they would all come, and they would all listen, trying to get off their one-liners so they could relive them later over their grappa. That's the way I hoped it would work, anyway.

We checked over the top and saw her standing in front of the door, haranguing at the top of her voice. Then a light came on inside and Savario nudged me. We went back to the skylight and quickly pried up one pane of the heavy glass that projected out over the edges of the opening in the roof. It shattered but we had it muffled with a sack so it was only half-volume, only loud enough to waken half the dead.

I glanced around the roof once more and let myself down on the rope, clutching it between knees and clenched elbows so I could slip to the floor in one motion. I went down it like a fireman down his pole, so quickly that I was well inside when I heard the gunshots below me on the ground floor. Pistol shots. That meant Giacomo hadn't gotten off the first round. Which meant he was dead. I was only a yard from the floor when the rope above me gave way and I fell inside. Savario had cut the rope. I guessed he got scared by the shots. After I was dead he would tell his boss the rope had broken and he couldn't follow. Nobody would know different.

I rolled away from the drop zone. It was pitch dark but I had the flashlight stuck down my left sock. If I managed to get downstairs in one piece and find the back office I could check the story of the trapdoor. The hell with Savario.

I crouched against a pile of cardboard boxes, listening hard. No feet pounded upstairs. No voices shouted instructions at one another to go and check the broken window. All I could hear was the faint street sounds, flooding up the side of the building and spilling in through the broken skylight. It meant only one thing. Whoever had shot Giacomo knew I was in the building and was lying in wait for me. Probably at the foot of the stairs, waiting for the little mouse to stick his head out of his hole so they could blow it off.

I waited for about ten minutes but nothing broke the silence in the building. They could be just as patient as me. It was changing nothing. I had to move.

I hadn't had much time to look over the building as we drove by but I had noticed one very ordinary feature. The windows were placed above one another. It was the same back and front. That meant that if Herbie really was in a cellar inside the back office, he was accessible from the back office of this floor, given a rope and surprise. And I still had the rope.

Carefully I retrieved it. It was about thirty feet long, I'd been generous when I flopped it down the open skylight and Savario had done the cutting outside, between the skylight and the chimney we'd tied to. I coiled it over my shoulder and wormed back to the rear of the floor, listening for movement in the building. None came. I checked the offices. There were two of them, Victorian fashion, half-glass so the boss could look up from his desk and be sure all his elves were working. The doors were fastened with simple Yale locks and it took only one second with a credit card to open one of them.

I went inside and waited another minute, still straining my ears for sounds. Still nothing. I imagined the men's smiles would be turning into scowls by now but they would hold themselves ready at the stairs, superior in firepower and cunning. They would wait all night if necessary, guarding their prisoner. In daylight they would come up and if I'd managed to scramble out they would shrug philosophically. They'd done their job, they had Giacomo's carcass to prove it. I felt for the poor bastard. Guts is fine but it won't win over luck or training, preferably both.

There was no handy radiator to tie my rope to but the window was a casement and I was able to open it silently and knot the rope around the hinge. Nearly ready. Now I had just one thing left, a diversion, then I could move.

I felt my way down the middle of the floor, judging the path by the square of grayness that was the broken skylight. At the far end of the room there was an ancient cage-style elevator. I pressed the button and it groaned upwards.

I listened hard and it seemed that I could hear a shuffling going on, below the whining and scraping of the elevator mechanism. The boys downstairs were stirring, waiting for me to make my terminal mistake. The elevator reached my floor and stopped. I opened it, using a half-second flash from my light to locate the controls, then threw a cardboard box into it and pressed the down button, stepping back as it started to descend.

In the eight seconds it took to reach the ground floor I had sprinted on tiptoe back to the office, pushed through the window, and was ten feet down the rope, poised just above the lower window.

I heard the elevator stop with a whine and then two rapid shots, big flat bossy bangs from Giacomo's shotgun. And as the echoes rattled around me I slid another six feet, kicking away from the wall so I could pendulum back again, feet first through the glass of the downstairs office.

I chimed through the shattering glass, eyes clenched shut against splinters. The rope checked against the top of the window and I let go, landing on my feet behind a big old desk. There were lights on in the warehouse beyond the same half-glass walls I'd seen in the offices on the floor above.

At the far end of the floor three men were standing around the elevator, one of them with Giacomo's sawed-off pump gun, the others with pistols, their heads screwed around towards me. The man with the shotgun reacted first, starting to raise it but pulling the trigger a moment later than I did. I hit him in the face. He hit the guy next to him in the legs, blowing one of them off. The third guy threw down his gun and sank to his knees screaming at me with his hands clenched as if in prayer.

I came out of the office on the run, moving fast enough to throw any other gunman off a clean shot. But no shot came. There were only the three of them in the place. One dead, one dying, one paralyzed with fear. Then I saw Giacomo sprawled alongside the elevator, his looted pockets pulled inside out.

I rapped the fearful one in both collarbones with the barrel of my pistol and he collapsed, yowling. I whipped his belt off and wrapped it around the stump of the other guy's leg, twisting it tight with a cargo hook until the gouting blood slowed to a pulsing seepage. Then I left him and ran to the back office again pulling back the worn rug from the floor, checking for a cellar entrance.

There was nothing in the floor of the office I'd crashed. I went next door, smashing the glass with my pistol to reach through and turn the latch. I whisked the rug aside and found the trap door. I opened it and called down into the darkness. "Herbie, can you hear me?" I was too wary to shine my light down the hole. I kept to one side and called again and this time I heard a groan. I swung onto the edge of the hole and vaulted down the seven feet to the floor, avoiding the steps, landing in sawdust and rolling as I would have done after a parachute drop.

I ended up beside a man who was lying like an

abandoned pile of clothing. I could tell without looking that it wasn't Herbie. He smelt of garlic and urine and fear. And the words he was hissing at me were all in Italian.

I flicked on my flashlight and checked him over. His hands were tied behind him and his face was bruised shapeless, like an apple that's been used as a football by a grade-school class. One eye was shut and most of his teeth were gone but through all the damage there was enough to tell me that this was the guy who had approached Herbie and me in the restaurant, the day before.

▸ 13 ◂

I holstered my gun and pulled my knife, slashing the ropes off his wrists and ankles. He groaned and seemed to fall apart, flopping into a totally relaxed posture, fingers half open, legs sprawling, reaction against the cramp he had been suffering while he was tied. After a second or so he got control of himself and rolled up into a sitting position, rubbing his hands weakly. I grabbed him by the shoulder and hoisted him to his feet. "We've got to get out of here. Let's go."

He mumbled something and tried to walk but his feet were still numb and he fell. I threw him over my shoulder in a fireman's lift and headed up the steps to floor level. He moaned at each step I took and made a feeble effort to adjust his position over my shoulder. He had internal injuries I guessed. Whoever had worked him over had worked him all the way over, ribs and gut as well as the head. It had been a professional bashing, probably with a solid purpose, like finding out where Herbie was. And that made me think, even as I lifted him up and listened for sounds in the warehouse. Why had Carla's friends lied to me? Why hadn't they told me Herbie wasn't there? Had they just been afraid their own men would chicken out on the attack? It seemed they were right but I hadn't come to Italy to act as cannon fodder for the Mob. They could carry out their own bloody rescues if this was the way they handled things.

I paused below floor level, drawing my gun and snapping a couple of quick glances over the top and all around to check that the coast was clear. It seemed to be. I climbed the last five steps and toppled my find into the armchair. "Wait there," I told him, "I'll find us some way to leave."

His English was gone now, he was in shock but he nodded and said, "*Sí*," and sat still, too beat even to rub his numbed wrists.

I ran down the length of the warehouse and glanced out of the front window. Carla's car was down the block about fifty paces and I could see the glow of a cigarette on the driver's side. She was waiting like a good little mobster for the boys to come marching home. Fine. That much had gone right in the plan.

I went to the big door at the front. It had a little Judas door set in it and I half opened it and waved my flashlight at her, keeping my face out of sight. There was a thirty-second wait, and then I heard the car approach, then the door opening, and the tritch-tratch of her high heels crossing the cobbles.

She was saying something haughty in Italian until I reached out and grabbed her wrist and pulled her inside. That made her shriek, but it was only a tiny noise and it died when she saw my gun.

"We can talk later, sweetheart. But first I've got a sick man to move away from here. You're going to find us somewhere cozy." I let go of her and rebolted the Judas door. She made no attempt to run. Possibly she thought her boys were still in charge. She walked ahead of me, rapidly, unafraid, towards the back of the building and when we came to the blood and the bodies she gave only a tiny gasp. "Giacomo's been shot," she said, without turning.

"It's too late to help him. But the other guy needs a doctor, pronto. You can call an ambulance as we leave. If he gets help within twenty minutes he could make it."

She shrugged and walked on while the wounded man stared at her, open-mouthed in his agony, his eyes glazing, too shocked even to moan at her callousness. I stooped to check his tourniquet. The bleeding from the stump had stopped altogether now but the other leg was still bleeding steadily. I figured he was down to about fifteen minutes left.

Carla was in the front office, talking to the guy I'd found in the cellar, half-screaming a torrent of anger. He held up one hand feebly but she bored on. When I came in he said, "*Signor,* please. I need a doctor."

"Right away," I promised. "Carla, get his arm over your shoulder, I want you taking half his weight."

She straightened up, nostrils flaring like a blood mare. "Me, touch this, this thing?"

"Grab him and support him or I'll break your teeth," I said. I'd never come up against a woman as arrogant as she was. Tough, yes, some of the undercover women of Ulster had been even tougher, but hard as any of them had been they had always had compassion, at least for their own men. Not this woman, she looked at life as if it were a mirror, seeing nothing anywhere but herself.

She hissed her fury but not at me, nor the injured guy, it was a blind gesture of protest at Fate. She took his arm over her shoulder and we staggered him out to the front. I stuck my gun into the front of my belt, and unlocked the Judas door.

I reached across the back of our burden and held Carla by the wrist, locking her thumb under mine so that she couldn't pull away. "You're going through first. If there's anyone out there, you start laughing and acting drunk. Got that?"

"Let go of my thumb," she said.

"When you've been a good girl. Cross me up and I'll

tear it off for you." I was angry. She'd got me into this and I'd been lied to and I'd been deserted under fire. I wasn't going to take any more nonsense from her or anybody else.

She stuck her head out of the door, then tugged at my hand. "It's clear, come on."

I stooped to lift the man's feet over the foot-high lip at the bottom of the door, then followed him out and pulled the door shut behind me. We covered the fifteen paces to her car and I propped our man against it and let go of her wrist. She jerked her hand away. "You sonofabitch," she hissed.

"Give me your keys." I held my hand out and she reached into her bag. I knew what was happening before she could complete the move and grabbed her fingertips, my thumb underneath them, fingers locked on top, and rolled the heel of my hand upwards, putting a near breaking strain on her hand. She yelped and flopped down and the gun she had been drawing clattered out onto the stones. I picked it up with my left hand and released her. "I want your keys," I repeated. In the dim light of the street I could see that her eyes were filled with tears, fury probably, I hadn't hurt her. She was as proud as she was beautiful and I had gotten right under her skin.

She gave me her keys and I opened the door to push the man in but she said, "No, there are roadblocks. He must go in the trunk."

"Where the hell are we taking him?" I asked her. As we were talking a pair of lovers came down the street, arms around one another's waists. I let our man's head sag and turned him so that I was between his battered face and the kids, who weren't watching us anyway. Carla picked up her cue like a movie star. She came up to me flirtingly and laughed and put one arm around my neck, obscuring our prisoner still further. She whispered to me, teasingly. The kids must have thought she was making romantic promises. She wasn't.

"You've just killed a man. If you let the police get to

you you'll rot in jail for the next thirty years. Got that?"

I beamed at her, for the benefit of the kids, and said through my big happy smile, "It was self-defense."

"Marvelous," she cooed. "You kill a man after you've broken into the premises to commit a felony. That's murder."

"I wasn't going to commit any felony, I was going to spring this sonofabitch, thinking it was Herbie."

"That might work in Canada. Here you're just another foreigner running around with a gun. That makes you either a crook or a terrorist. Either way you'll be sixty-five before they let you out."

She may not have been right. Maybe I should have gone to the police and taken my chances, and my lumps. But the *maggiore's* warning was still fresh in my head. No guns. No violence. Let the police do it. I didn't have any friends down at headquarters. And I hadn't recovered Herbie so I couldn't expect Kate Ridley to go to bat for me. "Okay. So what now?"

"Do as you're told and we'll get the kid back and you get off the murder charge," she said.

It sounded better than her first suggestion so I unlocked the trunk and when the kids were safely past I rolled the man into it. "Lie quiet, we're taking you somewhere safe," I told him and shut the lid. Then I gave the keys to Carla. "You drive."

She went around the car, not lifting her eyes from mine, it was as if she figured her gaze was a dental drill and I was a rotten tooth that was going to cave under pressure. I just made sure she didn't run off. When she sat behind the wheel, I got in and slammed the door.

"We need somewhere to stay overnight, somewhere we can get a doctor to look at the guy in the back. What do you suggest?"

She twisted the key in the ignition, holding it after the engine started so that the starter motor whined. "Just stop ordering me around," she said. "Remember that I'm the one with the answers and keep your mouth shut and we'll get on just fine."

That didn't sit well but she was right so I just waved one hand at her and sat back in the seat as if this whole thing was my idea.

She pulled away from the curb, honking at a Vespa scooter with a couple of kids on it who seemed to be trying to consummate their courtship while driving sixty miles an hour.

"We cannot go to my place, that's impossible."

"Why, are those other scumbags going to be looking for you?"

"It is not in my plan," she said.

"What plan?"

"You don't need to know the details. But I will tell you a little of it, just so you understand where you fit in."

"Go ahead. Maybe it'll make more sense than what's been happening so far," I said.

"Understand that I am in charge of this kidnapping. Me." She took one hand off the wheel and pointed a finger at her bust. "Me," she repeated. "Not Scavuzzo, not Tassone, me."

"Okay. You get your name above the title when they make the movie. Then what?"

She flicked a glance at me and it seemed that her mouth turned upwards in amusement but her tone was serious. "There are things to do. Other people heard of the ransom. Other people took the boy away. We have to get him back. When we do, I get the money, you get the boy. You take him back to his parents and the police forget about that dead man at the warehouse."

"They'd be more likely to forget it if I get the kid back before the money is paid out," I said.

"You have no choice," she said simply. "If you try to use force on me I will lead you to the wrong places and you'll get blown away. Work with me and you win, work against me and you end up dead or in jail. Take your pick."

"Look, let's see how serious you are. There's a man

in that warehouse who'll die if you don't call him an ambulance. Do that right away and I'll consider what you're saying." That was part altruism, part cunning. I needed time to think things through, to work out just how deep in trouble I already was.

"All right." She slammed the brakes on. "There's a phone in that restaurant, I can use that. Wait here."

"Nice try," I told her. "I'll come with you."

She slammed the car door and then walked quickly into the restaurant, smiled a million dollar's worth of charm at the maître d', and picked up the phone. I watched her dial 0 and then chatter rapidly, including the word *ambulanza*. She could have been stringing me along but it was enough for me. I didn't owe the guy in the warehouse anything more friendly than a bullet but I hate to see wounded left untended, anybody's wounded. And if the ambulance arrived soon he might make it.

We went back to the car and got in. She drove off more calmly this time, thinking hard. I didn't interrupt her. I was doing some thinking of my own. I was in trouble. The *maggiore* had warned me not to go anywhere, raise any hell. Capelli had turned a blind eye to it but since then I had killed a man. If I'd found Herbie in the basement I could have got away with it. But now my best bet was to steer clear of Capelli for a few days, trying to find Herbie on my own, with whatever help I could squeeze out of Carla and the guy I'd found down the hole in the floor.

We crossed the river and I glanced at Carla. "You're heading out of town?"

"It's the only choice."

She reached the end of the bridge and turned left. Ahead of us I saw the roadblock, a couple of "road-up" trestles, holding the outward bound traffic down to a single lane. A pair of uniformed cops were standing there, looking bored. They brightened when we drove up. From thirty yards away, down the beam of the headlight, you could see their faces get more animated as they made out our car, something out of the run of Fiats and vans.

"Keep your mouth shut, just smile and nod," Carla told me out of the corner of her mouth.

She stopped beside the policeman, wound her window down and asked "*Che?*" which I knew meant "What?" and was about as polite. It worked. The coppers were younger than she was. I could see them glancing at one another, preparing the comments on her beauty that they would make to one another after we'd gone. But in her presence they were like little boys in front of their grade school teacher. They fell over one another to be nice, explaining everything to her. One of them made the mistake of leaning down and putting his hand on the frame of the open window. She stiffened and he moved his hand as guiltily as if it had been on her thigh, which she had been careful to leave half uncovered. After a minute they saluted her and she paid them off with a smile and drove by.

"Nice going. What would you have done if they'd wanted to look in the trunk?" I asked casually.

"There is no secret to controlling policemen, any men," she said snootily.

"Not for you. I'll give you that much. You're not just a pretty face."

"God!" she said. "Do any of you ever grow up?"

We drove for thirty-five minutes through the dark, past a cheerful Italian muddle of vineyards and olive groves and small fields. We went through a couple of villages, places with only a few lights still on this late. Then we came to an old stone farm with a wall around it. Carla swept through the gateway at forty miles an hour and jerked to a stop, inches short of the midden. "Come on," she told me and got out.

I followed her towards the farm door, which was opened by a woman, dumpy and sixtyish, dressed in the inevitable black.

She and Carla exchanged shrieks of Italian that would have seemed angry if they hadn't ended up kissing one another on the cheek. Then the woman spoke to me but I stood and smiled in the darkness, letting Carla explain how dumb I was. In the meantime I was checking the farmhouse as a defensive position. Unless the enemy used mortars, a couple of men could hold out here for days. The wall around the barnyard was eighteen inches thick, the house itself was solid. Carla had chosen well.

Now we were safe I asked Carla for the keys. She handed them to me, not even looking at me, and I opened the trunk. The man groaned and eased himself out. That was a good sign. If he was well enough to move on his own, he might get away without doctoring. I knew he needed a tetanus shot but if he'd ever had one before he would manage.

The women rattled on some more and then Carla told me, "Take him inside, I'll put the car away in the barn."

"I'm sticking with you," I told her. "For all I know, this could be another setup."

"For Jesus' sweet sake," she hissed but she didn't argue when I leaned the wounded man against the farmhouse wall and sat in the car as she drove it into a barn. I helped her shut and bar the big door then we went back to the house. The woman had the wounded man on a chair in the kitchen and was heating water on a gas stove. She chattered at Carla when we came in, and Carla told me, "She says this man has been beaten, did you do it?"

"Tell her no, I've got enough enemies on the go for one night. I don't need her after me."

She lifted her face and laughed, the first honest sound that had come out of her all evening. "You're scared of an old woman?"

"Terrified." I grinned at her. "I'm hoping she's going to feed us and I keep remembering that Lucrezia Borgia was from around here somewhere."

"You know your history," Carla said and made an approving little nod. If it was intended to soften me up it was a failure. I just wondered what she had in mind for me. Was a posse of men in black shirts with white ties coming to blow holes in me? That was about the only event I could imagine that could make Carla spontaneously cheerful.

She said something else but I ignored her, watching while the woman sponged away the blood and dirt from the cuts in the man's face. He was tough—I gave him that—he didn't flinch; but then, she was moving carefully, the way a milkmaid washes the udder of a restive cow. Any attempt at gentleness had to be heaven against the hell he'd gone through in that hole in the ground.

"Who kicked you?" I asked him and he blinked as if coming back into his body was a task almost too much for him. I repeated the question and he spoke at last.

"One of them was the man with his leg gone. I think God punished him for what he did."

"If God worked the way you think, *signor,* the world would be full of one-legged men," I told him. "Why were they beating you?"

"It was about the boy. They thought I knew where he was."

Another possibility shot to hell, he didn't know where Herbie was either. "What's your name, your real name?"

His voice suddenly changed, as if he recognized how much less a wheel he was now than he had been yesterday morning. "I am called Giovanni Mazzerini," he said.

I sniffed. Carla was watching me out of her big emerald eyes, wondering if I was smart enough to remember the original cover story. I was. "That's supposed to be your warehouse, is it?"

He shook his head, gently, flinching as he bumped his face against the gentle fingers of the old woman. "I do not own warehouses, *signor,* I am a little man."

"Somebody thought you were big, or else they thought you were lying to them, which was it?"

He shrugged again, a tiny movement, like a baby's first uncertain steps. He was going to get better, once he started talking with his whole body I would know he was fit.

"I was with the men who took the boy from you this morning." He gave an officious little gasp and his hand came up to make that stroking motion down his cheek. "You were a tiger, *signor.*"

"You got away with the boy. Where is he? What happened, I thought you guys were all shot?"

Now he was recovered enough to strut a little for me, still reclining on the old faded couch but his body stiffened; if he could have stood up he would have swaggered. "Nobody shoots me," he said.

"You ran like hell, I guess," I said. I liked him better devalued, it wouldn't pay to have him striking poses.

"I escaped," he said primly.

"Then you must have seen who got the boy. Tell me or I'll take over where those other guys left off, and I'm stronger than they were."

That deflated him. He shrugged again but it was defeated. "They were just men, ordinary men, with guns."

"More than one?"

"Two men," he said, proud again at his escape.

"Two men with guns and you got away without being shot? You're lying to me, Giovanni, and I don't like liars. You were part of the plan, weren't you?"

"No," he almost screamed it. The old woman turned and scowled at me and muttered something but made no attempt to interfere. She looked old enough to remember the war. Maybe she'd seen the Germans working over a partisan, maybe right here in this kitchen. Her face told me she figured I was no better. I smiled at her and spoke to Carla. "Tell this old trout that I saved this man's life, will you?"

Carla spoke and the woman answered and the man tried to chime in. It was like having a seat at a new opera. I got annoyed. "For Christ's sake, I don't need the last act of *Pagliacci.* I just want to pick this guy's memory a little."

Carla held up her hand and the woman stopped speaking.

Giovanni said, "I am telling you the truth, *signor*. I got away. I ran, they shot at me, they missed. They did not miss my friends."

"If you don't know who shot at you, you must know who kicked you."

He flicked a glance at Carla. "I think the *signora* knows the men better than I do."

I straightened out and turned to Carla. "You and I need to have a little, chat, Carla. We can do it here or we can do it in private. Which would you suggest?"

She stood there, as proud as a lioness. "If you hurt me my friends will kill you."

"Spare me the drama. Let's talk."

"Come," she said, flicking her head imperiously towards the door. I followed her and we went out of the kitchen into the family parlor. It was crowded with furniture, big stuffed chairs and a horsehair couch and religious pictures on the walls, the Sacred Heart, Saint Sebastian, the Madonna. I hoped it made Carla feel like confessing.

I indicated a chair and she sat, crossing her knees primly.

"Okay, what did he mean by saying you knew the men who were kicking him?"

She flared. "You listen to scum like him?"

"Frankly I don't know who's lying and who's telling the truth. But something isn't kosher. Your friends lied to me, certainly. They told me Herbie was in that warehouse. Why would they do that?"

She shrugged. "You were there. You were useful. They sent you. I suppose that chickenshit Savario ran when he heard shooting."

"Like a rabbit," I agreed. "But how come you didn't whisk me back to the old homestead? Then we could find out where Herbie is from this guy we've picked up and go get him."

"I don't want to share the information with them. We don't need them anymore, now we've got a line on where the kid is," she said.

"But I thought you were working with them."

She smiled a taut smile, the kind you see on the faces of aging movie stars afraid their makeup will chip. "If you're crossing a river you need a boat. But when you're across the river and climbing a mountain, why carry the boat?"

"Okay. I'm impressed. You took a course on comparative religion and studied Zen. What the hell does that have to do with Herbie?"

"Given a few minutes with that garbage in the kitchen I will know where the boy is," she said. "I no longer need the help of my former friends."

"That's great, but what if somebody else finds out before you do?"

"They will be killed." She looked at me like a kindergarten teacher looking at the class dunce. "You have to understand, Locke, there's big money at stake here."

"Big money nothing. His father is just a run-of-the-mill millionaire. In fact, less, he's spread too thin. He doesn't have a whole bunch of cash to slap around on ransoms. That's all an illusion."

Now she sneered. "You are still a soldier, aren't you? You'll never be anything more. Didn't your employer ever tell you that he took out five million dollars' worth of kidnap insurance on his son?"

▸ 14 ◂

It must have amused her to see my chin hit my chest. Five million dollars' worth of ransom insurance? He had never mentioned it to me, the bodyguard, and yet these wolves knew all about it. That meant only one thing. Ridley was working some kind of scam. He had arranged the ransom money, and then arranged for the kidnapping. The Mafia picked up the kid, he paid up, and they would split the cash. Smart, or what?

"Then he's in this thing, up to his scummy eyeballs," I summed up.

Carla shook her head, pityingly. "You're a slow study, Locke. Of course he is. That's why he hired a bodyguard for the boy, to make it look as if it was all legitimate."

I moved a pace closer to her, close enough to be menacing but not close enough that her artfully crossed leg could swing up and put me out of the game. "Then what's to stop me clobbering you and driving back into town and giving this news to Capelli? Or is he in on this as well?"

"What's stopping you is that you've killed a man." She waved both hands, all Italian again. "Oh sure, you'd get an interested hearing from Capelli. Then the father would deny it and they would get around to counting bodies and find you were guilty. I don't think you'd like an Italian prison. A blue-eyed WASP surrounded by a thousand horny little Italian men for twenty-five years."

She was probably right there but that didn't matter. I wasn't anxious to spend time in anybody's jail, however well run. I backed off a pace and perched on the big soft arm of a chair. It looked as if I was a fugitive. If I had to cover up the killing of Giacomo I'd already left it too late. The police would have questioned the guy I'd spared in the warehouse. He would have sung the entire score of his favorite opera. I was a marked man. I'd been bested.

"Has the old bird next door got anything to drink around the place? This is getting a little heavy," I said. Clever, Locke. No sense irritating the fair Carla anymore. She was the only key to the prison door. If she could help me find the kid and put his father away, people might listen to me.

"They make their own grappa," Carla sneered. "It's not the kind of fancy drink you'd order but it may get your heart started again."

"A Christian sentiment," I told her, grinning like Stepin Fetchit.

I didn't even bother following her out of the room. I was in her hands for the next little while. I needed time to think.

She came back with a bottle of what looked like lighter fluid and two tiny thick glasses. "I think I'll join you," she said cheerfully. "This is the most fun I've had in a long time."

"The John Locke Protection and Entertainment Committee. We aim to please," I said and poured the drinks.

She raised hers mockingly. "*Cin-cin.*"

"May your shadow never grow less." I raised mine and took a glug. It was the real stuff. You could have run a jeep on it. I noticed she took hers down without a blink. I wondered if she could fight as well and drive a tank. She seemed tough enough, for all her beauty. I poured myself a second dram of white lightning and offered the bottle to her. She nodded and I topped her up. As a junior officer it had never been my job to plan strategy. Tactics yes. The only tactical move I could see filling the bill here was to get her drunk, that way she couldn't sell me downriver.

"The way I read all this, Ridley has an arrangement with your friends. They take the kid, he provides the money and they divvy it up after the smoke clears, right?"

"Right," she said and raised her glass again. Maybe it was the exhilaration of seeing me behind the eight-ball, maybe she was a wino, I'm not sure, but she glugged it down and handed me the glass. I refilled.

"The only fly in all this mutually profitable ointment is the fact that some ringer has grabbed the kid, right?"

"Right again," she said. She raised her glass then pointed to mine. "Hey, what's the matter, can't you handle a real drink?"

I threw mine back and had thirds, a half second before she was after her fourth glass. Nice going, Locke; two more of these and she'll be on her ear. Then all I'd have to do would be sneak past the last of the Borgias outside, hotwire the Mercedes, and head for the border. I could dump it there and take a train. Once I got into Germany I had some friends who could make me invisible.

I discarded the idea even as it rolled through my mind. No way was I running out on my job. I had to find Herbie. Dammit, I'd lost him, I had to get him back or break my contract and that was not my way of working.

"Maybe I can be useful when your soldiers find where the kid is being kept," I suggested. "I seem to be sharper than the bulk of the Mafia hoods around here."

She sat up straight and slammed her glass down on

the arm of the couch, bouncing it in the softness, jolting the contents out in a fine spray. "Mafia," she hissed. "That's the way you see it, isn't it? I'll bet you just loved *The Godfather,* didn't you?"

"I never saw it. I was in Oman, making like an Arab when it played."

My humor didn't humor her. "You live with clichés, you smug goddamn WASPs. You hear a word once and every Italian is tarred with that brush."

I held one hand up, making a pantomime of it, acting as if the liquor had hit me a lot harder than it had so far. "Look, no offense intended. Yes, it's a cliché, but this is Italy and Capelli told me that your father and your late husband were both killed by what he called Mafia people in the U.S."

"Wrong," she said.

"I'm only repeating what I heard. Sorry if it offends you."

"It angers me," she said, and there were tiny pinch marks on each side of her nose. "It angers me because it's wrong and it's glib."

"What did happen?" I asked gently. I wanted to understand her and she seemed close to speaking the truth.

She looked down into her glass, squeezing it tight enough to make all her knuckles white. "What happened was that my father married me off to a man he wanted to make a deal with. My own father treated me like a chattel, because I was his daughter, not his son."

"And then what?" I was coaxing, as if I was trying to talk her in from a window ledge.

"And then his deal didn't take." She looked up at me with her eyes blazing, but filled with tears. "My beloved husband killed my father with the help of some people from Italy."

"I'm sorry, Carla."

"Don't be. He got his, a week later," she said, pronouncing each word hard and separate.

"What happened? A gang war?"

She laughed, and dashed her tears away with the back of her hand. "That's what the police thought. Only they're wrong. I arranged it."

Deep waters. I just shook my head and looked sympathetic.

She stood up, holding her glass in both hands. Then she drained it and set it down on the table. "You're the only man I've ever told that to. Just you."

There was still nothing to say. I sat there on the arm of the chair and tried to look duly grateful.

"Yes, I went to New York. Yes, I came here and found my way in with this scum whose name you probably heard from Capelli." She turned and glared at me, nostrils flaring. God she was gorgeous.

"It all sounded plausible," I said apologetically. Maybe we were going to get some truth here. Or maybe it was amateur theatricals night and she was putting on a star performance.

"And of course, being a superior, blue-eyed sonofa-WASP-bitch, you believed him," she accused.

"I took note of it," I told her. "What the hell do I know? It seems nobody has said one word of truth to me since I got to Florence."

Not strictly true. Kate Ridley was straight but I didn't want to remind this woman of her.

She turned suddenly and picked up her glass and thrust it at me. I filled it and made like I was topping up my own. "Yes, I did those things," she said softly. "I did that and I slept with that greasy bastard for three months. You want to know why?"

A cue for the well-timed protest. Look shocked, Locke, look shocked, it could pay off with some real information. "No, you don't have to explain anything to me, Carla. I'm truly sorry for your loss."

"You may be, but Scavuzzo isn't. Not yet. He was behind my father's death. Him and my late husband. And I'm going to get even with him."

An imaginary light bulb flicked on over my head, filling my brain with blinding light. She was on my side!

That was why I hadn't been backshot. She wanted me whole so I could help her get revenge on Scavuzzo. I tried an obvious suggestion. "The way to get him would be to take the Ridley boy away from him and deprive him of the money."

She nodded, then sat down and sipped her liquor as if we were little girls playing tea parties. She lowered the glass and smoothed her skirt. "Agreed. But it has to be timed right. We have to wait until the money is paid, then get the kid and the cash."

"I like the way your mind works," I said, trying a hearty, army officer chuckle.

She looked up and smiled at me, sweetly as any of the Madonnas in the Galleria Uffizi. "Yes," she agreed again. "And then you kill him."

She meant it, I knew.

"That's liable to get me into even worse trouble than I'm in now," I said quietly. "At least if I'm arrested I'll be out before I'm old and gray. Scavuzzo's boys won't let me cop a plea. They'll kill me in return."

"Not if you're clever." She reached out and pushed her drink onto the edge of the table. "I think you can handle it, make it look as if somebody else did it, or like an accident. From what I've heard of the SAS they know as many rough tricks as the Cosa Nostra."

She was looking at me calmly now. She had laid down her hand, five aces. It was up to me to beat it or pay up.

I sipped my drink. It was a mistake. With grappa like that you have to short-circuit your tastebuds, whack it straight into your stomach and you manage fine, otherwise, you're aware of what you're doing to yourself. I frowned and said, "If we're going to do all these clever things, we're going to need a plan. The first thing I suggest is that we start trusting one another. I'll lighten up on you and you treat me like an ally not an enemy. Deal?"

"Deal," she said but she didn't smile or hold out her hand.

"How are we going to find out where Herbie is?"

"We can find out. All it takes is a little squeezing on that guy in the kitchen. He knows something. Either he was part of the second gang or else he recognized somebody. I can tell." Her voice was low and rough. It would have sounded sexy except for the subject.

"A number of guys have worn out their shoes trying to get him to talk. How do you think you can do better?" I asked.

"Their brains were in their feet," she said. She stood up. "Come on, let's get started."

She led the way and we went back into the kitchen where Mazzerini was sitting up on the sofa nursing a shot glass like the ones we'd been using. He looked up out of his lopsided face and tried to smile ingratiatingly.

Carla walked up to him and backhanded him across his biggest bruise, hard enough to send him sprawling. The old woman said something but Carla gave her a short burst of Italian and she backed away, nodding in agreement. Carla watched until the woman was out of the kitchen, then she turned back to Mazzerini.

"You think you're tough, don't you?" she hissed.

I wouldn't have thought I was, not with her staring me down. He was even quicker to agree with her.

"No, *signora*. I am not tough. I couldn't tell those men anything because I didn't know anything. It is the truth."

"Yeah, and I'm the Mona Lisa," Carla said. She turned to me. "Get me a knife, Locke, there has to be one somewhere around."

It was my chance to enter the masquerade. I took out my claspknife, clicked it open and handed it to her by the blade.

"Thank you," she said primly. I could see Mazzerini watching the knife. That was a mistake. You watch the eyes, not the weapon. The eyes drive the attack.

Then Carla crouched and caught hold of his pants by the crotch. She dug the blade into the fabric and pulled upwards quickly. I keep the blade sharp enough to shave with. It peeled the fabric apart like a split paper bag. He was wearing red shorts and he slammed both hands down over them. She stabbed him lightly in the back of both hands and he took them away, babbling, but before she could reach for his crotch again he talked.

"*Signora,* no. I will tell you everything."

She raised the knife blade and held it under his nostril. He pulled his head back as far as it would go but she moved with him. One false move and he knew what would happen.

"Names," she said.

"Vasoni," he said, and then burst into a torrent of Italian. I watched her as she listened, the knife still poised to slit his nose. She had to be the toughest woman since Ma Barker, no denying it. Once or twice she prompted him with short hissing sentences, then she straightened up. Mazzcrini made an effort to sink to his knees in front of her but she kicked him casually and turned away, handing me back my knife.

"We move in the morning," she said.

▸ 15 ◂

"Where to?" I pressed the lock on my knife and flipped the blade shut. Carla held one finger up to silence me and went through the door the old woman had taken. She closed it behind her and I heard the rattle of Italian conversation. I turned back to Mazzerini and asked him instead. "Where's the kid?"

"He is at the house of a man who works for Signor Vasoni." The backs of his hands were bleeding, welling up slow globules of dark blood that he sucked away. "She is a devil, *signor*. She said she would cut me."

"She'd have done it," I assured him. "It's a good thing I'm around or she would have killed you after you told her what she wanted to know." Standard interrogation tactics, courtesy of the SAS or any other agency. Get the prisoner to fear one of you, love the other. I didn't know how much good he could do me but it never hurts to go by the book.

The door opened and Carla came back, with her arm around the old woman. She introduced me. "John Locke" was all I could make out. Then the old woman said something and I took her hand and made a little bow. She beamed and said something else and Carla laughed.

"Maria's father worked for my grandfather," Carla explained and I smiled again at the old lady. "I've explained what happened and she's on our side. She's got a place we can lock him up until we go. I think he'd be better if you tied him up, but that's up to you, why not look at the place first?"

I followed the old woman out to another room on the ground floor, her wine cellar. It had a thick door with a big bolt on the outside. I wondered whether she used to lock her husband in when he climbed too deeply into the homemade grappa but in any case it would have held a bull. And when I looked inside I saw it had no windows.

"Bene," I told her and was rewarded with a quick spatter of talk. I went back to the kitchen and got Mazzerini to stand up straight. He held his side and moaned but I figured he was well enough to spend the night in the cellar. Too well, maybe, perhaps well enough to jiggle the bolt loose some way. "Is there any cord around? It doesn't have to be heavy—bootlaces, something like that."

Carla spoke to the old woman and she went off and came back with a roll of coarse string, the kind you would use to tie up a parcel. I thanked her and cut off a yard. Then I turned Mazzerini around and tied his thumbs together behind him. I didn't crank up the pressure. I just wanted him hampered in case he started feeling better through the night. Then I took him out to the wine cellar and locked him away. I did him the favor of filling a jar that stood there with red wine from a barrel and putting it where he could get his mouth on it and tilt it towards him if he needed some refreshment.

The women were still standing in the kitchen when I came back up. "Right, do we move now, or rest or what?" I asked.

"We rest," Carla said. "Maria's son is away. She has a spare bed."

"Fine. I'll crash on the couch," I said and moved towards the other room.

Carla laughed. "She thinks you're my husband, you dumb bastard."

That startled me but I covered it. "Dandy. I'll do my best to live up to my obligations," I said.

Carla laughed and kissed the old woman and then took my hand. When in Tuscany do as the Tuscans do, Locke. I didn't go as far as kissing the old lady, not being sure what the custom might be, but I beamed at her and followed her up the stairs.

The son's room was strictly utilitarian. It held a truckle bed that wouldn't have been out of place in a barracks, a wardrobe, and a crucifix. When we got there the old lady made a quick pronouncement, Carla responded and then turned to me. "Maria insists we have her bed, this one is too small."

"You're the boss," I said politely. I was waiting for the other shoe to drop. Maybe she planned to use my knife on me instead of Mazzerini. God alone knew how her medieval mind was working.

The old woman's room was equally simple but it had a bed big enough to bring forth a dozen children on, and procreate any more you fancied. Carla nodded and laughed with the old woman. I did my best to look modest. Beautiful women do not usually arrange things so cozily for me. I wondered whether the grappa was behind all of this license. And if so, where could I get a hogshead of it?

There was a bathroom down the hall and after some florid goodnights which left Carla and the old lady giggling like schoolgirls we all got comfortable and I was alone with my brand new wife.

"What's she going to say when she finds out you're lying?" I asked as I hung my shirt over the back of a chair.

"I'll worry about that," Carla said. "You worry

about earning your keep."

"That's not going to be a problem," I assured her as she unbuttoned her blouse and slipped her skirt off. She was enough of a courtesan to leave her lingerie until the last, watching the effect she was having on me. "Has anybody taken the trouble to tell you how truly spectacular you are?" I asked.

"Words are cheap," she said and got under the sheet and single thin quilt.

I put my gun under my pillow and climbed in beside her. She laughed. "You won't need a gun. I'm doing this to you, not the other way around."

"That's to discourage voyeurs," I told her. "I'm a blue-eyed WASP prude at heart."

We lay facing one another, my arm under her neck, my other hand stroking her. She was smoother than satin, a fine, taut body that thrilled me to touch. I kissed her gently and she responded, just as gently. Then I kissed her throat and she sighed and I craned down and gently rolled her nipple between my lips. And then she took over.

She was like a woman just out of prison, dominating me, demanding. If we had been dancing instead of making love, I'd have been the one going backwards.

At last she was sated and drowsy. I lay beside her, one hand cupped around her breast, listening to her breathing.

"Why me?" I asked her, softly.

"You're here," she said.

"Not the most flattering speech I've heard in my lifetime, but what the hell."

She gave a little bounce that turned her body towards me. "Does it bother your male ego? Is that it? Did you ever wonder how a woman feels when some man picks her up and passes time with her?"

"Well, no, but you've gone a long way to evening up the score," I told her.

"Good," she said firmly. "Now let me get some sleep."

"Look, I know you like to love 'em and leave 'em, but I need to know what's happening tomorrow," I whispered. "A plan will work much better if we're both in on it."

Now she uttered a shorter, more grumpy sound. "Won't it wait?"

"If we have to move in the morning I need to know what's happening. Are we leaving at four A.M.? Or are we going back to town after breakfast?"

"Sleep," she said firmly but I sat up. This was not a time to be dominated.

"It's more important than that. Whoever these people are who snatched the kid, they've had the boy since noon, that's about twelve hours. They've probably already made their ransom demands and they're waiting for the money to arrive. The best time to catch them off balance is over the next four hours, before dawn. They'll be tired and low. After that it's anybody's game. And they have us outnumbered."

Now she sat up, whispering in an angry hiss. "I told you I knew what was happening. You have to trust me."

"I've trusted people all my service life, starting from the tests I took when I joined the SAS. One of the things they do is run you to the top of a cliff and tell you to jump. You don't know what's below, you don't know if they're even aware you're on a cliff. But if you hesitate, you're out. They send you back to your unit."

"Exactly," she nodded. "That's what I'm talking about. I'll take care of the safety net, you just jump when I tell you to."

"No," I said. "I'm just as anxious as you are to sort this out. You can have the money. You can have Scavuzzo as well. But I'm a soldier not a gangster. I need a plan of action."

She reached up and pulled the light cord that dangled from the ceiling. The light from the colored chandelier washed down over her face, making dark hollows under her eyes, accentuating the angry downturn of her mouth. "Look," she said. "I've told you what's going to happen. You're working for me, remember."

I laughed. I wasn't amused but it was time to burst her bubble. I didn't mind playing dollies with her, all that had been enjoyable, but when she wanted to put my neck at risk, I had to take charge.

"You're the amateur, Carla, not me. You've got an address and you think you've got it all solved. There's more to it than that. You need a floor plan. You need a guess at least as to how many men are inside, how they're armed, where they're holding the kid. You need a diversion. You need professional planning otherwise you'll be dead and I'll be dead and Scavuzzo will have the kid, the money, and the last laugh."

It was a long speech but it registered. She was bright, and her folks had come from this part of Italy, the birthplace of Machiavelli. She knew about cunning.

Her shoulders slumped. "Can't we do all this in the morning?"

"We should have done it first, then taken our R and R," I told her. "We have only two guns, mine and that .32 of yours and I'm low on ammunition. If you've got contacts to get some more arms, I need them. Or else, how about a better idea?"

"Like what?" She reached for her cigarettes which she had set aside on the night table. She lit up and waved the match out, a big angry gesture.

"Like getting the police to help us spring the kid." She took the cigarette out of her mouth and opened it to start yelling at me but I held up one finger. "It's not so dumb. I know Capelli. We can set you up as the go-between with the cash. You drop out of sight with the suitcase and Scavuzzo comes after you. That's when I move in and set him up."

I was making this up as I went along. Capelli would get me off the arrest hook if I came back to him with the news of this man Vasoni's involvement. If his department worked like any I'd ever been involved with, he would know how to handle storming the house. And if the Ridleys had kidnap insurance the money was meaningless, just a counter to play with. If the counter rolled off the table and was lost, Capelli wouldn't be too worried. Oh, he'd go through the usual business of treating the loss as a theft, but he'd be a hero for solving Firenze's first kidnapping and he wouldn't worry about the cash.

"You put a hell of a lot of trust in Capelli," Carla said at last. Her skin was damp with perspiration and she shivered and pulled the covers up around her. "Nothing has changed since you killed Giacomo. You're still a marked man."

"What's changed is that we've got the information he needs. That buys us a legal place at the table. We can sit in on the game again and get the kid back. He'll let you handle the cash, he can even suggest it. He can use you in place of the boy's mother."

She reached out and stubbed her cigarette in the ashtray, an angry little hammering motion. I waited and slowly she began to talk. "When my father, and then my husband, were killed, they put the Chicago police and the FBI on the case. They went underground, they got close to the people who did it, but they never made an arrest."

"That was the States. The laws over there are all in the criminal's favor. They don't judge the criminals. They judge the police on how they got their evidence. Italy's different. It's nominally a socialist state but they've never forgotten how well Mussolini made the railroads run."

She lay back, pulling the covers around her. "So you think we should run right into Capelli's office and start all over again?"

"No." My head was working well. The liquor I'd drunk and the lovemaking were all burned away, I was back on patrol in the dark in the Falklands, moving in on the Argies' artillery, ready to spike their guns. "No, we go back into Florence and I call him and ask for help. I get him to provide me with men to tackle

Vasoni. We'll rendezvous somewhere neutral and proceed from there. At the same time, if he's already had a ransom demand, I offer you as the go-between."

Her eyes glittered in the overhead light. "You think he's going to go for that?"

"All he wants is to get the kid back and look good in the newspapers. If we can help him, he'll use us and pay his debts later. For me that means a quick pardon for the business at the warehouse, for you it means five million bucks and Scavuzzo's head on a platter."

She lay and looked at me, frowning slightly against the light. "You're making sense," she said at last. "When do you think we should move?"

I lay down again and slipped under the covers against the warm satin of her skin. "If you really want the money, we should wait a few hours. Ridley senior will be here by morning. He won't have the money with him but his people in Canada will have arranged it. That means he should be free to get hold of it by, say noon. If the kidnappers know he's got ransom insurance, they won't move too soon. They'll get in touch, but they won't make their demands until about midday. They'll probably want to work in darkness, that means they'll ask for a delivery after nightfall."

She turned to face me and I put one hand on her hip, my thumb in the delicious little hollow against her belly, massaging her with my fingers. She gave a little moan. "Ummm, that's nice."

I stopped doing it and she opened her eyes again. "I know, business first. Okay, how would you handle it?"

"Mid-morning we borrow the old lady's car, or truck, whatever, and drive back into town. The *Polizia* will be looking for that heap of yours, it's conspicuous."

"Then what?" Her voice was soft, seductive.

"Then we call the Rega and get some help organized through Capelli. We arrange for you to make the money drop before the police go in after the boy. That's to lull the kidnappers. And it means you're free to disappear with the cash. I go ahead with the troops and get the kid. Then Scavuzzo comes after you and we nail him."

I was lying in my teeth. Killing Scavuzzo was not on my agenda. That was her battle, not mine.

"Sounds good to me," she said drowsily. "Can we sleep now?"

"Are you in that much of a rush?" I asked and then kissed her and reached up to tug the light cord.

I was awake at daybreak, four hours later, and lay looking at Carla. That's always the moment of truth with a woman. You've seen her under artificial light, made up for the evening. You've loved her and grown through the experience. And then daylight comes poking its unromantic nose into the proceedings, letting you see the truth, the whole truth and nothing but the truth. With Carla, the truth was still beautiful.

After a while she woke and looked at me, her face as soft and trusting as a child's.

"Good morning," I said and kissed her on the nose.

"Good God," she said and shut her eyes again.

I laughed. "That's not very flattering."

With her eyes still shut she said, "What kind of time is this to wake up?"

I checked my watch which I'd dropped on the night table. "Quarter to six. I'm usually up and running by this time of day."

"This isn't day, it's the middle of the night," she said and rolled over.

I patted her flank and got up, slipping into pants and shirt and heading for the bathroom. There was no shower but I sponge-bathed and looked in the cupboard for a razor. The only one there was a dull old cutthroat but there was a strop behind the door so I honed it a few times and scraped my face, managing to avoid cutting myself. Then I went back to the bedroom for the rest of my clothes, and my gun, and went downstairs.

The old lady was in the kitchen, making coffee. We

exchanged smiles and *buon giornos* and I took two cups of coffee and went out to the wine cellar. The door was still bolted and I opened it carefully and found Mazzerini asleep against the barrels. The wine jar was empty, still where I had left it. I woke him and cut the string from his thumbs. He sat up, rubbing his hands painfully.

"I need to make water," he said and I led him upstairs to the john, standing over him so he couldn't make a break for it through the window. Then I took him back down to his cell and gave him his coffee. He thanked me and sipped it gratefully. His face was still swollen and he was stiff but he looked a little better.

"Who are you working for, Vasoni, who?" I asked him.

He flicked a worried glance at me, wondering if he was in for more interrogation. "I work for nobody. A man asked me to come and see you and the boy in the restaurant, I came. Then he asked me to drive the car to pick up the boy. I drove the car."

"Then how come you weren't shot, like the others in that car?"

He shrugged. "It is not always easy to know your friends. I did not trust the man who asked me to drive. So I made a call to Mr. Vasoni and his men were waiting. They let me go."

"Let's hear it for Machiavelli," I said.

He frowned and asked, *"Che?"*

"Before your time," I told him. "He wrote the book on ruthless. Now tell me where this house is where they're holding the kid."

"I'm not sure," he said immediately, his eyes flicking to my face and away again, fearfully.

"Signor Mazzerini. Do I have to remind you that the *signora* is upstairs. I have come to talk with you on my own because I know she is still angry. If she plans to turn you into an ox, she can still do it, if you do not please her. Tell me the address and you will not be hurt."

He sighed and then gave me an address. The name meant nothing to me so I asked him, "What kind of house is this? Is it big? Is it on its own, or in a street with all the houses joined together?"

"In a street," he said. I couldn't tell for sure but he looked too scared to be lying.

"And what makes you sure that the boy is there? Did they tell you where he was going?" That didn't sound feasible to me. Hoods are more close mouthed than that.

He shook his head. "They did not tell me but I heard one of them say, 'we can drive right into the garage at my place and take him out the back way.' "

"Very convenient," I said, then flicked my coffee cup, slashing the dregs onto the earth floor. "And where in Florence is there a house in a street with a garage in it? I think you've seen too many American movies. You're lying, Mazzerini, and I'm losing my patience."

He was over quota on pain. He flinched away and put his hands up in front of his lumpy face. "*Signor,* do not hit me, please."

"You have ten seconds to tell the truth," I said and started counting backwards. I got as far as eight before he broke.

"Is not a house." He was trembling. I said nothing, just looked at him and wrinkled my nose as if he were filth.

"Is not a house," he said again. "Is a *fabbrica.*" He stopped and waved his hands seeking the English word. "A *fabbrica,* where they make coats, purses, things out of leather."

"A factory?" I still wasn't buying. Most of the production in Italy goes on in people's homes, under the counter where the taxman can't see. They don't have many factories for things that women can make on the kitchen table.

"*Sí.*" He nodded eagerly. "A factory."

"Which one? And you'd better know the answer; my

patience is running out."

"Sí." He nodded and mugged at me, showing the gap where his front teeth had been in happier times. "*Sí,* is a *fabbrica,* Belladonna."

I picked up the wine jar and filled it. He looked at it the way kids look at candy bars but I leaned back against the barrel and sipped. He tried to conceal his disappointment.

"Tell me, how come you spill your guts to me without any pain, and yet those guys yesterday kicked you around and you didn't talk."

He licked his lips. "Signor, some wine, *per favore."*

I held out the jar and he grabbed it and glugged half of it down. A waste, it was good wine, a musty dry red.

When he lowered the jar I took it out of his hand ans said, "You told them everything you've told me, didn't you?"

He sank to the floor and buried his bruised face in his hands.

"Sí." He was almost sobbing. "I tell them everything and still they kick me."

▸ 16 ◂

I locked him in again and went back to the kitchen. Carla was there, drinking coffee and laughing with the old woman. I smiled at her and said, "Well, I hope you can stop yourself crying, because I can stop you laughing."

"What's happened?" she asked, still smiling as brilliantly as an also-ran on Academy Award night.

"The other guys got to our prisoner before we did. He told them everything yesterday. We're too late."

She didn't stop smiling. She was cleverer than that. "Look happy," she instructed me. "The old lady has radar, she can sense what's going on."

I beamed and held out the coffee cup I'd brought back with me. The old lady poured for me and I said *"Grazie mille,"* and she commented to Carla who laughed.

"She says you must have been studying Italian in bed."

I stretched my weary grin a little wider. "Very smart. Now we have two choices. Either we go and storm this place, on the off chance the kid is still there, or we send you back into the lion's den to see where Scavuzzo's people have taken him. You decide."

The old lady turned to the cupboard and got out bread rolls. There was no butter but we beamed some more and ate, Carla dipping hers in her coffee. God. What a woman. She would be equally at home in the finest house in the country but she was acting exactly right for this place and time.

When I could see she didn't intend to answer, I said, "I think it's too late to run to Capelli and tell him we know where the kid is. The other guys probably collected him last night while we were making music. The only card we have left to play is to send you back to your buddies to see what you can find out."

"Really. And how do I account for the time I've been missing?"

"Good question. You can tell them I grabbed you and held you hostage. You got away while I was asleep."

"Any Italian will think we slept together," she said.

"Tell them it was my idea, you had no choice. They want to murder me anyway by now, that just gives them another reason." Easy, Locke, I thought, there's no need to be this helpful. You don't really need a posse of angry Mafia guys carrying out a vendetta even to save the fair lady's name.

She dunked her roll again and said, "I told you yesterday, I know what I'm doing. Just because you're in the dark doesn't mean you have to panic. Just trust me."

"Do you know how they say 'screw you' in Hollywood?" I asked her.

She shook her head impatiently. "What game are you playing?"

"The way they say 'screw you' is 'trust me,'" I persisted. "So don't expect me to roll over and put all four paws in the air when you make the same comment."

She sipped the last of her coffee, ignoring my high humor. "You're too late, suggesting I go back to those guys. They won't trust me again. They're never going to tell me where the boy has been taken. And even if they did, I wouldn't be able to get back to you with the information."

She was making sense. And the more I thought about it, the less hope I had. Capelli was already one step ahead of me. The unwounded man I'd left at the warehouse had probably told him everything. That left me with no bargaining power. And I'd killed a man, and he knew that too. I was still behind the eight ball. I accepted another roll and sat and thought.

Carla broke the silence. "What we're going to do is go to this place where Mazzerini says the boy was taken. If he's still there, I should be able to find out. If not, I might pick up some indication of what happened."

"That's going to be dangerous," I cautioned. "If the people at the factory are criminals, they'll recognize you. You're moving in very prominent circles. I'll bet every two-bit hood in Italy knows your pedigree."

"That won't matter," she said matter-of-factly. "You'll be coming with me."

"Chances are I'm already on the 'most-wanted list.' Every cop in Florence is going to be looking for me."

"You flatter yourself," she said. "No Italian man will give you a second glance if I'm with you."

She had a point there. As long as her face hadn't been circulated on the same wanted poster we were probably safe together. "Okay, let's go. But what about Mazzerini? We can't take him with us, can we leave him here?"

Carla turned to the old woman and spoke quickly. The old woman answered and Carla smiled. "Her son will be back tomorrow. He'll let him out then. She won't be in any danger."

I stood up. "Come on then, time's a-wasting."

The old woman had a truck. It wasn't much but I brushed the chicken feathers off the seat and Carla got in and we headed back to Florence. I watched for landmarks and signs, ready to tell Capelli exactly where the farm was when it came time to level with him. I didn't think it would make trouble for the old woman. She hadn't done anything wrong, just given hospitality to a friend, but I was going to need some evidence of the story I would have to tell the police.

It was a typically beautiful Tuscan morning. People were working in the fields, bending over their vegetables under that blue, blue sky. When we stopped for a main road I could hear a man singing not far away, a big, round, untrained voice singing the famous tenor part of the duet from *The Pearl Fishers.* In the States he would have been listening to a ghetto blaster. I glanced at Carla. "Some time when all this is over, I'd like to spend a month at a place around here, getting back to basics."

She laughed. "Don't write me a part in your day dream. I hate any place that's not paved over."

"Pity," I said, "We could have got to know one another a lot better under this kind of sky."

"Sunlight is death on your skin," she said and lit a cigarette, which is just as bad for your hide if you believe the surgeon-general.

Florence isn't like a North American city, not in any way, but most of all in its lack of a commercial strip on the road leading in. There are no motels or chicken joints or burger stands, one minute you're driving in the country, the next you're there, the way you might have been if you came here on horseback five hundred years ago, looking to beg Lorenzo to lighten up on the taxes because there was a murrain on your cattle.

We passed the same roadblock on the way into town. A couple of bored policemen were going through the motions, waving every car through without a search. I figured they would pull out before the day was through. They were convinced Herbie was still in town. The fact that they were right didn't make their actions any more creditable, not to me. I've worked a lot of roadblocks in Ulster. You don't quit because you don't succeed within twenty-four hours.

In town the streets were jammed but I had found the secret of driving in Italy on my first trip. You drive *con brio*. If you want to make a U-turn against six lanes of traffic, go for it. The right of way belongs to the boldest driver. People may swear and wave out of their windows at you but they let you through and admire you for trying.

It took forty minutes for me to find the street Mazzerini had told me about. It looked promising, as if he could have been telling the truth. The buildings were big and unpretentious and could well have been the Florentine version of factories.

"Park there," Carla told me suddenly. She was pointing at a corner where some tiny Fiat was pulling out. It didn't leave much room for the truck, or any for pedestrians who might want to cross but she got out with her head high, ignoring the anger on the faces of people who had to walk over our bumper to get past.

"Come," she said and led me back down the street to a big plain building.

"Is this the place? I can't see any sign."

"It's the place," she said firmly. Then she stopped and stared straight into my face. "Remember what I told you last night. I know where the cliffs are. If I say jump, just jump. Don't think. Don't question anything I do or we're both dead."

I threw up my hands, not even answering, and she walked away to the building. She didn't pause in front but swept right in, up the three worn marble steps to the door. I took the time to glance around and notice that there was a garage door in the front, big enough to allow a vehicle to enter. Herb Ridley could have been driven inside without getting out of the kidnap car.

We found ourselves in the kind of sweatshop you see in movies about making it on the Lower East Side in

1910. There was a desk with a plain girl answering two phones that never stopped ringing, and behind her a clutter of sewing machines with women working non-stop, heads down over pieces of leather.

A balding young guy with a mustache big enough to have sapped all the strength from his scalp was darting about with a clipboard, bellowing instructions to a slow-moving workman who was loading a trolley at the women's worktables. Carla bore down on him and when he saw her he stopped and did a wonderful Latin double-take. How could anything this radiant be happening to him on a Tuesday morning?

I hung back. The way she was acting, it looked as if she knew what was happening. I assumed she had some way of checking out the factory and seeing if there was any sign of either Herb Ridley or of anyone she knew. And whatever she was saying it was working. She picked up a purse from a pile of work, flipped it open, pointed to a seam and tossed the purse aside, talking nonstop.

The bald guy tried to cut in but she overrode him, galloping into another speech without drawing a breath. She moved off down the aisle between the sewing machines, picking up work indiscriminately and rejecting it. He trotted after her, clipboard waving, saying what must have been the Italian for "But lady, listen up." I followed them both at a distance that looked respectful but was really just careful, my right hand in my jacket pocket, nursing the neat little automatic I'd taken off Carla. I worked as if I was on a Belfast street patrol, stopping from time to time to check behind and around me for men bearing me ill will. I couldn't see any.

When she got to the far end of the room, Carla stopped and listened to the young man for about thirty seconds, then gave him a smile he would remember all his life. She looked over his head, something she could do without craning up, and beckoned to me. She spoke

Italian and I made out *"Avanti"* but the wave of her hand was clear enough anyway, I came up to her. Again she spoke in Italian, telling me something. I made a bored little nod and she waved the bald guy ahead. He opened the door onto a corridor that led to an office. He ushered us ahead, into it.

It wasn't much. The furniture had been there since Mussolini marched on Abyssinia and it was dusty and cluttered with boxes almost to the ceiling. In fact it's only remarkable feature was a man, standing up and reaching for a gun that lay on the desk in front of him.

The fact that his piece was on the desk told me he wasn't a cop. That meant he was another hood, possibly one of Carla's good buddies, possibly not. Either way I had to act tough. I stepped into him, past the desk, catching my pocket on the corner and ripping it slightly, but I didn't stop to examine it. I slammed the heel of my hand under his chin, knocking him cold. As he slithered down I turned and sunk my fist into the bald guy's gut. He folded, gasping, and I knelt by him and put pressure on his carotid arteries with my thumbs. It took only a few seconds and he was out cold.

The whole thing had taken less than half a minute but in that time, Carla had gone. I wondered if she was searching for Herbie, or if she'd disappeared but I didn't waste any time over it. I frisked the guy with the gun and found a ring of keys. I also picked up his gun. It was a Browning 125 automatic, an adequate piece but its chief charm was the fact it used the same 9mm ammunition as my Walther. Corn in Egypt! I slipped out the magazine and put it into my pocket.

Then I went out, locking the office on the two sleeping beauties and pressed on down the corridor, opening all the doors. All of the locked places were storerooms, filled with cartons of what I assumed to be their purses. No Herbie. It took me about three minutes. Then I came back to the office. Skintop was waking up but when he saw me come in he immediately pretended to be asleep again.

I stood for a few seconds, topping up the magazine of my Walther with the bullets from the other guy's gun. Then I took a chance on using the telephone. I was lucky, you didn't have to dial 9 to get out, and I called the Rega and got through to the room.

Kate Ridley answered, her voice strained. She spoke Italian and I cut in immediately.

"Hi, Kate, John Locke. Is the *tenente* there?"

She was flustered. "John, where are you, what's happening?" but then there was a rustling on the line and Capelli took over.

"Where are you?" he demanded.

"Right now I'm at the Fabbrica Belladonna. It's a leather factory." I gave him the street and number. "There's some hood here who was expecting me to arrive. He had a gun."

"What have you found out about the boy?" His voice was all business but I could imagine his helpers dispersing right now to send cars over here and collect the guy—and me, if I stuck around.

"It's been set up by the father," I said. "He took out five million dollars' worth of insurance on the boy before we came here. The gangs here knew all about it. Apparently Ridley senior plans to split the ransom money with them."

I realized that my call was being taped but I didn't know who was listening on extra lines attached to the phone. It seemed that Ridley was. I heard a roar at the other end, then a scuffle and then Ridley was bellowing at me. "You lying bastard. I'll sue you for every penny you've got."

"Cut the crap," I told him. "Cooperate with the police and they'll go easy on you."

He began to shout again and then there was another scuffle. I guess a couple of Capelli's men were wrestling the phone away from him. They won. The next voice I heard was Capelli's.

"Where did you hear this?"

"From Carla. She's known about it all along. That's why she approached me on Sunday. Also there's another guy, Mazzerini, he was the driver of the kidnap car. He was in that warehouse we sent the ambulance to last night. Right now he's locked up in a wine cellar in a farm north of the city. I think he told everything he knew to the men you found at the warehouse but if you want to talk to him, you go east from Pedanto a kilometer and a half, turn north and look for a farm with a wall around the yard. There's an old lady there. You'll also find Carla's car in the barn."

"Wait where you are, we must talk." Capelli had a dead man to account for and he wanted me in his office making a statement. I didn't think that would make any contribution to finding Herbie so I refused.

"No dice, *tenente.* I'm going to find where the boy is, I think I know where to look. If I get close I'll call you for reinforcements. In the meantime, stay on top of Ridley, he's behind all of this."

I hung up, wondering if Herbie had ever been here. Mazzerini had sent me here knowing his buddies would catch me. The only thing I couldn't work out was why Carla had run off. Was there some new fifth or sixth dimension to this crazy kidnapping? Time would tell but I would find out sooner if I was on the outside, reading newspapers, than if I was down in one of the *maggiore's* cells waiting for Ottawa to get off its bureaucratic backside and send me a lawyer.

None of the women in the plant even looked up at me as I walked out. They were all too busy churning out piecework on behalf of Belladonna. As I passed one of the tables I noticed a rack of needles and thread standing on it, where some finisher was making minor repairs and adjustments to finished coats. I smiled politely at the woman working there and picked up a biggish needle and a spool of thread. My pants were fixable if I could get a few moments of privacy.

I didn't see Carla anywhere and the girl at the front was still taking telephone calls so I nodded to her and walked by, ambling easily, trying not to look as if the police would be pouring in here within another minute, asking if she'd seen the *turista*. I couldn't wait around for that. I had business to attend to.

▸ 17 ◂

The truck was still standing on the corner and I walked past it to check if Carla was inside. She wasn't. It didn't surprise me, she was conspicuous enough without playing Beauty and the Beast by driving that rattletrap. People were still climbing over the bumper to cross the street and I did the same, ducking away down a maze of crowded side streets where no police car could move faster than I could run. Behind me the familiar see-saw note of the sirens approached the Belladonna and stopped as if some giant had grown angry with the noise and wrapped steel hands round their steel voiceboxes.

The *Herald-Tribune* was on sale and I bought a copy and carried it casually in my right hand, covering the rip in my trouser seam, until I came to the first tourist attraction I could find, the Museo di San Marco. It was jammed to the walls with tourists, most of them Americans, and I became the closest thing there is to invisible while I mingled, looking for a washroom where I could fix my pants. I found one at last, and sat in the cubicle stitching away while the accents of Texas and New York boomed outside with comments on Fra Angelico's *Annunciation* and the exchange rate on the dollar and the impossibility of finding a good steak in Italy.

It took me about ten minutes and I was presentable. The thread was stiff and thick and chestnut brown. My repair job would have broken every heart on Savile Row but I felt spiffy again and I flushed the toilet and left, to the relief of a pale-faced man who was crunching down a Lomotil and shifting from foot to foot outside. "You've sure taken your time," he snarled and dived for the cubicle.

I knew what I was going to do next but I had no idea how to do it, so I spent half an hour going through the museum. It was hard to get up the staircase to the second floor because of the crush of people, women mostly, in front of the *Annunciation,* but the gentle stop-and-go movement of the crowd gave me a chance to get my thoughts in a straight line and by the time I had spent a minute looking at the fresco, which was so beautiful it almost took my mind off my problems, I knew what to do.

I went back out and found a quiet restaurant on a corner where there was a good view up and down all four streets. I felt safe enough there to order an espresso and I shook out my paper to see what the world knew about the kidnapping. There was a small story on the front page but it didn't mention anything that I didn't already know so I turned to the sports and checked how the Blue Jays were coming. Better than me, it seemed. They'd edged past the Yankees five to four the day before and were six games ahead of the pack in the pennant race. As I read the news a small part of my mind was flying high, looking down on the whole problem, working out what to do. It all came down to finding some way to get back into the house I had been in yesterday. But that was easier said than done. The people inside would be wary now. They had one man dead, and Carla and I were missing. They almost certainly blamed me for all their trouble. If I just knocked on the door they would have a gun on me before it opened. I needed a disguise, camouflage, something.

I paid for the coffee and moved on towards the center of the town, looking for a florist. I found one, small and expensive seeming, on a street close to the Duomo. It had a wonderful wreath in the window, the kind of thing a WASP would never buy, even for a state funeral. I went in and the owner came up to me. He was small and businesslike. Bad news was good news in this line of work.

"Hi, how much is the wreath in the window, please?"

"A friend of yours has died, *signor?* How sad!" Sure, I thought. I could see the calculator flashing in his eyes. How sad was I feeling? He decided on eighty thousand lire.

I pulled out some of the Ridley family expense money and paid him and he brought the wreath out of the window, working on it, tilting individual leaves and blooms just so. I thanked him and went outside to look for a cab.

The first two refused me but the third one was a Volvo and he opened the trunk and laid the wreath in it, leaving the lid up. The driver spoke enough English to understand me and I directed him to the house where Carla had taken me the day before.

When we came to the end of the street I paid him off, reclaimed my purchase from his trunk, and set off towards the house, holding the wreath up in front of me like a riot shield. There was enough space between the flowers for me to squint out and ahead, but no chance of anyone's seeing my face. Ideal.

People moved aside as I walked, the younger ones joking, the older ones respectful. One old woman even crossed herself when she saw the wreath. I hoped she wasn't a fortune-teller, I was feeling vulnerable.

I got to the door and knocked firmly, a no-nonsense deliveryman's knock. Still holding the wreath high I turned sideways into the doorway and drew my gun, making sure nobody on the street saw me.

After a few moments the door opened, letting out a blast of bad language, unmistakable, even though it was in Italian. And through my cover I saw Savario, just as natty as the day before, resentful at having to play doorman.

I moved forward into the house. He objected but, just as I thought, he didn't get into a shoving match, in case he damaged the blooms. He just cranked up the volume on his complaining.

When we were clear of the door I closed it with my heel and lowered the wreath. He gasped when he saw my face, and shut up completely when he saw the gun. I set the wreath down on the bottom of the stairs and motioned Savario to lean against the wall. I patted him down, taking his gun and a five-inch switchblade. I unloaded his gun, then opened the switchblade and stuck it into the newel post on the stairs and snapped the blade. That made him flinch. Chalk up another to good old Freud, in his terms I'd just turned Savario into a capon. I nudged him with the muzzle of my gun and he moved ahead into the room where I had waited the day before.

It was empty so I got him out again and marched him back to the office where the boss man had told me his plan. Bingo. He was there again, smoking the twin of the cigar he'd lighted the night before.

I gave Savario a shove into one of the chairs then pointed my gun straight at the older man's heart. His mouth came open, the cigar falling onto his leather desktop where it smouldered, smelling like a burning car tire. He seemed to have stopped breathing.

"Hi. Remember me?" I asked him.

He started to say something but I didn't listen. I reached across the desk and backhanded him across the head, hard enough to send him sprawling into the corner. It wasn't out of revenge, although I owed him one. I just wanted him off balance, all his carefully acquired prestige wiped away. Then he would talk.

He lay there, licking the blood of his broken lip, his

eyes wide with horror. I doubt if he'd felt any pain since his father gave up clipping his ear for him, fifty years earlier.

"Get up," I said, and he did, slowly, his hands half up, not quite surrendering but pleading silently that I wouldn't hit him again. I waved the gun at him. "Come around this side of the desk," I told him and he came, nervously. I backed away from him and turned the key in the door.

Boss Man was in front of the desk now. He seemed to have shucked it, the way a dispossessed turtle might shuck his shell. The dislocation had made him shrink. I was aware that he was only about five foot three, with a blue chin and dyed hair. I reached out and spun him around, slamming his face first against the paneling. I frisked him all over. He was clean and I spun him around again and told him, "Take your pants off."

His eyebrows raced up to his Lady Clairoled hair. "What?"

"You heard me. Take your pants off."

He did it, a nervous tremor starting in his hands and racing through his whole body. This was the worst insult in the world, which was why I was doing it. I didn't have time to use any fancy interrogation techniques. I wanted facts, fast, with a minimum of violence. This way works. A man takes off most of his sense of manhood and all of his self-confidence when he takes off his trousers.

I reached out and took his trousers away from him. "Good boy. Now sit on the floor with your hands on your head." He did it, trying to avoid Savario's eyes. All his pride had vanished. He was mine. I went around his desk and opened it, carefully.

There was a gun fastened under the knee slot that he would have used on me if I had wasted any time striking postures in front of him. I pulled out each drawer in turn, glancing at the papers then emptying them on the floor, checking underneath the drawer for anything attached, any secret compartments. He watched me, not speaking, fear and anger fighting in his eyes. Fear won. He stayed silent.

There was nothing that made sense to me. A lot of ledgers full of figures, some letters, but that was all. There was nothing in English, nothing with a name I'd ever heard of. I emptied the last drawer, checking underneath it to see if anything was taped there. Nothing was. Then I took out the wallet I'd removed from the man with the gun at Belladonna.

"I'm just going to ask you once, then I'm going to start kicking you," I told him. "Who is—" I read the name from the license in the wallet, "Giorgio Speroni?"

Savario's mouth opened but the boss spoke. "He works for a friend of mine."

I embroidered a little. "Right now he's in the hospital with a team of doctors trying to put his jaw back together. I broke it for him."

He licked his lips but didn't speak. I went on, smiling the way he had smiled at me from this side of the desk the night before.

"He tried to shoot me. That was after somebody else tried to shoot me, last night when you set me up alone in that warehouse. You'd better tell me what's going on or the doctors will have to work on your jaw as well."

He started to speak, slowly, obviously making up his story as he went along. "You are a very dangerous man, Signor Locke. We were afraid you would hurt us. You are working for the boy's father. When you took the woman last night and disappeared, we had to put you out of the fight."

I came around the desk and kicked him on the shin, not hard, just swinging my leg as if I was bored. But my toe hit him precisely on the nerve. He yelped and rubbed the hurt, his eyes clouded with pain.

"Who are you working for? Is it Scavuzzo?"

"I do not work for anybody," he said angrily. I'd reached his pride. He considered himself a wheel. Good. I would use that.

"Don't lie to me. Scavuzzo sends his woman to your house to give you orders."

He looked as if he was going to spit. "That American whore. He sent her to me because he was tired of her, he thought she would amuse me."

I wondered if he was telling the truth now. It would explain Carla's anxiety to make Scavuzzo suffer. But she wasn't some kind of white slave. She was a Mafia princess, she could have gone back home if things didn't work out here. Couldn't she? I felt like I knew all the players now but I couldn't tell which team they played for, not without a program.

"Where's the boy?" I asked him. He shrugged but it was a micro-second too slow. I could see he was lying and I snapped the question at him again. "Where's the boy? Tell me now and you'll save yourself a lot of pain."

"All I know is that the man who drove the car and the boy were in that warehouse yesterday, when you went there with Savario. And poor Giacomo."

"Don't lie to me. The police already told me that all the men in the kidnap car were killed, shot."

He lifted his hands from his head to gesture. "Three men were dead, that's what they found. But Mazzerini was not one of them. He killed the other two men and the man who let them into the garage where the car was found."

Was Mazzerini hard enough to carry out that kind of action? He didn't look tough to me, but maybe knowing how much ransom was involved he had worked up whatever guts it takes to back-shoot three colleagues. Honor among thieves? Tell me about it.

"Then why wasn't the boy with him when I found him in the warehouse?"

"They moved the boy before you got there." He shrugged and went to lower his hands but I tapped his shin again and he yelped and put them back on top of his color-corrected hair.

"How do you know that?"

He glanced at Savario, then at me, then licked his lips. *"Signor.* That man there went into the building when you came out. He spoke to the man you left there. They told him everything."

I glanced at Savario. He looked as if he was afraid of wetting himself. He was more scared than he should have been. But he spoke no English, it was no good working on him. I continued with the boss.

"You're lying," I said. "I am going to have to get the truth out of you some way."

"I tell the truth. Believe me." He was starting to sweat, his forehead glistening.

"I wouldn't believe you if you were on fire and shouting for help," I told him. I reached down and grabbed his left hand off the top of his head, rolling his fingers between finger and thumb so he shrieked and sprawled towards me, trying to ease the pressure. "Tell me where the boy is or I'll break your fingers, one at a time."

It had happened to one of my men in Ulster. Not an SAS man, he would never have fallen for the trick, a young Guardsman, innocent enough to go for a quiet beer without making sure he had five or six buddies with him. The Provos had trapped him, using a girl to suggest he go home with her. He had gone, and had ended up in a basement being interrogated by four of them. They were after the names of his officers, me and my lieutenant, so they could send their gunmen calling later when we'd been rotated back to England. They had broken seven of his fingers before we found him, but he hadn't talked. I didn't think this man was as tough.

He didn't answer and I cranked up the pressure, not to the breaking point, but just inside it, where he could feel the joints stretching.

"I'll take you there," he sobbed.

"Good." I let go of him and he collapsed full length on the floor, rubbing his fingers with his other hand, holding back his tears. I threw him his pants. "Get these back on, I don't want any bare-assed clown driving me around."

He scrabbled himself back into his pants, not looking at me until he was dressed again. I'd been right. His suit was his authority. He was calm again now, taking big slow breaths to overcome the fear he'd suffered. He glanced at Savario who lowered his eyes. I wondered if he would survive, knowing that the boss man had been humiliated. Pride is the biggest motivating force in Italy. It would be cheaper to shoot Savario and hire another soldier than rebuild a shattered image.

"Where is the boy?" I asked again.

"I will take you there," he repeated.

"You will tell me first." I drew back my hand lightly and he flinched and covered his face. "I want some of my friends there when we arrive."

He grinned, an ingratiating little flick of the corners of his mouth. "Then they will say that you did not find him, that they found him," he said.

"No matter." I wondered why he was playing games. The most obvious reason was that he planned to lead me into an ambush. Handling him was like milking a cobra.

"He is here," he said slowly. "Now will you believe me?"

"I will when I see him. And he had better be unharmed." I waved my gun towards the door, "Unlock the door with your left hand, keep your other hand on your head."

Savario was still sitting on the couch. I looked at him, debating how to keep him quiet. Even if we locked him in this room he would go out of the window, or just shout. He looked at me, fearfully, then away. I hit him, with the butt of the gun, in the temple. It's the only knockout place on the head. Miss that one spot and you could beat a man's head to mush without putting him to sleep. I was right on. He groaned and collapsed. I laid him flat on the rug and waved the gun towards the door again.

"Let's go."

He opened the door and I stepped behind him, crouching, in case some family retainer was waiting outside to nail me with a bullet. None was. We went back along the hall, past the broken knife and up the stairs. He stopped in front of the door of one of the bedrooms and pointed to it, silently.

I made a turning gesture with my free hand but he didn't touch the door knob, he tapped, three times, then a pause, then twice.

There was a rustling inside and the door opened. I grabbed my man by the hair, stuck the gun into his neck and pushed him forward, through it.

The man inside gaped at us and in the moment of his surprise I hit him with the gunbarrel and he fell down. Herbie was lying on the bed, his hands and feet tied, his mouth taped. His eyes were huge, almost bursting out of his head as he wriggled, trying to attract my attention.

I let him wait while I checked the room, behind the drapes, in the cupboard, making sure there was nobody else there. Then I kicked the senior hood in both collarbones. He screamed but muffled it by burying his face in the carpet, thankful that I hadn't shot him.

Now, with no threats to worry about I shoved my gun back into its holster and pulled out my knife, slashing the ropes on Herbie's hands and feet. He pulled the tape off his mouth, weeping with relief and excitement. "Oh, John, I was scared."

I bumped him on the shoulder. "You were entitled, Herb. But it's over now. I want to take the old guy here with me, then we'll head for the hotel." I pulled my gun again and led the way downstairs. Herbie came behind me, silently, moving like a soldier on patrol, checking around with every step. I wished I'd given him a gun.

At the bottom of the stairs I stepped over the wreath

I'd delivered and turned to the back of the house, Herbie behind me. I reached the door of the office and was about to turn the key when I heard a woman's voice say, "Freeze, Locke, or we kill the kid."

I turned around, very slowly. Carla was standing in the front doorway, between two men, one of them holding a shotgun trained on Herbie. The other one was a middle-aged man with a gun and a grin. I recognized him immediately from the photograph Capelli had shown me. It was her boyfriend from Milan. Scavuzzo.

▸ 18 ◂

The gun was trained on Herbie, not on me. Carla said "Drop the gun or he dies." She knew I would have gambled if it had been just my neck on the line, but I couldn't be sure that the guy with the shotgun wouldn't pull the trigger reflexively, the way Savario had. And if he did he would tear Herbie in half.

I dropped the gun and said, "Okay, now what?" still watching the shotgun, waiting for the guy holding it to get careless and lower the muzzle. I could have dived for my gun and put a hole through him before he could lift his aim again. But I didn't get the chance. Scavuzzo said something in Italian and Carla translated.

"Try anything funny and we shoot you. You got that?"

"Yeah. I've got that. But what about the boy?"

She smiled, first at Scavuzzo, who looked at her like a proud father watching a bright two-year-old, his ugly face splitting in a grin. "We want to thank you for getting him back for us," she said.

"You mean you knew he was in here but you didn't come in for him?"

"We had no way of getting into this place without starting a small war. So we waited around and when you came in, I used my key and saw what you'd done. You're good. D'you know that?"

"Thank you fair lady. Now let me take the kid and go home."

I don't know how much English Scavuzzo spoke but he heard that. He dropped his grin like a dirty handkerchief and clattered out a quick sentence in Italian that Carla didn't need to translate. But she did. "He says you can go when the ransom is paid, not before."

I felt a little surge of relief. I didn't believe my survival was high on their list of priorities, but at least they weren't going to kill me out of hand. I had the chance to come up with something between now and zero hour.

Scavuzzo put his own gun away and spoke to Carla again. She answered in Italian then told me. "Come on. Come with us. Do as you're told and you live."

"That sounds like the kind of offer you can't refuse," I said and nodded to Scavuzzo to let him know I was knuckling under. If I was really lucky they wouldn't frisk me and find Carla's gun.

She pointed down the hall to the office. "Come on in, both of you and we'll make the phone call."

"What phone call?" I was acting dumb, waiting for the shotgun to waver, but it didn't. If I stepped out of line, Herbie was meat.

I unlocked the study door and went in. Savario was coming around, holding his head with both hands. The others came in behind me and he straightened up when he saw Scavuzzo, trying to stand up but passing out again with the effort. Carla stepped over him and picked up the phone. She held it for a moment and then turned and looked through me, her focus far away as she worked out what she wanted me to do.

"I'm going to ring the Rega and get through to the room. Then you take over. You tell them you've found the boy, then let the boy speak to them for a moment, then you ask for the ransom. Tell them to hold off on any arrangements they've made so far and wait for more instructions. You got that?"

"Sure. You want it to look as if the new ransom demand is my idea. You want me pegged as the kidnapper, right?"

"Now you're catching on," she said. "But remember, if you do anything cute like telling them where we are right now, we shoot the kid, then you. So don't try anything." She waited for my nod before she began to dial.

My head was racing. I knew that incoming calls would be taped. Any clue I could give would be analyzed and used. But how far could I go? I would have to say something Carla didn't understand but which was obvious to Capelli and Kate Ridley. I had to translate the words "Fifty-four Via dell' Angelico" into a code they could work out before Carla did.

Carla spoke into the phone and then handed it to me. Kate Ridley answered, speaking Italian. I cut in, as breezily as if I'd bumped into her at a party. "Hi, Kate, John Locke here. Good news. In fact this has been a good day all around, hasn't it? I mean, did you see the paper? The Blue Jays clobbered Los Angeles 5–4 yesterday." I hoped I'd put enough emphasis on the score to catch her attention. I was hoping Capelli would be well enough trained to analyze every word I said. An anti-terrorist agent would have been—but maybe not a city cop. And I already knew they weren't as sophisticated as they are in the States. There they would have used a computer phone that printed out the number from which every incoming call was dialed. Capelli didn't have that kind of backing—but could he take a clue when I gave him one? We'd see. In any case, my words sailed right by Kate Ridley.

"For God's sake John, what are you talking about?" Her voice was ragged with tension. My code had whistled over her head unnoticed.

"Oh, well, more important, I have someone here to

speak to you. Herbie, say hello to your mother."

He took the phone and said, "Mom?" and then the tears gouted from his eyes and he chattered like a child for ten seconds before Carla pulled the phone away from him and handed it back to me.

Kate Ridley was saying, "Herbie, Herbie, are you there?"

"He's here and he's safe and sound. I'll have him back to you very soon. But there's just one holdup. The people who have him want the cash."

"The cash? You mean the ransom?" Her voice ran up the scale almost to a scream. "You said he was safe, that you had him."

"I do. The only problem is, some people have me and they want the money. They said you were to discount any instructions you've had already and to wait for new orders about the money. In the meantime, don't worry, I'm with Herbie, looking after him."

Carla's hand reached out and depressed the button on the phone. She was looking at me carefully. "What was that about baseball?"

"I'm a Blue Jays fan, so is Kate Ridley. I just wanted to act natural, that's all."

She looked at me carefully, the ice in her eyes thick enough to sink another *Titanic*. "Just don't screw me around, Locke," she breathed, "or you're a dead man."

I held both hands up, palms towards her. "Believe me, I want to get out of this alive and well." Nothing like the truth for sounding sincere. I just didn't bother adding that I wanted to see Scavuzzo and the rest of his scumbags in jail first. And it still might happen, if I was lucky, if we would stay put, right here, and Capelli could work out my code and come riding to the rescue. I wasn't holding my breath but I'd tried. They could put that on my tombstone.

Scavuzzo spoke to his gunman, then took the shotgun off him, still training it on Herbie. Carla told me, "Turn around and put your hands behind your back." I did it, there was no arguing with her tone. The gunman moved in and clicked a pair of cuffs on my wrists. Then he patted me down, gingerly as if he didn't want to offend me. That was a bad sign. It meant my reputation had gotten around. He was scared and he would be extra careful. Careful enough to find Carla's gun and my knife.

Carla took the gun back but he kept the knife, playing with it happily. It's a good Buck clasp knife with a catch you have to depress before the blade will open. It impressed the hell out of him and he chuckled to himself and played with it, like a kid on Christmas morning.

I smiled at him and said, "Take care of it, I want it back later." Carla looked at me disbelievingly and laughed. It was my death sentence. There wasn't going to be any later for me, I had to get out of this as best I could. I guess my part was over. I'd rescued Herbie for her. Now I had to die. It made me wonder about the way she had savaged me all night in that farmhouse. Did she get a charge out of making love to condemned men? Had she been as violent with her husband, the night before his car blew up?

Scavuzzo ejected the two shells from the shotgun and broke it down into three pieces. That meant we were leaving. More bad luck. I might have had a chance if we'd stayed here. Capelli might just have cracked my code. Now it wouldn't help. I watched as Scavuzzo handed the pieces of the gun to the man who had been holding it on Herbie earlier. He went outside to the hall, coming back with a briefcase. Marvelous, just the present for the hood who has everything. I wondered if it had a calculator and a calendar built in.

Carla said, "Listen up, Locke. We're going out the back door. All three of us will have guns trained on you. If you try anything fancy one of us will kill you. If the boy runs we will shoot you first, then him."

Herbie said, "I'm not going to run. You don't have to shoot John."

I turned and winked at him, it was all I could do. He looked grim but not afraid. I think his terror had burned itself out over the last twenty-four hours. He was a soldier, milk-faced and untried but angry enough to be an ally if we got the chance to do something. I hoped they put us together, without company. I had an idea.

In the meantime I played dumb. "Look, I'm not going to try anything. My job's done, I've found Herb, he's all right. As soon as you get the money we go home. Right?"

Carla glanced at me, then away quickly. "Of course," she lied.

She led the way, out of the office and down the hall.

Carla turned at the back door. "You're going outside now, Herb. I'm going to walk behind you, I want you to go nice and easy and get into the red car that's parked right ahead of the door. Get in the back seat and sit in the middle. Okay?" He nodded.

Now she turned to me. "You're going to sit in the front where I can keep my gun on the back of your head. One move I don't like and I'll blow it off, you got that?"

"Is it my mouthwash? What?" I asked her but she swore. I checked over my shoulder. Scavuzzo and his soldier had guns in their hands, Scavuzzo's under the flap of his suitcoat, the soldier's under the briefcase. Both guns were cocked, both pointed at me. That made the odds too long. I would have to wait for a better chance. Maybe in the car. I might be able to roll out of it, especially if we went through the middle of town. In heavy traffic I could maybe attract some cop's attention. Maybe.

And maybe I would win the lottery. The odds were no longer. This bunch was taking no chances on losing me, or Herb. Their car was right against the door. They kept me covered by pretending to lean against me, one arm around me, the other down low, holding the gun in my ribs. She was smiling and talking. We looked like a lover and his lass. With a hey-nonny-no. Hah!

They moved out and into the car like soldiers carrying out a drill movement. Herbie in the middle at the back, Scavuzzo on one side of him, Carla on the other. The gunman got in the driver's seat with me beside him. Just to put an end to my daydreaming he pulled the seatbelt across me and clunked it in. I was trapped until he decided to let me go.

Carla leaned over the back of my seat, craning around the neck rest, one hand holding her gun in my temple. I wished she would take it away. Perhaps I would have a chance to goose the gas pedal in traffic and get us into an accident. It would give Herbie a shot at freedom. If there were enough cops around, I might even make it myself. I tried to talk her down. "You can put that gun away, sweetheart, the name is Locke, not Houdini."

"Let's say I feel happier like this," she said. "Just so that you don't get any ideas."

"Spoilsport," I said and sat quiet, waiting for us to get started. Only we didn't. Scavuzzo spoke to the gunman and he nodded and went back into the house. I wondered what he was planning to do. Then I heard the first faint bang, the flat authoritative bang of my Walther. Then there was the sound of a man's voice shouting and a second bang, and a third. Then a thirty-second pause, and a fourth.

"Now you're really in trouble," I said but Carla laughed shortly.

"Not me, you. That was your gun he used. You'll have some more things to explain now, won't you?"

"I look forward to getting the opportunity."

Herbie said, "What's going on, John? Please tell me." His voice was hoarse and strained as if he had sung too many verses of "ninety-nine bottles of beer" around the camp fire. I hoped he would get to do it some time. Right now I didn't like his chances.

"You have to learn from this experience," I told him. "Never judge a book by its cover. This pretty lady with her gun in my ear isn't a movie star. She's a hot-pants Mafia princess."

That was as far as I got before she rammed the muzzle of the gun into my ear, trying to force it all the way through my thick head. Then Herbie said, "Stop that. Stop hurting him," and the pressure came off my ear as he tugged at her gun hand. I just hoped he wouldn't squeeze the trigger for her.

I craned around as far as I could in my harness and saw Scavuzzo holding his gun silently to Herbie's head. No wrestling, no sweat, just the immediate promise of death if he didn't stop fighting. He did.

"Nice going Herb," I told him and Carla rewarded me with another jab in the head. It hurt but I only said, "All right Carla, I promise I'll take you to the school formal."

"You bastard. I'm going to smash your teeth out," she promised. Then their boy got back into the driver's seat. I noticed that he was wearing gloves. Damn. My gun would have only my prints on it. And its bullets were in three dead men. How do you explain this, Signor Locke? Drink your nice castor oil and let's go over it again.

The driver backed out of the alleyway, moving very slowly, doing everything with pinpoint precision, like a man who has just realized that he is drunk. I knew what was happening. His memory was playing back the images he had created inside that house, men pleading, cursing, dying, rolling away from him with their mouths round with surprise as their lives seeped away.

He drove by the book, giving way when he had to, going for the breaks when they came. We stayed away from the center of town, out among streets of low houses, as ordinary as they get in Florence, which means they've been around for only a few centuries. For about a minute I watched every move, checking for street names, landmarks, directions, anything to guide me. Then Scavuzzo said something to Carla and she took off her scarf and flipped it around my eyes, doing her best to crush them out of the sockets. I didn't say anything. The mood she was in she could have blinded me without a second thought. I just hoped Herbie would keep looking. He was coming out of this a better, tougher guy than he had gone in.

We stopped at last. Everyone got out of the back seat, then the door on my side opened and the driver unclicked my seat belt and Carla tugged my arm until I half fell out of the car. I could tell it was her from the presence of her perfume but her hands were as strong as a man's.

She jerked me upright and I felt concrete under my feet, or old stone possibly. In Florence you couldn't be sure. Then someone slammed the car door and it echoed. We were inside something. I wondered what.

Carla shoved me, steering by the pressure of the gun in my back. If I hadn't been blindfolded I would have swung at her, Herbie could have distracted Scavuzzo and I might have had a kick at the other guy. But if we were inside something, then someone outside the car had closed the outer door after us and if he was still present, the odds were too long.

I heard a door being opened ahead of me, then Herbie said, "What, in there?" in a surprised tone and the next moment I was shoved against a door jamb and inside some smaller space. I could tell it from the echoes, that was all. Herbie was still with me, that much was good.

"Stay there quietly," Carla said, and a door shut behind us.

I stood, listening carefully for about thirty seconds. Then I asked Herb. "Can you take this blindfold off me?"

"Sure." His fingers were trembling but he untied the knot and I could see again. There wasn't a lot to look at. We were inside an unlighted, windowless shed about thirty by twenty feet. Three walls were wood, the other was stone. I guessed we were up against some ancient wall, inside a tool shed of some kind. Only there were no tools or useful objects around that I could see.

Herbie's face was just visible, pale in the gloom. "What are they going to do to us?"

"They're going to sell you back to your folks. Don't worry," I told him cheerfully but he didn't reassure so easily.

"I don't think so. They're talking like they're going to kill us." His voice was trembling but I overrode it, heartily. Let's hear it for military command training.

"We're not dead yet. Now come here and feel carefully into the left lapel of my jacket."

"What am I feeling for?" He was bright enough to start looking before he started asking questions. That was a good sign.

"You're looking for a darning needle, about an inch and a half long. I stuck it there earlier on today, I know it's there."

He prodded the lapel until he found it, the hard way, the point in his finger. He hissed annoyance but didn't beef.

"I've got it. Now what do I do with it?"

"Hang on to it. If you drop it we'll never find it in this gloom." I turned around so that my handcuffed wrists were towards him. "This is difficult, so take your time."

"What do I have to do? Pick the lock?"

"No. Take the right cuff, now, can you see, or feel, which way the ratchet is working?"

He could and slowly I coached him through sliding the needle down into the ratchet, flipping the catch up so that he could unfasten the cuffs, one painful click at a time. It took us about one minute per tooth and my hand was only halfway to freedom when we heard the sound of voices outside.

"Stick the needle back in my lapel, out of sight," I whispered and he did. "Right, now stand behind me, in case only one of them has a gun. I can take a run at him."

He wanted to protest but there was no time. A lock clattered and the door swung open. Carla was there, with the gunman. She stood in the doorway and called to us. "Herb, come out from behind Locke."

He didn't move and Carla shrugged and said, "Have it your own way, I'll just tell Pietro to shoot Locke in the legs."

I wasn't sure whether she meant it but I didn't argue when Herbie walked to one side of me. She didn't seem to have a gun. That meant we had a chance if Herbie could hold her while I kicked Pietro's lights out. Not a good chance, but a chance.

He was too careful for me. Carla told us, "Come on out, Herbie, keep your hands on your head." And as we came to the doorway he backed off, out of striking range but plenty close enough for his gun to do its job.

"Sit down," Carla said. "You don't have to come all the way out." I was close enough to the door to see that we were inside a covered courtyard, old but not distinctive in any way. It was paved with flagstones. I couldn't see any doorway but when I sat down on the ground, like a good little prisoner, I could see the inside of the roof which was covered with the familiar baked tiles of the region. That meant that if we could climb up the wall we could break out. Good news.

Carla was carrying a purse and she opened it and took out a tiny Phillips tape recorder. "Time to say your lines," she said, smiling as if she meant it. She was wearing a light blouse and skirt and a whisper of perfume and I could feel Herbie yearning for her as we both waited to see what new nastiness she had dreamed up.

"I've written out what you're to say, don't make any mistakes with it," she said. She held out the paper to Herbie. "Read it through, then read it into the machine."

He read it to himself, frowning, then nodded and Carla handed him the machine. "You talk into there," she said, then pressed the Record button and motioned to him to begin.

"Hi, Mom and Dad. I am well and safe as long as you

pay the money like the people tell you to. Please don't try to catch them or anything because they're going to kill me if you do."

He handed her the recorder and she switched it off and said, "Good. Now let's see how your kidnapper can handle his part."

She was crouching to be at our level and she pivoted on the ball of her foot so that she was facing me, her perfect breasts on a level with my eyes. She held out the piece of paper for me to read and I glanced through it and looked up into her wonderful brown eyes. "This is pretty smart, think of it yourself?"

"Just read it, and don't add anything," she snapped.

She held out the tape recorder and I read the words from the paper. "This is John Locke. Herbie will be fine as long as the money is delivered safely. We want five million dollars in United States one hundred dollar bills. Put the money into your matching leather suitcases, Mrs. Ridley, and go with the bellboy, out to the street with the moneybags on a baggage trolley. A car will drive up and the driver will ask if this is the Ridley luggage. You will say yes and get into the car. The money will be put into the trunk and the car will leave. Tell the police not to follow the car or to plant bugs or try any tricks of any kind. You and the boy will be released twelve hours after the ransom is paid."

Carla pulled the tape recorder away and rewound the tape and crouched listening to it like a teenager grooving on a Mick Jagger offering. Then she stood up, frowning as she noticed the cuts on my ear, still bleeding from her efforts with the gun barrel.

"Your ear's a mess," she said almost indignantly as if it was my fault she was obliged to notice.

"The bullet hole you're planning to put through it will be even more untidy," I said.

"Don't jump the gun. We made our bargain last night," she said. "Nothing changed. I'm sorry about the ear."

"I'll remember that."

Suddenly she grinned. "Did you ever read *Alice in Wonderland* when you were a kid?" she asked.

"Of course. And since. Are you going to send me a white rabbit to steer me out of this mess?"

"No." She shook her head, smiling like Miss World. "No. But I guess you remember the Caucus Race."

I frowned and nodded. "I think so. 'All have won and all must have prizes.'"

"You're not just a pretty face, are you?" She laughed and shut the door on us.

In the darkness Herbie's calm evaporated. His voice was nervous as he asked, "What was that all about?"

"It means she's playing games with us, Herb. Maybe it's all in fun but I'm not sure I know the rules."

Herb was learning. He didn't waste time complaining or wondering why Carla was playing around. He asked, "Want me to have another go at your handcuffs?"

"Right on." I let him take the needle then turned for him to pick away at the cuffs. He freed one tooth almost immediately and was saying "Now we've got it," when I heard the tiny click of the needle snapping.

▸ 19 ◂

Herbie swore, softly. Then he said, "I'm sorry, John, the needle broke."

"It was going to happen sometime. Don't worry, can you use the broken piece?"

He fiddled with the cuffs some more before giving up. "No, it's too short, it won't reach the tooth on the ratchet."

"Let me try for a moment, see if I can wriggle my hand out of it," I said. "You hold the handcuff tight, I'll tug."

"Okay." He held the cuff and I struggled against it until my eyes were just about bugging out. The loop was looser and I could get my hand in almost up to the base of my thumb but not quite far enough to get it through. When my wrist got too sore I gave up.

"Okay, give it a rest. Let's take a look around, the best we can in this lousy light. See if there's a scrap of wire or a nail or something we could use to spring the ratchet. The ideal thing is the key from a can of sardines."

He was scared but he was happy to play my game,

pretending nothing was serious. He said, "A sardine can key? You're kidding."

"No, deadly earnest. If we come across the litter from some sloppy picnic, we're laughing."

"I'll bear it in mind," he said gruffly. The little bastard sounded so macho I could have hugged him if I hadn't been out of commission. I was starting to believe he should have been kidnapped years earlier, the experience was doing him good.

Our prison was almost completely dark and it took us about an hour to go over every inch of it, noses close to the walls first, then the floor, looking for anything we could have used to open my cuffs. There was nothing. By then, my eyes had grown accustomed enough to the gloom that I was able to see that the roof was boarded in. There was no chance of breaking out, the way we could have done through the tiles of the courtyard roof outside. We would have needed a jimmy bar. Some thing else we didn't have.

"Right, Herb, let's think what we do now," I said. "Since we're not going to get anything to eat, we might as well feed our fancy with revenge. How can we kick these bastards' heads in?"

"I thought you would have a plan," he said carefully.

"Oh I do," I lied, "But let's see what you come up with, good mental exercise. For openers, what's outside the courtyard or whatever it is that we're in?"

"It's a big garden. Roses, trees, flowers, nice grass. Like a graveyard only with no graves."

I wasn't sure that would still be the case once Scavuzzo had collected the cash. Herbie and I would fit nicely under one of his rose bushes. But despondency wasn't going to get us home safe so I breezed on.

"Good lad. You really took notice. Did we come in through a gate that had to be opened, or was it just a driveway?"

He had that one too. "There's a big iron gate and a

man there who opened it when he saw the car coming. I think he was waiting for us because he ran out and did it as soon as we turned the corner at the end of the street."

"What kind of street is it?"

"More of a road really, just a couple of other houses along it over the last half mile," he said. "Looked rich to me."

"Herb, you'd make a good soldier," I told him. "Did we cross the river coming here?"

"Yes." He was excited now, proud of remembering the details. "It seemed to me that we went back along the river on the other side for a couple of miles, then crossed and came back a bit towards town."

I sat still, weighing the information he'd given me. Big houses with gate-keepers and well-kept grounds probably meant there would be guard dogs running free, maybe little men with guns as well. Escaping wouldn't be as simple as just getting through one door and making a dash for it. I figured we would need a car. Certainly we would need firepower. Probably our best hope of getting away was to barricade ourselves inside the house and phone the police. I wondered if they were keeping tabs on the addresses where Scavuzzo could be found. And I wondered how long it would take them to respond if we did call in.

Herb stood up as I sat comparing our options. He went over to the door to squint through the crack beside the hinge. I saw his shoulders sag. Nothing out there offered any hope. Then he came and sat down next to me, resting his back against the outer wall of our shed.

"Maybe if I acted like I was sick. She might send that guy to get somebody, then I could grab her and we could make her let us out."

"Not bad. But it would be better if we could overpower the guy with the gun. If you can take off him then we've got some real leverage."

"Yeah." His voice was full of excitement but it all exhaled as he finished the thought. "Yeah, but how?"

We sat and thought about it for a while. "I think we should tackle them the next time they come in. We have to act early, before the money is delivered. They want us alive until then, in case your parents get cagey and ask them for proof that you're still alive."

"You mean that's all they're keeping us alive for?" he asked in a croak.

"Just being realistic. I don't think they're planning to release me. I know too much about who's doing what to whom. And being honest with ourselves, they may feel the same way about you."

He didn't speak for almost a minute. Then he said, "You really think so?"

"I'm afraid so, Herb. It happens in a lot of kidnappings, even when it's a child involved. With a guy your age, someone who just proved to me that he would be a good witness, they may want to play safe. But don't get despondent. All we have to do is overpower one man and get out of one door, that's all." Lies. Lies. But he had enough worrying to do without getting into details.

He was silent again and at last he asked, "Have you ever been, like, you know, closer than this to getting it?"

"Sure." Hell we were maybe hours away from death. I'd been within micro-seconds of it a time or two.

"When was the closest, for you?" Normally I don't tell war stories, but Herbie was asking the big question out of the big need, wanting to know how much space we really did have left in our lives. Without a valid comparison he couldn't understand.

"It was in the Falklands." I could remember the rain and the gunfire, the slow approach, on my belly over the wet ground. The damp cold eating into my joints while my heart raced as I anticipated the sentry seeing us and firing.

"Go on," Herbie said. "What happened?"

"Oh, it was a firefight. We won."

"Yes, otherwise you wouldn't be here. But tell me about it."

"Didn't I tell you that a gentleman doesn't talk about women he's known or men he's clobbered?" I asked him.

"Yeah, I remember," he said, "and I'm going to keep the rule, I promise, if it ever applies to me. But do me a favor, eh, I want to know." He wasn't looking for kicks. He was asking it in a flat, information-seeking voice, fearful for his own life. And because I wasn't sure I could save it for him, I told him.

"We were sent on a patrol against an Argentine base. Our objective was to overpower the sentries and destroy their guns, then retire with the minimum possible losses."

"And what happened?" I could make out the disk of his face, the eye sockets dark and deep as a panda's eyes as he stared at me.

"What happened was a screw-up at headquarters. Or maybe the cynical bastards thought they were helping us by making the enemy keep their heads down. Anyway, just as we reached the enemy position, our own mortars came down on them." I pressed my fingertips against the cool stone, beneath me, remembering the shriek and thunder of the incoming fire, the flashes that lit up my patrol as we squirmed the last couple of hundred meters.

"And a shell nearly got you?" He was probing gently, like a surgeon fingering an inflamed appendix.

"Maybe, but that doesn't count. When you look back somewhere and see a shell land and think it would have got you—if—that's just geography, you don't count that. What happened to me was that the explosion blew me up in the air, tearing my weapon out of my hands. I came down, half stunned and disarmed and found myself looking up at an Argie sentry. He'd been caught in the same blast but he still had his gun."

"And he shot at you and missed?" Herbie's voice ran up the scale almost to breaking point.

I shook my head. "Tighter than that." Closing my eyes I could still see it all. I had honestly looked into the eyes of death that night, into the terminal eye of a gun muzzle aimed point blank. "No, he shot me, only his gun barrel was stuffed with dirt from the blast and his weapon blew up on him. He was firing from the hip and the blowback drove the mechanism back through his gut."

He was quiet for a long moment then he asked me. "Did you kill him?"

"I didn't have to. He was gone." I could remember the whimpering that ended even before I retrieved my own H. & K. and went on, towards the guns.

He cleared his throat, nervously. "Listen, don't get me wrong, all right?"

"Shoot." I could guess what was coming.

"How many men have you killed?"

"That's classified. But the answer is, none that I could have avoided killing, I've always been a soldier, not a hit man."

I'd picked the wrong time for philosophy. He made a tight-lipped little joke. "I hope you're in the mood for soldiering right now."

"As much as possible with my hands behind me. But why don't I show you what to do, if you get the chance. Stand up and I'll give you a couple of basics."

He stood up and I talked him through a couple of strikes and kicks, nothing fancy, nothing that required elegant placing of the blow, just plain brutal tactics that might enable him to stop some overconfident thug from putting a bullet through his head.

He was sweating and excited when I stopped, anxious to learn more. The new knowledge had given him back the self-respect that had gone when the first hood had shoved the first gun into his side. He was ready to hurt them and anxious for the chance.

"Come on, this is great," he said, moving around me lightly on the balls of his feet.

"Practice what you know," I told him. "Practice and practice until it's second nature. You may never need to know any more tricks, fighting isn't about tricks anyway, it's about readiness."

"Sure, how's this?" He turned away from me and shadow-boxed the air in front of him for thirty seconds non-stop. Then he stopped, panting.

"That's the next lesson to learn," I told him. "How to keep on fighting until the other guy has collapsed with fatigue. You do that by keeping fit, working out and running every day of your life, even when it's thirty below and you don't want to get out of bed."

"I will," he promised. "I will. I'll go running with you every day we're here and I'll keep on when we get home."

Amazing, a few minutes' worth of technique and his fear of dying was over. That's the secret of building an army I guess, get 'em while they're young and tell them they're invincible.

Voices suddenly muttered outside the door. I shook my head at Herbie. "Don't do anything rash," I whispered. "Wait for the right time."

He nodded without speaking and then the door swung open. I blinked at the light and then focused on Carla, who was holding her little gun, and Pietro who had the family shotgun trained on Herbie.

"Stand where you are, both of you," Carla said.

"What's happening now?" I asked, trying to sound bored. I wondered if they'd got their money and were going to cancel us both and bury us in one of their big rosebeds. Maybe if I charged the guy with the shotgun he would aim at me while Herbie clobbered Carla and took her gun. At least he'd have a chance. It was better than rolling over and playing dead for them.

"I have a proposition for you," Carla said. She was looking at me, ignoring Herbie as if he was just a pawn on the board. Maybe he would get valuable later but it was me she needed right now.

"Didn't your mother teach you not to proposition strange men?"

"Cut the crap. We could use some help and you're the best guy for the job."

"What job? You need a Christian to feed to your lions? I hardly qualify. I haven't been to church in years."

"Shut up," she snapped impatiently. "Listen to me."

"Go ahead. Let's hear the latest scam."

"We've had word from a friend that the police are going to booby-trap the money. They're putting it in bags with explosives in it."

"Why would they do that? You've still got the boy, you just hold off on delivering him."

She sighed. "You don't understand the way the Italian mind works, do you?"

"Same way as a male dog's, I thought. If you can't eat it or screw it, piss on it."

She didn't even bother sighing. She just said, "Whoever gets the money will take it to the boss. The boss will open it. That's the way it is. Only this time, when the boss opens it, he'll be wasted. Then everybody will run away, the police move in on the sound of the bang and find the boy. Simple."

I shook my head. "That's garbage. You asked them to send Kate Ridley with the money, I know you did, I made the tape, remember? The police won't take a chance on harming her."

Carla looked at me very straight. "The *maggiore* has refused to send Kate Ridley. He's hard. She volunteered to come, anything to get her darling boy home safe, but he said no."

That was the first good news I'd had all day. At last somebody in the world wasn't giving in to these bastards. But there wasn't much hope that it would do me any good. I got back to my own situation, as tactfully as an Armenian rug dealer. "You mentioned a proposition."

"We want you to inspect the bags for us, to open them if possible."

"And what do I get in return?"

"Your life," she said quietly.

I laughed out loud. She was lying. All her brave talk meant was that they couldn't find a bomb disposal expert without calling in some veteran of the Red Guard who would want to corner a chunk of the take on behalf of the People—meaning him and his in-laws. As soon as I'd opened the bags they'd blow me away. But on the other hand, at least I would have my hands free while I was working. I might be able to overpower someone who had a gun. If I did, I could start reversing the odds in my favor.

"What's the matter?" she asked with a pout. "Don't you believe me?"

"I wouldn't believe you ever. But that's not the point. We're talking deals, I want the kid free or it's no dice."

She swung her head away, exasperated. "Don't talk nonsense. The kid's safe as a church. Once we've got the money, he's released. You know that."

"All I know is I've been lied to from the first time I set eyes on you." I glanced around at Pietro but he was concentrating on Herbie, neither one of us could have tackled him safely. Either I did a deal with them or we stagnated here until someone decided to pull the plug on us. I gazed at Carla, smiling politely and waited.

"I've promised you your life," she said again.

"And you'll cancel that promise the moment I've opened those bags, always supposing that I can open them without killing myself."

"Listen," she said carefully. "You're not the only guy in Italy who knows how to handle explosives. We can have someone else flown in to check the bags. That's what Julio wanted to do anyway but I suggested you."

"And he went along with that?"

She sighed, waving her arms in exasperation at my stupidity. "You're so dumb you make me tired, Locke. If he brings someone in, they'll want a share of the money. You won't."

"That's just part of the answer. The truth is, I'm expendable. If I blow my own head off with those bags you don't have any grieving widow to take care of." I was just feeding her the words while I asked myself all the questions about what she was saying. For one thing, would the police put the real money into an exploding bag? Surely they would pack the bags with old phone books or Italian soccer fans magazines. Why blow a fortune into confetti?"

And secondly, and more important, why would Scavuzzo accept the booby-trapped bags? That one bothered me. Why didn't they just insist the money was delivered clean?

And then the answer came to me. Whoever had told them about the booby trapping must be close to the police and the law enforcement system in general. He was a mole they had planted and if they acknowledged his information by balking at the delivery of the bags, they would blow his cover. Boy, was this Machiavelli's hometown or what?

"Since you have Herbie and me by the short and curlies, I'm going to accept your swell offer. Now, take the handcuffs off me and we can discuss it."

She looked genuinely sorry, Sophia Loren regretting that she had no pen to give a fan an autograph. "You know I can't do that, John. You'd just jump me and try to get away. I'm only here to sound you out."

"Then go in peace, my child." I moved away from her, backing, measuring the distance from my foot to her hand in case Herbie could get the other guy off balance and I could kick her gun away and give us a chance.

"I'll be back as soon as we get word on the money."

she said. She flicked a fast glance at Pietro. Then she whispered, "Listen, nothing's changed from this morning. You know that."

"Nothing's changed from where you're sitting. I'm stuck in a shed with nothing to eat or drink and my hands cuffed behind me so I couldn't answer the call of nature should she choose to whistle at me."

She shook her head quickly. "I can't change that. You're too dangerous to set loose. But I'll get you some food."

"Okay." I nodded at her. "And if I'm going to go through with the defusing, there's some things I'm going to need."

"Like what?"

"Like too many things for you to remember without a list. Go get a pencil and paper and I'll tell you."

"I'll come back," she nodded at me and spoke to Pietro. He listened to her without turning his head, like a well trained bird dog on the point, and nudged Herbie with the muzzle of his gun.

I saw the kid stiffen, then check himself, holding in his new knowledge of how and where to hit a man so that he stays hit. I took the pressure off him, calling out, "Back inside, Herbie, they're bringing us some food."

"I hope so," he said angrily. I was proud of him. Nobody would have guessed he was scared for his life.

I turned and followed him back inside the shed. As Carla motioned to Pietro to shut the door I faced her. "No dinner, no bomb," I said.

"Don't worry about your food. Just sit there and try to remember how to do your job," she snapped. And I laughed out loud as the door swung shut.

Herbie looked at me, almost invisible in the thick new darkness now that our eyes were used to brighter light. "What's funny?"

"She's hired me to defuse a bomb for her. I've never defused an explosive device in my life before."

He was about as amused as a wife would have been. "Why are you laughing? You could get killed."

"No chance of that, they won't use anything too complex. What it means is they have to free my hands and put a weapon right into them. We're as good as home free, Herbie, believe me."

▸ 20 ◂

Carla kept her bargain. She and Pietro were back in an hour with food for us, a good spaghetti Bolognese that would have set off every garlic detector south of the Swiss border. She wouldn't take the cuffs off me, so Herbie fed me, as neatly as possible but it's an embarrassing process and I was glad to call it quits after about half as much as I would have liked to eat. So far my time in Italy had been a culinary bust.

When we had finished eating, Carla wrote down all the items I told her I needed to defuse her booby-trap and then she shut us in again and left. We had already searched the shed twice for anything to unfasten my cuffs so we sat and waited without talking until they came back for me about an hour later. Pietro was dressed the same but Carla was wearing a set of baggy coveralls that hadn't been sewn by Bill Blass or any of that crowd. I still didn't think any good copper would mistake her for a man but it cancelled out the more spectacular aspects of her shape. I ribbed her anyway.

"Why, it's Rosy the Riveter," I said. "No dice, kid, you couldn't disguise that bod by wrapping it in a lifeboat cover."

"Not everybody is as relentlessly dirty-minded as you," she said with a touch of anger. I suppose she was feeling macho at the thought of lifting all that cash.

"We're on our way," she said.

"Good. These handcuffs are killing me."

"They stay on," she snapped.

I shrugged. "Have it your own way but defusing a bomb is hard enough with your hands free. Dressed like this I can't guarantee results."

"We'll undo your hands when you're shackled into the truck," she said. "You're a mad dog, Locke, we're not taking chances with you."

Herbie was looking at me, waiting for a sign, like maybe the Second Coming. In the meantime, Pietro was covering him carefully with the shotgun, there was no room to move. I gave Herb a microscopic shake of the head. Don't try anything, our turn is coming.

"What happens to Herbie while I'm off playing with matches?"

"He stays here."

"And what guarantee do I have that he's going to be safe?"

"You have my word on it," she said carefully. "Nothing will happen to him as long as you behave yourself."

"Your word." I laughed. "Which word will that be? I can think of about thirty-nine of them that apply to you. None of which is worth making book on."

"Shut your mouth. You come with me and do as you're told and you live. Any more of this crap and I'll shoot you."

"Now instead of later?" I shook my head and sat down. With any luck, Pietro would try to stand me up again. While he was trying that, Herbie could practice some of the tricks I'd shown him. But Carla wasn't buying.

"So far we've been treating the boy gently," she said. "It wouldn't take very much more of your aggravation to stop that. Like we could maybe beat him on the soles of his feet until you came along. Or we could cut his fingers off. I don't care. I just need you with me in that truck."

I didn't believe her but it seemed that Herbie was impressed. He cleared his throat and said, "Listen, I'll be okay John. You go ahead."

I winked at him. "Hang loose, it's me they want out of the way, not you. I'll call out when they bring me back, you'll know it's me."

Pietro scowled at Herbie and flipped up the muzzle of his gun, indicating the inside of the shed. Herbie shrugged and went in. I could see his fingers flexing as he moved. He would be ready if they came to kill him. I hoped so. That way I would have been a successful bodyguard, regardless.

I watched as Carla closed the door and clunked the big padlock shut. Then she hooked her head at me and I followed down the echoing courtyard which I saw now was lit with strips of flourescent lighting hanging on bare ballasts below the old beams that supported the baked tiles. Why was it covered in? Crime, certainly, Scavuzzo needed a spot out of sight to unload trucks or do whatever else needed doing. Like disposing of unwanted bodyguards. I would have to use my time well once they took the cuffs off me, otherwise I would be shuffled out of here in a bag when they'd got their money, despite what Carla was promising.

There was a van parked close to the big double doors of the courtyard. It was a nondescript rattletrap with no name on the side. Carla led me to it and opened the rear door. Pietro prodded me with his friendly persuader and I climbed in.

The interior was surprising. The sheet metal on the sides was thicker than I had assumed, quarter-inch armor plate I would have guessed. The rear windows were one-inch thick glass, bullet-proof portholes that could be swung out of the way to fire through if needed. The driver's seat was accessible from the rear of the van, the way it is in a recreational vehicle. And there were benches along both sides, room enough for ten men to sit while the van chugged through traffic.

"This thing's an armored personnel carrier," I said. "That's going to be useful if they decide to start shooting at us as well as trying to blow us up."

"Sit there," Carla said and pointed to the end of the seat behind the driver. I sat, obediently. It was the spot I would have chosen over any other. I would be able to put the driver out of commission from here. If Carla was dumb enough to take her gun off me for a moment once we were driving it was game set and match to me.

Carla lifted the lid of the seat opposite me. I could see two Armalites, the Browning rifles the Americans call M-16's. They were laid out in properly built braces. And there were magazines as well. If they were loaded I could resolve the whole situation once she took the handcuffs off me.

Carla opened an inner container and took out a set of leg shackles, the same design as handcuffs only bigger. She spoke to Pietro and he covered me from four feet away while she stooped, out of his possible line of fire and coupled my left ankle to the post that ran up behind the driver's seat. Then she said, "I'm going to take your cuffs off now. Don't try anything cute or Pietro will shoot. I promise you that."

"Sounds like the kind of promise you'd enjoy keeping," I said. "Here, help yourself." I turned away from her, pushing my wrists out where she could work on them. She tried the right wrist first, then swore.

"Try the other one. I'll undo the right."

She unsnapped the left cuff easily and I brought my hands in front of me, flexing my elbows, sighing with pleasure at the end of the cramps. The cuffs were still dangling from my right wrist.

"Let me see the key a minute," I asked her, smiling politely. Manners cost nothing, especially when someone has a shotgun pointed at your gut.

She handed over the key and I pushed the right handcuff shut one click, then banged it on the seat beside me. I saw the tiny shard of steel from the broken needle flip out. After that the key worked perfectly and I handed the cuffs and the key back to Carla and sat rubbing my wrists and flexing my arms, getting ready for the biggest challenge of the day. Because I'd made my mind up. There was no way I was going to do any bomb disposal work for them. At the first opportunity I would break the driver's neck and grab Carla.

Pietro gave Carla the shotgun and stepped out of the van. He opened the big courtyard doors. Outside it was a lovely afternoon, hot and perfumed with flowers. I could see ahead of the van down a long driveway to a closed double gate made of thick iron bars. There were no dogs in sight but there was an eight-foot wall around the whole property, dogs could have run free throughout the grounds, answering to commands on a silent whistle. It would make no sense to come back over the wall and attempt to get in and rescue Herbie. When I came I would have to come armed, or better still, with armed reinforcements.

The only feature I didn't like was the two-way radio Pietro was using. For the fiftieth time since this job had started, I wished I spoke Italian. From his tone it sounded to me as if he was talking to his boss. That meant someone with the power of life and death over young Herb. I guessed that if Pietro didn't make his calls on cue, they would move Herb away from that house, even kill him. If I was going to try something, I would have to wait until we were almost back here before I tried to take Pietro out.

Pietro got into the driver's seat, parking his walkie-talkie on the seat beside him and drove slowly down the roadway between the flowerbeds to the front gate. Carla sat opposite me, nursing the shotgun over her knees.

A tiny old man came out to the gate and opened it before we got there. Pietro drove out, waving at the old guy, moving at a comfortable speed, not fast or slow enough to attract attention. I sat with my hands on my knees, bending forward so that Carla wouldn't see that my feet were braced against the side of the bench ready to lunge at her.

I glanced out of the front window, past Pietro, seeing that we were driving down a slight slope between vineyards that ended raggedly against the road. Then I looked back at Carla and she held my gaze, fixedly, as if she was trying to beam me a message by ESP. Slowly, moving so carefully that Pietro couldn't have caught it in his rearview mirror, she raised one finger towards her lips, an unmistakable signal to wait. I narrowed my eyes at her, questioningly, and she winked. I still didn't trust her, but there was no doubt she expected me to make a move and wanted me to wait for her signal.

Pietro passed a small car, glancing back at it in his mirror, then beaming to himself. When he had settled again, staring ahead oblivious to what was behind him, Carla silently mouthed four words, "First, Get, The, Money."

I didn't move. I just sat hunched forward, forearms resting on my knees, still wondering what was best for me and for Herb Ridley. If I acted now I could possibly put both of them out of action. But if Pietro failed to make his appointed calls, they might kill Herbie out of hand and run. I would have to wait for a while anyway and see what Carla's plan was, if any. Otherwise I would take over the van once we were close to the house on the way back. Bide your time, Locke.

It took us half an hour to get back into the thick of town. I sat there, cooking quietly in the heat. The one thing the van's designers hadn't considered was heat dispersal. As we sat in the afternoon sunlight the temperature rose until perspiration was running off me and I could smell the ghost of every garlic-eating mouth-breather who had ever sat in the van throughout its history. It was getting bad enough to cloud my judgment. I was almost ready to go ahead and take Pietro, trusting that the people at the other end would think the radio was on the fritz. Then I saw the Ponte

Vecchio. We were almost at the Rega. I might as well wait and see what Carla had in mind.

She reached into the pocket of her coveralls and pulled out two ski masks. She pulled one of them down over her own face and handed the other to Pietro. He was stationary in the traffic and he pulled it on without taking his eyes from the car ahead. And still I waited. There was something about Carla's certainty that fascinated me. She had a plan. If it was dumb I'd ignore it but first I'd do things her way.

The traffic flows one-way, west along the Lungarno. We drove in the left lane, slowly enough to exasperate a number of drivers who honked and passed. Pietro didn't even look in his mirror at them. He stopped in front of the Rega and sounded his horn four times, two long, two short.

We were parked in front of the door so that I couldn't see what was happening, but after thirty seconds he got out of the van and went around the side. Then the back door opened and the bellboy from the hotel struggled to lift three suitcases into the rear. He was trying to look like he was minding his own business but I could see his eyes darting nervously. Capelli had him primed to notice everything. I made sure he saw my leg shackle. If he did, he didn't editorialize on it with his eyes. He lifted and sweated and then stood back. Smart. Carla had the shotgun trained on him the whole time.

Then Pietro slammed the back door and came around to the driver's seat. He picked up his radio and made a three-word announcement. There was an equally crisp answer and he laid down the radio and drove off, watching the rear mirror with great care.

I was looking over his shoulder, ahead. That was where Capelli would have put his cars, spaced this side of every intersection for the next quarter mile. No matter which way we turned, we would have one of them behind us and the others closing in.

Maybe it was all out of my hands anyway now. They

couldn't get away, not if Capelli wanted to hold them. The van stood out like a sore thumb. By now, every cop in Florence knew its license and description.

I glanced back at Carla. She had moved away from where I could reach her and set the gun aside. She was kneeling beside the biggest suitcase, holding the toolbox she had prepared for me.

"Don't touch anything, there are tests to do first," I snapped. Even a small blast inside this steel coffin would pulp all three of us.

She looked up at me and said, "Don't believe everything you hear, John, you'll spend your whole life worrying." Then she took my clasp knife from the toolbox and slit the fine leather of the case, cutting first longways, then across, opening a big L-shaped hole. She put her hands inside and hooted with laughter. "Got it," she said triumphantly. "Five million bucks and it's all mine."

I guess my mouth must have been hanging open like a kid's on his first trip to the circus. "You said those bags would be booby trapped."

She laughed, happily, musically, genuinely amused for the first time since I met her. "Oh, they're going to be, that's where you earn your keep."

▸ 21 ◂

"What the hell for?" I threw up my hands. Blame the spaghetti Bolognese, I don't usually act that Italian.

"To make sure that I come out of this free and clear." She was digging deeper and deeper into the bag, bringing out handfuls of bills. "Look at all these lovely hundreds," she said and laughed again. Pietro took his eyes off the road to glance back, rolling his ski mask up with one hand, laughing, cockeyed happy at the sight of all that loot.

I looked from one to the other of them in disbelief. They were as excited as kids in a toy store, chattering and laughing. They had all the lovely money and they weren't going to let that nasty old Scavuzzo take it away from them. So be a good boy, John, blow his head off for us.

My first impulse was to tell her to go to hell. But that would have meant staying chained to my post with Carla's shotgun trained on me. Once I got out I could change the rules. It seemed that was the way everyone was playing this game. "Okay, set me loose first," I said, but Carla wasn't paying any attention to me, she was digging deeper and deeper into the case, dredging up more and more thousands of wonderful tax-free dollars, laughing and rocking to and fro like a backward boy on his first pony ride.

"I'm going to need this thing parked. I can't work in a moving vehicle," I shouted. I had to shout. She was laughing and Pietro was calling out over his shoulder. It was all premature anyway. The first police car would be on our tail by now.

Carla looked at me as if suddenly remembering my presence. "Don't worry, we'll find you a quiet place to work."

"Yeah," I said. I half stood, checking out the windshield first, then back, through the porthole in the rear door. The usual Florentine crush of traffic was clamping us in, there was no room for a dash. We would be stopped by the police within minutes. I sat back and relaxed. There was no need for me to do anything more than survive until the first roadblock. Then I only had to hit Pietro and take his gun, disarm Carla and I was free—to make the rescue bid on Herbie and then start the long explanation to Capelli. That last thought sobered me down. There was no room to be smug, not yet.

But I had reckoned without Carla. Suddenly she was all business. She half stood, checking the traffic behind us, then snapped a command to Pietro. He stopped talking and made an abrupt left turn. I still wasn't impressed. I knew we couldn't outrun a flotilla of police cars. And we wouldn't have done it, without Carla.

She unflipped the catch on the porthole and lifted it slightly. Then she held a handful of hundred dollar bills out of it and let them go. I watched them flutter back in a spiral that lasted ten seconds before the first car jammed its brakes on, causing the car behind to smash into it. Carla laughed and dropped more bills and I saw the traffic behind us slam to a standstill as drivers and Vespa riders abandoned their vehicles everywhere and tumbled over one another to grab the money. Greed was going to get us away where stealth would have failed.

Carla stood there, calling out to Pietro who turned

left and right three or four more times while she shed more money at every corner. I watched her, fascinated. She looked like an angler playing a trout, giving just enough line to tire the fish. Behind us first one then several police sirens started sawing the air but the way was blocked, even the sidewalks had cars on them. The streets were a mass of shoving people, too engrossed with collecting cash even to look up at where it had come from. Carla had won, she had bought her way out of an impossible situation.

As we turned away from the center of town she stopped dropping money and closed the porthole. "We're going to park and you can work then," she said. "I've put everything you need in your tool kit. Plastic, detonators, timers."

"It will take me about twenty-five minutes. Can you account for the time?"

"Leave it to me." She was still grinning. With the ski mask rolled up on her forehead and her baggy coveralls she looked like some beautiful impish child with nothing naughtier on her mind than a raid on the cookie jar.

"I'm not working on explosives while I'm chained to this post," I said.

She tugged the ski-mask free of her hair and tossed it aside, shaking out her sweaty hair. "Don't worry, I'll unlock you."

"Give me the key." I held out one hand but she ignored me. She was unzipping her coveralls, down to the waist. I could see she was wearing only a brassiere and panties underneath. Her skin was glistening with sweat. I didn't like the fact that she took no notice of my presence. It could have been simply because we had slept together or else because she knew I was what the Irish refer to as a dead man walking, with her own gun waiting to put an end to the walking part. The only consolation was that she had set the shotgun down on the floor, pinning it under one negligent foot. I was safe for the moment anyway.

Carla took a dress from one of the compartments and

slipped it on, then called something to Pietro and he answered, over his shoulder, still laughing, intoxicated by the intangible scent of money that seemed to fill the truck. He turned a couple of times, down smaller and smaller streets. Carla stood at the back of the van, still holding a handful of hundred dollar bills, fingering them the way a dress designer might have felt velvet, staring past me and Pietro, through the windshield. Then she gave him another command and he stopped in front of a parked car.

She undid the rear door and he got out and came around to the back. She spoke to him and gave him a car key. He was back in thirty seconds with a heavy suitcase, the twin of the one she had slashed open. He slid it in, gasping at the weight. She spoke to him and he nodded and stepped up into the back of the van, moving past me. He was level with me, watching me warily as he stepped by when Carla took her little pistol out of the pocket of her abandoned coveralls, and shot him twice through the back, then once through the head.

He fell forward, blood pouring out of his mouth, trying to focus his eyes, trying to speak, finally, trying to cross himself, and died.

I looked at her face. It was just as beautiful but blank, like a mask covering the ugliness inside. She blinked once then reached in her pocket and brought out a key which she tossed to me. "Get yourself loose."

I did, unsnapping the shackle on my leg and refastening it around the pole, where it would be harder for her to stick it back on me afterwards, if she decided to, if she wasn't going to treat me the same as Pietro.

"Get in the driver's seat," she said impatiently, not even looking at the dead man. He was just garbage, cluttering up her doll's house. I didn't argue, she had her gun trained on me. Besides, I'd have a better chance of escaping once I was next to the door.

I slid into the seat and adjusted it backwards to fit my legs. Pietro had been short, I realized. Funny, holding a gun he had always seemed a little larger than lifesize. Now he seemed smaller.

"Where to?" I asked, watching her in the rear mirror.

"Turn right at the end of this street, then keep on until you come to the next light." She had moved up closer to me, the gun still the most prominent feature. Now she sank down on the seat I had been chained to, the gun very close to the back of my head. I wasn't sure how close, she was lost from my mirror.

I drove carefully, signaling properly and turning right then keeping on for almost a mile down a road that was obviously taking us out of town, westward, towards the sun that was sinking, splashing shadows long enough to darken the side streets we passed.

We reached the light and she said, "Left here, about three hundred yards on the right side. You'll see a gas station, it's closed. Pull in."

She was right. The station had been closed for some time. The windows of the little garage on the lot were whitewashed over. She nudged the back of my neck with the gun barrel. It was still warm from killing Pietro.

"You're probably planning to make a break for it now," she said. "I don't have the people I need to stop you but you've got to know that if I'm not back within the hour they're going to shoot the boy. You should also know that he's been moved again. It's no good storming back to the palazzo and making like the SAS. He's gone."

"Why should I believe you?"

She gave a little sigh. "Why would you doubt me? You saw what happened to him." The gun muzzle moved, downwards, I guessed, pointing at its last target.

"Okay. What do I have to do?"

"Get out and open the garage door. Here's the key." I felt the end of it sticking into my neck close to the gun muzzle. I reached back and took it, carefully. No sense giving her any kind of reason to shoot. She didn't need much. I got out of the van and opened the door. Traffic was passing on the street behind me, cars and people coming and going carelessly. I guessed they hadn't heard about the hundred buck blizzard that had been blowing around the city core. All the drivers had on their minds was business or the eveining's assignations. The Good Lord willing, maybe I'd be one of them again by later tonight.

Inside the garage there was a car parked. A nondescript red Fiat with Milan plates. Whoever had organized this caper had really organized, this car was invisible.

I got back into the van. Carla had moved back from the seat she had been occupying. There was no chance to grab her. "Drive it in and close the door," she said.

I did and the dimness of the light seemed to cut us off from the noise and presence of the world, like being underwater.

Carla got out of the back of the van, holding the shotgun in one hand, the pistol in the other. "I don't want to use a gun. I like you and I want you to live, but I must have this suitcase booby trapped. Will you do it?"

"Unquestioningly," I lied. "Where's my box of tricks?"

"Under the seat you were on." She backed off a pace while I got into the van again and crouched over Pietro's body to unlatch the cover of the seat I'd occupied first. Inside it was a box and inside that were padded partitions that contained fuses, electrical wire, a timing device, batteries, detonators, everything except the explosive.

"So far so good. Now where's the plastic?"

"This end of the seat, in a cooler chest."

Good thinking again. Plastic is stable even in tropical heat but it tends to smell stronger when it gets warm. It's harder to camouflage the bomb.

The chest was packed with ice and the explosive was

wrapped in plastic bags, two charges about half a pound each. Enough to wipe out Scavuzzo's whole family tree. "What's the scenario? Are you planning to leave the room when he opens this case?"

"I want a blast big enough to kill him and shred the paper in the case but not bring a goddamn house down. Can you do that?"

"Your wish is my command." I opened one pack of the plastic and started to knead it. It was enough to kill a whole roomful of people, although I didn't think she would recognize that.

"I'm going to use a friction detonator. When he opens the lid of the case it will break a circuit and trigger the blast."

"Good. Get on with it." Her voice was harsh and tight. Reaction, I guessed, to the death of Pietro. She hadn't felt it while she was still high on the smell of money. Now she was realizing what she had done. Probably she would start to shake in a few minutes, and then probably weep. It would make it easier for me to get the upper hand. I couldn't risk hitting her. If I knocked her out I wouldn't find out where Herbie had been moved to.

I stood outside the van now, leaning down over the suitcase Pietro had moved in before he was shot. "Is this one already booby trapped?"

"No. I packed it myself," she said. "Go ahead and open it."

I did, snapping the catch and opening it carefully, listening for the telltale click of a mechanism. I would probably be too late but if I rolled under the van I might survive with nothing worse than ruptured eardrums.

There was no sound. I raised the lid of the case very carefully, crouching to look through the crack as I did. I couldn't see any wires dangling, anything suspicious. "Come on," Carla said impatiently. "I told you already. It's not booby trapped."

"There are old bomb experts and there are bold

bomb experts," I told her. "But there are no old bold bomb experts."

She made an impatient hissing noise through her teeth. "Come on for Christ's sweet sake."

I opened the lid all the way and looked down on the contents, a thick pile of newspapers. The one on the top was dated the previous day and had no news of the kidnapping on the front page. It probably meant she had packed it before the kidnapping happened. Talk about organized.

I rolled the plastic thin, like a kid's plasticine snake, and pressed it against the lower lip of the suitcase cover. Logically the person opening it would have that side towards him. The density of the packed newspapers would force the blast towards him, pulverizing his whole body. Then I picked out a detonator and an electrical relay mechanism, a simple burglar alarm switch, the kind you can pick up in an electronics store for five bucks. I hoped it was well made. There was no room for error now.

Part of the kit I had asked Carla to pack for me was an ammeter. I used it now, testing all the electrical components. They were working well. I coupled the detonator and relay in place and taped them inside the body of the case, tearing out enough newspaper from the contents to accommodate the mechanism. Then I did the same with the batteries, in the lid of the case. Connecting the two was a wire with a current running through it to hold the relay back. When the case was opened the circuit would be broken, the relay would relax, driving the plunger into the detonator, which would in turn set off the booby trap. The kind of job any rough and ready soldier would do, not fancy but deadly.

The only thing I didn't do was couple the battery properly to the relay. Everything looked good but the mechanism wasn't armed. I figured to get a crack at Scavuzzo anyway. I didn't need him blown up.

"Right. That's it," I said and straightened up, wiping

the sweat off my forehead. Working with explosives is harder on a man than digging coal.

"Good. Put all the suitcases in the trunk of the car. This one on top," Carla said. She was still waving the pistol around but she had set the shotgun aside, confident that I would come along like a good boy to the rendezvous with Scavuzzo. I just hoped Herbie was going to be there.

The bags exactly filled the trunk and they were heavy but they didn't squash the car down on its axle the way I'd expected. I glanced at Carla who had relaxed completely now. I could have snatched the gun off her with no trouble, if I'd been sure she would lead me to Herbie after I did it. "What have you done to the car? Heavy duty springs?" I asked her. Just a dumb male, making conversation.

Her answer surprised me. "Of course. I've been organizing this for a long time."

She waved the gun at me. "Open the door and then back out, but don't try taking off without me."

I did it, every move by the book. But she didn't know that my ethics were suddenly fighting a tough fight with natural greed. Five million U.S. dollars spelled freedom for the rest of my life. I could take it off her and skip town. Disappearing would be no trouble. Five million bucks buys a lot of invisibility. A beard, a new passport and I could live like a lord.

But on the other hand, Herb Ridley might not make it through and I would wake up nights with his trusting face in front of me. I sighed and opened the car door for her as she closed the garage.

She had the gun low beside her, on a line with my right kidney. Unless Italian hospitals were better run than any other business I'd encountered in Italy, one shot would kill me, slowly, over a painful couple of weeks. So I drove carefully, at the limit, listening to her instructions.

She headed me out of town, south now so that the shadows of the houses beside the road splashed over us as we traveled. "Where are we headed?"

"To a rendezvous," she said, clamping her mouth shut as if extra words might spill out on their own if she didn't bite them back.

"And then what? Scavuzzo opens the case and departs this vale of tears. You shoot Herbie and me and drive off into the sunset."

"Partly right," she said and now she allowed herself a ghost of her earlier glee. "The first part is right. Scavuzzo gets his head blown off, I take off in this car and you and the kid head back to Florence and live happily ever after."

"I saw you kill Pietro," I reminded her. "Once you've got what you want, Scavuzzo cleanly dead, what's to stop you shooting Herb and me?"

She had her right hand across her lap, training the gun on me, but now she laughed and set her left hand down on my groin. "You're worth more than that," she said.

I looked at her and grinned. "You think and act like a man," I said. "Only you're a very special woman." Clever, Locke. What was it Somerset Maugham said? Give the plain woman a hat, the clever woman a book.

"That's the first real compliment any man has ever paid me," she said and her anger was only a millimeter beneath the surface. "To the men I grew up with I was just a good-looking piece of tail. Maybe if I'd been born ugly they would have taken me seriously. But none of them did."

"They will now," I promised. "You're a genuine empress of crime. Maybe the first ever." Oh you smooth-talking bastard, Locke.

"To answer your question, that's why I won't shoot you. I think you understand me."

"I wouldn't claim that, but I sure as hell respect you."

"Even better," she said.

I drove in silence for a couple of minutes, respectful as hell. Then I asked her, "Can you tell me what's going on? I mean, it's just about over now. I'd like to know."

I guess she'd never had the same security lectures I'd been given and the law of *Omertà* that the Mafia talks about isn't quite as watertight. She snorted and said, "Haven't you worked it out?"

"Not so far."

"I came to Italy to set this up. I knew I needed foot soldiers so I got next to Scavuzzo. That pleased him." She said it unselfconsciously, her beauty was a commodity to be used. "So he allowed me to go ahead. He put me on to that scumbag I took you to yesterday."

She was silent for a moment and I wondered whether she'd had to sleep with him as well. Her memories were angry.

"Then what?" I prompted gently.

"Then he got greedy and wanted to take over. He set up the phoney double-cross, shooting his own guys and taking the boy away from where he was supposed to go. Only Mazzerini cheated him, then was picked up by someone else. That's why he wanted to lead us to the Belladonna."

"How did you find that out?"

"The Belladonna is one of my own safe houses. Those guys there hadn't seen Herbie. They were still working for Scavuzzo, like always. Mazzerini was one of their own. He'd lied to us. So I took off to get hold of Scavuzzo again and go back to that house. Only he didn't have enough men left to get Herbie out. That's why we had to wait for you to turn up, so we could get the plan back on the road."

I just shook my head. "You're smarter than any of them."

She gave a quick little laugh. "I know," she said.

We drove for three quarters of an hour, first down the main road, then west again, with the sun flooding the windshield as we climbed a long slow hill.

"Turn left," she told me and I did. We were on a small road, barely wide enough for two vehicles to pass.

We came to a track running up to the right, towards a sharp little hill that was lit from behind by the setting sun, glowing like the Christ child in the Renaissance paintings Herbie and I had come here to see.

"Pull in at that house," she ordered, all business again, jabbing me with the muzzle of her gun.

I pulled up about fifteen yards from the house, next to a freshly dug patch of garden. Before we could even get out of the car, the front door of the house opened and Scavuzzo came out, carrying a gun.

He spoke to Carla who did not get out of the car until I was out, safely away from the wheel, no chance of burning rubber back to town with all her cash on board.

I kept away from him. A pistol isn't very accurate, unless you're a good shot. If not you'll miss a moving target at twenty feet and if he raised the gun I planned to be the fastest moving target in Europe.

Carla unlocked the trunk of the car and indicated the case. Scavuzzo moved to open it but she pulled his hand away, laughing and said something that made him turn and glance at me. Then she said, "Locke. Carry this inside."

"Yassuh, massah," I said. He wouldn't shoot me until I'd finished the donkey work. We had another minute before I had to jump him.

But he didn't give me the opportunity. He hung back, away from me as I lifted the heavy suitcase and walked it into the kitchen of the house. It was a bare, simple place but it warmed my heart. Young Herbie was there, standing with another man, fiftyish and roughly dressed, the farmer, and unarmed. I winked at Herbie and set the case on the table and waited as the others came in, first Carla, then Scavuzzo.

Now he reached to open the case and as he did so Carla dived for the door. He stopped in mid-movement then followed her. I waited long enough to hammer the farmer on the temple with the heel of my balled hand, sending him sprawling, out cold. Herbie was ahead of me, just one pace behind Scavuzzo. As I came out of the door, Scavuzzo was standing aiming at Carla who was scrambling into the car. Then Herbie tackled him, roaring and slamming into his back like a football player on his own five-yard line. Scavuzzo fell forward into the newly dug dirt but rolled as I leaped for him. He fired, pointblank into my chest. I fell on top of him, stunned, shaken, my face cut with tiny shards of something. But he was dead, his face caved in.

I picked myself up and wiped away the blood that smeared my own face and hands, dulled by the roar of the explosion, wondering why I wasn't dead. Then I heard Herbie talking in a high, hysterical voice. "It worked, John. It worked."

My ears were ringing so loud his voice was a muzzy echo in the back of my head. "What worked?"

"The gun. Like you said. It dug into the dirt when I hit him. It blew up."

I reached out and shook his hand. He grabbed mine and pumped it as if we'd just won the Superbowl. "We did it. He's dead," he said. And then he broke down and started weeping like a baby. And beyond us, down the same little track, Carla's red Fiat roared into the dusk, hidden in its plume of choking dust.

▸ 22 ◂

There was no car or truck on the farm. Herbie said there'd been another man but he'd left in the car he'd been transported in. That meant he could come back any time so we didn't wait. We left, jogging into the dust as it settled, jogging until Herbie was panting for breath, then walking briskly then jogging again until we reached the highway. It was dark by then and I let a couple of cars pass us, wanting to be sure we wouldn't get into the wrong car by mistake and find we were riding with somebody else who worked for Scavuzzo. Then a big tractor trailer came rumbling north and we flagged it down. The driver swore at first but I pointed to Herbie and said, "Signor Ridley. *Polizia, per favore.*" And he washed us down with eight gallons of Italian of which the only word I recognized was "*Si.*"

By then that night we had been passed from the highway police to the city department and we were sitting in Capelli's office with Herbie's parents and the *maggiore* who had come from some official function wearing more decorations than the average Christmas tree.

Herbie and his mother were sitting close to one

another while his father sulked and smoked Camels, finally bursting out with, "What about my goddamn money?"

Capelli was deathly tired. He looked as if he hadn't slept since the kidnapping. He said, "I thought it was insurance money, signor."

"It should have been. But they're raising questions. They're going to sue me to get it back. What are you gonna do about that?"

Capelli shrugged. "We will catch this Fontana woman, sometime. She will have the money with her. No doubt you will get it back in time."

"In time?" Ridley sneered. "In Italian goddamn time. Just look around this dump, will ya? Nothing's changed since Pluto was a goddamn pup."

The *maggiore* spoke to Capelli in Italian and Capelli stiffened and nodded respectfully. "You will come with me, please, Signor Locke."

"Of course." I stood up. The *maggiore* had already left the room and Capelli was hovering at the door. I spoke to Kate Ridley. "If they want to arrest me for anything, please notify the embassy and arrange a lawyer, would you do that?"

"Of course. But don't worry, everything is going to be fine."

I just nodded and followed Capelli out. Everything probably looked rosy from where she sat, with her arm around her kid. She hadn't killed a man or had her gun used to kill three other people.

We went back to the *maggiore*'s office. He seemed to expand when he entered it. His demeanor more grand, his decorations more believable. He pointed to a chair. I sat, hands on my knees as I would have done at a royal reception. Capelli stood. The *maggiore* ignored him.

"Signor Locke," he began, then paused like Laurence Olivier, "since you came to Firenze we have had more crime than in all the years before."

He knew it wasn't my fault but I knew I wouldn't get

to heaven for reminding him of that so I sat and looked respectful.

He looked at me and permitted himself what he must have thought of as a smile. "We have perhaps eight men dead or dying."

I figured that was a cue. "All of them were criminals, *signor maggiore.* You have eight less to worry about."

Now his face did crack a genuine smile, it came and went like the flicker of a camera shutter in the old days when people told you to watch the birdy. A twenty-fifth of a second. Hilarity, in his terms.

"Unfortunately the government does not take such facts into account," he said slowly. "Each man requires his own weight in papers." A joke! The room brightened and Capelli and I smiled. The *maggiore* went on. "But that is what policemen are for. I am hoping only that you have seen enough of Firenze. Perhaps you can go and look at the paintings in Venice. Or Roma. There are many paintings in Roma."

"I would be very glad to leave, *signor maggiore,*" Lord! Was I sincere. Even if it meant leaving the Ridley family without my services, I didn't want any time in jail.

"Good." He stood up again. "You understand I cannot tell you to go." I nodded, but he didn't wait for an answer and went on. "I can, however, have you arrested and held for questioning."

"I assure you that won't be necessary, *signor.* I'll be out of Florence first thing in the morning."

He smiled again, the same flicker on a face that nobody had said "No" to for as long as he could remember. "Good," he said and reached across his desk to shake my hand, somewhere to the left of the marble Caesar's ear. "Arrivederci, Signor Locke, and, on behalf of the people of Firenze, thank you."

Capelli whisked me out of there and took me upstairs, away from the Ridleys and the confusion of his office, into the big echoing squad room where a couple of uniformed policemen were eating sandwiches. They stood up when we entered but Capelli waved his hand at them and shook his head and they went back to eating and talking while he sat me down and leveled with me.

"The *maggiore* is right, John. You must leave. But your visit has cleaned our city." He thought about that sentence for a moment then amended it. "It has swept away some bad people from other places, you understand?"

"Perfectly. Scavuzzo's gone, so has that other hood at the house plus half a dozen soldiers dead and five more in jail."

"And all it cost was five million dollars," he said with a straight face. "Now let me say I do not doubt what you say about this American woman, Fontana. She got away with the money, you got away with the boy. Good, the money doesn't matter to me. But," he paused and bit his forefinger, staring at me the whole time out of those ringed, weary eyes. "I am wondering how dangerous she will be, how much work she will give the police."

"I don't think she'll show up around here anymore. Maybe not even anywhere at all in Italy. I think she'll head back to the States," I said, "but believe me, she means trouble wherever she goes. She wants to be the first empress of organized crime. And she's gonna make it. She thinks and acts like a very bad man."

He looked at me closely, wondering perhaps if I had enjoyed that beautiful body. I said nothing. I may be a sonofabitch but I was once an officer and I try to be a gentleman. Finally he gave up prompting me on ESP and asked, "Do you think she will succeed?"

"Hard to say. She's totally ruthless. She shot Pietro without thinking twice. And she's organized. The way she told it to me, she brought the proposition from North America over here, got next to Scavuzzo just so she could have some help setting it up."

"And he let her do this?" Capelli knew more about Latin men than I did, he was cynical.

"He was probably intending to get rid of her later. Not shoot her, that would be a waste. He might have sold her to some Arab or put her in a brothel somewhere, I don't know. Either way she hated his guts and planned to kill him."

"She sounds very organized," Capelli admitted, nodding slowly.

"Believe me. I mean, she not only set up the troops she needed, but she fixed all the details. I told you about the garage she'd rented and the car. But what impressed me most was the suitcase. She had the matching suitcase ready, had it done before the boy was snatched."

"What are you saying?" His policeman's brain was still ticking over. Was I making some kind of accusation here? And if so, against whom?

"I'm saying that she must have known in plenty of time a. that Kate Ridley was here, b. that she had blue leather matched luggage, and c. where to get a duplicate of that case. That took organization."

He took out cigarettes and offered them to me. I waved them away and he lit up and pulled a cluttered ashtray towards him to park the match. "We have recovered the suitcase from the farmhouse. It was made in Firenze. It would have been easy to get a replacement."

"Made where?"

He blew a long, tired stream of smoke, like the little engine that could. "Belladonna. The *fabbrica* where you went this morning."

"Small world," I said.

"Small world," he agreed. He stood up. "I have a long night ahead of me, then I will sleep three days together. Only I must ask you one thing. Do you know where the money is?"

"No. I give you my word as a—former—British officer. I know that Carla took it, but that's all."

"Good." he said. "Then I won't bother telling my men to search your luggage before you leave for the airport in the morning."

"No need. All I have is most of ten thousand dollars in traveler's checks."

"Spend it wisely,"he said. "Come. I will give you back your pistol."

That exchange took another ten minutes and then I went back to the hotel while Capelli talked to the Ridleys again. It was flattering to me. I'd been off in the middle of the whole caper and yet he trusted me completely. Ridley senior, no. Herbie and Kate, yes, but he kept them while Herbie told his own story one last time.

It was close to midnight now, all the restaurants in town were closing. I could have got the dregs of their stew pot but that wasn't the way I wanted to remember my last evening in Florence. So I bugged the hotel people for a bottle of good red and some crusty bread and cheese. Then I sat and ate and watched Italian TV just as happily as if I had brains.

The suite had been made up again now that the police had gone and the cot in the living room had gone with them. So around one-thirty I threw a blanket over myself and curled up on the couch. Kate and Herbie came in at three but they didn't disturb me. At least, Herbie didn't. Kate came over before she got into bed and kissed me gently on the forehead.

I opened my eyes and said "Hi."

"Hi." She smiled at me. "If you don't object, this sleeping arrangement suits me just fine tonight. But I wanted to thank you for taking care of my son."

"Pleasure," I said. "He didn't really need it. All he needed was someone to show him how to act. He's going to be fine now."

"Thanks to you," she said and kissed me again, softly, on the lips, and left.

I woke early, as always, and headed out to run. I'd set out my gear the night before so nobody else woke up. There was a uniformed policeman outside the bedroom and he beamed when he saw me, even going so far as to salute me. I told him *buon giorno* and trotted on down the corridor. There was another policeman downstairs trying to make time with the beldam who ran the breakfast shift in the kitchen. She was snapping his head off, probably annoyed that he wanted coffee and not her superannuated favors. I looked at him and grinned, remembering what Cahill had told me once, "It's a poor policeman who lets himself get cold, wet or hungry."

I ran with real enthusiasm that morning. All the fears and anxieties of the previous day boiled out of my system as I doubled my usual distance, putting in twelve hard miles in a little over an hour and a half. By the time I got back to the hotel the day was started for everybody. The lobby was full of departing guests who elbowed one another and tried to point me out without looking obvious. The bellboy was busy, too, trucking a pile of cardboard cartons into the elevator.

I got in alongside him and he smiled and we exchanged all the civil grunts. Then he got out at my floor and started along the corridor the same way I was going. I went ahead and let myself in but before I was across the room he was behind me, tapping on the door. I opened it and he smiled and said, "Signora Ridley, *per favore, signor.*"

"Sure, come in." I let him by and called and Kate came out of the bedroom, toweling her hair.

She said, "Good morning, John, did you have a good run?" before she noticed the delivery. It made her tut and wrap her towel quickly into a turban for her hair. "This could have waited awhile." She found her purse and pulled out a bill for the bellboy, addressing him in rapid Italian. He nodded and unloaded the boxes into the bedroom. I left them all behind me and took my shower.

When I came out of the room, Kate was ready for her day, crisp and businesslike. Herbie was just out of bed, sitting in his dressing gown looking grumpy. Not a morning person.

"Hi, have you two decided what happens to me now?" I asked.

"Herbie and I were just discussing it," Kate said, too brightly to be true. "I was wondering if he wanted to spend some more time here but no, he wants to go on and see some other places, with you along, if you don't mind."

"Nothing would please me more, but I'm sure he'd like to spend time with you as well, can't you come with us?"

"I'd be delighted," she said, then mouthed a little disappointed moue for us. "Only I'm still a working girl. I have to get my merchandise bought and shipped."

"Well, can't you join us afterwards? We're supposed to be spending only a week in Rome but maybe we could spend the time there that we were supposed to spend here."

She shook her head and the action really made her look the executive. I could have imagined her with a cigar. "Not possible, I'm afraid. I have to be home to supervise the arrival of the goods, then shipping to the stores and pricing and all the other things for the fall season."

"Well, okay, Herbie. You and me against the world. Why not go and shower and we'll have breakfast, hire a car and hustle off to Venice where the car won't be a damn bit of good to us?"

"Yeah." He stood up, relaxed now. I guessed he hadn't wanted to stay around Florence any longer. All the beauty in the art world wasn't going to wash the bad memories away. He seemed relieved. "Yeah. See you in fifteen minutes, I have to shave."

He left and Kate smiled. "Shave! Would you hear him. I'll bet he hasn't shaved a dozen times in his whole life yet."

"He's not a kid anymore," I told her. I figured she was taking her son too lightly. "He stopped me from getting killed last night. He saw three men killed the day he was kidnapped. If he wants to make a thing about shaving, he's entitled."

"I guess," she said. She was standing awkwardly in the middle of the room. I thought perhaps she was still feeling grateful, there was no need for that. I'd performed as advertised, no better.

"Listen, why don't you go on down to breakfast, I'll bring Herbie down when he's ready and we'll have a *caffelatte* with you."

"No." Her voice was high and nervous. She sounded dry-mouthed. "No, that's okay, thank you, we'll all go down together."

"Well don't feel you have to talk to me. Why not look at your goods that arrived, what are they, samples?"

"Yes," she said, smiling brightly. "Yes, samples of stuff I was buying before this business started."

"Well go ahead. Here, I'll help you." I stood up, taking out my knife. She moved in front of me, trying to look casual.

"No, don't bother now, I'll only have to pack them again."

I put one hand under her chin and tilted her head up so she was forced to look into my eyes. "What's in there, Kate?"

"Purses," she said. "Just purses."

"Good. I need a present for a friend in Toronto, let me see what an expert has picked out."

She leaned her strength against me but she would have needed to be the size of Mean Joe Green to keep me away from those boxes now.

I slit the tape on the top box and pulled out the excelsior from it. Inside was a fine leather purse, cut square and simple. Maybe it was meant for a man to carry, I don't know, but it looked like quality. "What's a thing like this worth?" I asked her.

"To me, twenty-five dollars American. In my store, two hundred."

I took out my billfold, still there, intact, after all my

adventures. "I'll give you one hundred. I figure you owe me a deal," I said.

She pushed the money away. "No. Your money's no good, John. But I wouldn't want you to settle for one of these. Call your friend and tell her to go into any of my stores and pick out the best bag in the place. That way you know she'll be getting exactly what she wants."

"And this way I'll be getting exactly what I want." I said and opened the purse. It was like all new purses, shiny and crisp and smelling of leather and packed with crinkly paper to keep its shape. The only difference was that this crinkly paper was in the form of crumpled U.S. one hundred dollar bills.

She looked at me, then reached out and took the purse out of my hands. "Now you know," she said.

I stood there and shook my head. "No. Spell it out for me. You and Carla set this whole thing up? What?"

She sat down on the edge of the bed. It was opened and rumpled and her pale blue nightdress lay negligently across the pillow. She picked up the nightdress and folded it, mechanically, like a nurse preparing a dressing.

"If you had ever lived with his father, you'd know why I wanted to hurt him, financially, the only way he understands," she said.

"Go ahead, break my heart. But this was your own kid you're talking about here. Didn't that matter? Were you willing to take blood money for your own son?" I guess my voice had roughened. I was talking to her the way I would have spoken to a soldier under my command who had put other soldiers at risk. But she didn't crack. She kept folding that nightgown tighter and tighter.

"You have to understand that I hadn't seen Herbie for four years. Not since the divorce. And anyway, it was going to be over by the time I got involved. All I have to do is move the money back to Toronto."

I looked at her without speaking and she could read my anger. "Look, I wasn't talking about my son when this thing was proposed to me. I was talking about a stranger, a boy who groped servant girls and stole cars. He was just another possession of a man I hated. Then, when Herbie got here and I met him, it was too late to change anything. I tried to contact Carla but she was adamant. She wanted to get her own revenge on this man Scavuzzo." Now she paused and looked up at me, staring into my eyes for the first time since I opened that bag. Her voice became almost a hiss. "She wanted to revenge herself on all of you arrogant bastards."

There was nothing to say. I guess a lot of men hurt a lot of women but the reverse is true as well. I just wondered for the thousandth time what makes people think life is going to be fair. In the meantime I needed distance from this woman. Her hatreds were corrosive. I shut my clasp knife and turned away. "Tell Herbie I couldn't wait. I'll be downstairs in the dining room."

As I moved to the door she said, "John, John. Don't let's part like this." And when I didn't speak she ran after me and put her hand on mine as I reached for the doorknob. "What are you going to do?"

"Nothing," I told her. "Not a damn thing." And I went out, closing the door carefully behind me, leaving her with tears of shame spilling down her face.

▸ 23 ◂

After that first morning the trip went well. Herb and I had breakfast and hired a car and drove over to Venice. The place was bulging but I have connections there, a retired British spook who keeps a little pension to boost the pittance he got when he quit spying. He gave us a room to crash in and I showed Herbie the sights.

I didn't push culture on him too hard. He needed time to overcome his battle fatigue. The first couple of nights he woke up in a panic, but he settled down when I sat and shot the breeze with him for a few minutes. That was all it took, a couple of nights.

On the third day we were eating lunch in a side street off the Piazza San Marco when a busload of Norwegian students pulled in. They were mostly girls, mostly knockouts. It worked out well. Herbie teamed up with a sixteen-year-old and I hit it off with the teacher. None of us got much rest over the next few days and by the time their bus left for Rome, Herbie was in love. So we broke the pattern we'd set ourselves and followed their route for another week and a half, including four days in Florence. Herb and I stayed outside the town and

Capelli and his boys didn't see us, or if they did they left us alone.

When the kids went back to Norway, Herbie wanted to follow them but I talked him out of it. Being in love was good for his art appreciation, and for the rest of the time we drove around the country studying the art of the Renaissance like a couple of Jesuits. Okay for him, but I was starting to get restless. However, celibacy finally did to Herbie what Freud promised. He began to sublimate. He bought himself some paints and started in to copy the works of some of the world's greatest. He was dedicated and he had talent. It looked like his grandmother was right.

The only change we made in our overall plan was to take a side trip to Trondheim before coming back home. Herbie saw Ea and promised to come to see her again, the next year. It looks as if he might. He's serious about art and so's she, and the first blush of romance at a distance leaves them extra energy to put into their painting.

Anyway, six weeks to the day I was back in Elspeth Ridley's house, dropping off Herbie who was going to live with her while he attended art college. She poured me a Bushmills and I reported.

"It's a good job you were along," the old lady said. "My son had taken out that insurance without telling anybody. It would have looked very suspicious if you hadn't been there and been so efficient."

"What are they doing about it?" I asked politely.

"Nothing, yet," she said. "It's posing quite a problem for Herbert. He's experiencing financial difficulties and this added five-million-dollar debt, if he has to pay it himself, that could be the last straw."

"At the risk of sounding nosy, ma'am"—I threw in the "ma'am" as an apology for bringing up the grubby subject of money—"where does that leave you? Will your income be affected?"

"It could be," she said gravely. "But I have taken

certain steps over the years that will insulate me from a company loss, even a company failure."

"I'm glad to hear it." I wondered what they were. Rejecting my father's lifestyle had meant rejecting any understanding of how the wonderful world of wealth really works.

"But that's not important," she said in what was suddenly a frail, old-woman's voice, different from her normal brisk tone. "The more important question is, do you think Herbie was harmed by it?"

"No. He came out of it unharmed, in fact it improved him. Kind of a tempering process," I said. Smooth, Locke. Maybe they were paying a bonus for performance above and beyond safe delivery of merchandise.

"Yes," she said, in the same tone, looking at me over the rim of her gin and tonic. "The improvement is remarkable."

"You can put down part of it to his falling for a very sweet little art student," I said.

"Yes," the old lady said drily. "He showed me her photograph the moment he came in. Very pretty, for a policeman's daughter."

Well how about that. The old lady was a snob. An Achilles wheel on her wheelchair.

"He's an inspector and her mother is a doctor," I said.

She sipped her drink and frowned at me. "Oh come on, John. You know what I'm talking about."

I sighed. "Frankly, Elspeth, I don't. If you're coming on snobbish, I've misread you. Take it from me, this is a nice girl. Herbie may not end up with her but if he did she'd make you proud."

She set her drink down and reached out for my glass which was not quite dry. "You just did it again, John. Let me get you another drink."

I didn't yield the glass. "Did what?"

She took my glass anyway and sloshed in the Bushmills. I was glad I had come in a cab, straight from the airport. Ontario's new drinking and driving laws weren't written to accommodate Elspeth Ridley's hospitality.

"You passed another test." She handed me the drink. "Here I was trying to find out whether you were a yes-man, eager to go along with whatever I said."

"So you don't disapprove of the girl?" I left all the other inferences alone. I may not be a yes-man but I'm not a no-man when there's chance of a bonus.

"Of course not. She's a sweet-looking little thing, like the young Garbo."

Herbie sauntered into the room. "I'm set up in the back bedroom," he said. "I hope you don't mind, Granma, it's got a north light. That's going to be better to work in."

"Work away to your heart's content. Only don't get your oils on the rug, it's an antique."

"I already rolled it up." He grinned. "It's okay, I guess, for something non-representational."

She pretended to throw something at him and he ducked and laughed. "I hope you'll be comfortable here," she said. "Now be a good grandson and go away for a moment while I finish talking to Mr. Locke."

"Yeah, sure." He straightened, then came over and stuck out his hand. "S'long John."

"So long, Herb. You still want to come running in the mornings?" I shook his hand and he hung on.

"Maybe till fall," he said. "I'm not big on slip-sliding down the Rosedale Ravine on the ice."

"I'll be by for you Monday morning at seven. See you outside."

"For sure," he said and winked and left.

Elspeth watched him go then turned back to me, no sentimental sighs, all business. "How much money do you have left?"

I turned to the flight bag I had brought in with me and pulled out a folder. "Here's the whole list of expenses. It came to sixty-three hundred and forty-eight dollars. Here's the rest of the traveler's checks and some change, thirty-six hundred and fifty-two."

She shook her head. "That's not enough," she said.

I stiffened. "Every nickel is accounted for, ma'am. Have your accountants look it over." I stood up but she waved me down again, smiling apologetically.

"No. No. Don't get on your high horse. That came out wrong. I meant it's not enough for what I had in mind. I wanted you to have a bonus. Here, keep the traveler's checks and I'll have my banker send you the balance of your pay and another fifteen hundred dollars."

"You mean you're giving me a five-thousand-dollar bonus? That's extremely generous of you, Elspeth." Clever work, Locke. Don't switch to calling her Mrs. Ridley now or she'll own you.

"You've earned it." she said. "Guidance therapy for way-ward boys is expensive. Even more so in—what do they call them—life-threatening circumstances."

"Thank you again," I said and dug deeper into my flight bag, coming up with the present I'd bought her in our second spell in Florence.

"Why thank you, this is unexpected," she said. "Whatever is it?"

"It may not be appropriate but it seemed like a good souvenir of what happened," I said as she unwrapped the purse.

She held it up, delightedly. "Well, isn't that thoughtful of you. Thank you. Where did you pick it up?"

"In Florence," I said and her eyes flicked at my face and away in a sudden flash of alarm. I felt my stomach contracting but I twisted the knife I had unknowingly dug into her. "It was made at Belladonna," I said and she gasped and dropped it as if it were hot.

I stood up over her. "You're part of it, aren't you?"

"Part of what?" She whimpered in her old lady voice.

"Part of the plot. What happened? You figured the family trust was going belly up? You figured to grab a chunk of it before it all went down the tubes, is that it?"

"I don't know what you're talking about," she said,

her voice strengthening and coarsening as her throat dried up on her.

I put my glass down. "Don't worry," I told her. "I'm not going to say anything. If I do, it shatters young Herbie's way of life. You go to jail. His mother goes to jail. His father goes belly up. I can't do that to the kid."

"I don't know what you're talking about," she said again, fluttering her hands.

"Goodbye. And don't bother arranging bonus checks. I don't want any stolen money. I'll take the rest of my contract out of your traveler's checks and give the balance to your banker."

I turned and left, not looking back.

The cabbie who came for me glanced at the bags and brightened. "Airport?" he asked.

"No, just got back. Clifton Road, please."

He slammed away, annoyed that the fare wouldn't be in double figures. I rewarded his bad manners by tipping him a quarter. He left, swearing, and I walked up the back stairs to my apartment.

The two queens on the ground floor were throwing plates at one another. Typical Saturday night. But on the second floor I could hear Janet Frobisher's stereo playing. I was glad she was in. If the gods were good to me, this would be the night we finally got together. I had done some soul-searching on the airplane while Herbie mooned over the photograph of his girl. What I needed was some stability in my life. A regular girl like all the other regular guys had. Janet would be ideal. She was intelligent and beautiful. I could settle down with her. No roses around the door or anything, but a good steady relationship that lasted longer than it takes a dozen long-stemmed roses to wither.

I couldn't place the music she was playing, it wasn't Mozart but some kind of folky thing. No matter, we could play the classics later after a welcome home dinner.

I knocked on the door. It was opened by a tall, lean

man. I looked at him and my heart sank. "Hi, Bruce. Is Janet home? I'm her neighbor."

"Yeah," he said, in his pinched Australian drawl. "G'day. Come on in." He turned away and called out, "Hey, Jan, it's one o' the poufters."

"I'm from upstairs, not downstairs," I said dully. I had identified the song on the stereo. It was "Click Go the Shears," an Australian boozing song.

Janet came to the door, holding a glass of red wine. By the look in her eye and the degree of décolletage she was sporting I guessed it wasn't her first of the evening. "Welcome back, John. Come in and have a drink." She waved at me but I stood my ground. I hadn't flown four thousand miles to play gooseberry on her reconciliation.

"No, this isn't the time. Tomorrow maybe. I picked you up a souvenir in Italy. I just stopped by to say hi and ask if there were any messages."

"Nobody's been calling," she said.

Her bush ranger had opened a beer and he stuck it into my hand. "Have a beer," he commanded. Like most Australians he was able to split the word up into two-and-a-half syllables.

There was no way to refuse so I sat and watched them nuzzle one another for the few minutes it took to demolish a Molson Golden then said goodnight and wended my way up to bed.

The music lasted well into the night when it gave way to shouts that went on until something clanged. It sounded to me like a skillet hitting a hard head. But that's me for you, an incurable romantic.

MATT SCUDDER THRILLERS

BY

LAWRENCE BLOCK

Matt Scudder. He's as tough as they come. The unorthodox detective gets his inspiration from a bottle.He's not a cop. He's just a man who won't stop until he finds the truth—no matter what the price!

_A STAB IN THE DARK	0-515-08635-5—$2.95
_TIME TO MURDER AND CREATE	0-515-08159-0—$2.95
_EIGHT MILLION WAYS TO DIE	0-515-08840-4—$3.50
_WHEN THE SACRED GINMILL CLOSES	0-441-88097-5—$3.95

Available at your local bookstore or return this form to:

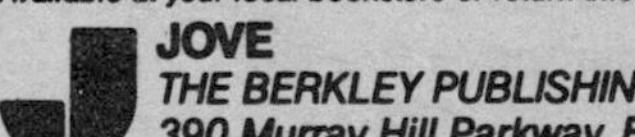

JOVE
THE BERKLEY PUBLISHING GROUP, Dept. B
390 Murray Hill Parkway, East Rutherford, NJ 07073

Please send me the titles checked above. I enclose ______. Include $1.00 for postage and handling if one book is ordered; add 25¢ per book for two or more not to exceed $1.75. CA, NJ, NY and PA residents please add sales tax. Prices subject to change without notice and may be higher in Canada. Do not send cash.

NAME______________________________

ADDRESS______________________________

CITY______________________ STATE/ZIP______________________

(Allow six weeks for delivery.)